An Indomitable Woman

Tabitha & Wolf Historical Mystery Series

Book Seven

Sarah F. Noel

ISBN-979-8-9916088-9-3

Cover design by: HelloBriie Creative
Printed in the United States of America

Also By Sarah F. Noel

Tabitha & Wolf Historical Mystery Series

A Proud Woman

A Singular Woman

An Independent Woman

An Inexplicable Woman

An Audacious Woman

A Discerning Woman

An Intrepid Woman

A Patient Woman

An Enigmatic Woman

A Valiant Woman

An Anointed Woman

The Continental Capers of Melody Chesterson

A Venetian Escapade

Mischief In Morocco

The Amsterdam Engima

ACKNOWLEDGEMENTS

I want to thank my wonderful editor, Kieran Devaney and the eagle-eyed
Patricia Goulden for doing a final check of the manuscript.

To my dear friend, Diane Frick.

Foreword

This book is written using British English spelling. e.g. dishonour instead of dishonor, realise instead of realize.

British spelling aside, while every effort has been made to proofread this thoroughly, typos do creep in. If you find any, I'd greatly appreciate a quick email to report them at sarahfnoelauthor@gmail.com

PROLOGUE

The sharp blade sliced through the young woman's jugular as easily as if it were cutting through butter. Her killer looked at the young woman's body, the blood flowing from the fresh wound on her neck. She was clearly dead, but that was not enough. It was never enough, and so he moved down to her abdomen and began his grisly task.

CHAPTER 1

London 1898

Miriam Tuchinsky straightened her cravat, smoothed down the front of her jacket, and looked up at the huge Mayfair house she was standing in front of. Turning to the large, imposing-looking man standing a step or two behind her, the woman said, "Wait for me out here, Shlomo."

"You sure?" the man asked.

"I'll be fine. Lady P is no threat to me, far from it. You remember that Lord P saved Bubbe's life. This isn't Brick Lane; I don't need protection in Mayfair." With that, Tuchinsky walked up the marble steps to the grand, oak front door with its well-polished brass knocker.

Miriam Tuchinsky wasn't a woman normally lacking in self-confidence. You didn't grow up in the hardscrabble East End of London, amongst the often-despised Jewish immigrant population, fighting your way against all odds to be a successful and feared leader of a criminal organisation by second-guessing yourself. However, she was very much out of her element in this part of London. That she had a personal connection to the grand lady who lived in the mansion didn't lessen her awkwardness at presenting herself at its front door.

"What is wrong with you, Tuchinsky?" she muttered under her breath. "Lady P told you that she was a private inquiry agent, and your money is as good as anyone else's." Taking a deep breath, Tuchinsky rapped on the brass doorknocker.

Tuchinsky had never met a butler and had no point of comparison, but when Manning opened the door, she had to stifle a chuckle; he was the tallest man she had ever seen, and rail thin. The butler had the normal inscrutability that the upper classes expected from a man in his role, but Manning had always managed to flavour it with his own particular dourness. Tuchinsky wasn't sure why such an attitude in someone who would not look out of place in a freakshow seemed so absurd, but it was all she could do to control her facial expressions and not offend the man before she said a word.

Manning took his position as the butler to the Dowager Countess of Pembroke very seriously. Beyond the dowager herself, no other person alive was as in awe of the woman's intellect, standing in society, and family heritage. He also knew of her recently proclaimed intent to be a private inquiry agent. His mistress had warned him that there might be visitors who were not from her usual aristocratic circles. Indeed, it was not so many months since Mickey D, the Whitechapel criminal, and his wife Angie, had been dinner guests. It would shortly be the dowager's turn to host the monthly luncheon for the Ladies of KB, an eclectic group of madams the dowager had encountered on her first foray into solo investigations. Manning assumed that the bizarrely dressed woman standing in front of him was yet another of the rabble and riff-raff that the dowager countess now insisted on engaging with. He inwardly sighed.

"How can I help you..." Manning paused, taking in the woman in front of him in the well-tailored men's suit, bowler hat set jauntily on top of her dark, curly bob. "...madam?" he concluded.

Tuchinsky had been called far worse things in her time and merely smiled. She had long found that the dissonance caused by her pretty feminine features, which she didn't try to mask, and her penchant for dressing as a moderately successful businessman put people on the back foot, particularly men. This wasn't why she wore men's clothes, but it was an interesting and useful side effect.

"My name is Miriam Tuchinsky, and I would like to speak to Lady

Pembroke, the Dowager Countess, if she's available," Tuchinsky said, trying to inject suitable deference into her voice.

As it happened, the name Tuchinsky was familiar to Manning. At the climax of her first solo investigation, the dowager had found herself in the middle of the East End, on Brick Lane, surrounded by Jewish immigrants, which is how she had first met Tuchinsky. Welcomed into Tuchinksy's grandmother – Bubbe's – kitchen, the dowager had been so taken with the old woman's chicken soup that she had begged for the recipe. Bubbe had insisted that the recipe alone was not sufficient to replicate the delicious flavours and had offered to take the dowager's cook, Mrs Anderson, to the kosher butcher to buy boiling chickens, and then to host her for a cooking class. The outcome of this class had been that, not only was Bubbe's chicken soup now regularly served at the dowager's table, but so was something called lokshen pudding and some interesting Jewish bread rolls, called beigels, that Mrs Anderson had returned from Brick Lane with, and which Bubbe periodically sent out to Mayfair.

Neither Manning nor any of the dowager's servants knew the full story of how the dowager had ended up at Brick Lane and became associated with the Tuchinsky family. Still, they had heard Mrs Anderson's tales of cooking side-by-side with the old Jewish grandmother and had all come to enjoy the chicken soup that the cook now made regularly. Manning again sighed inwardly; he would have loved to have turned this bizarrely dressed woman away, but he knew better than to make decisions on behalf of his increasingly eccentric mistress. Instead, he stood back and indicated that Tuchinsky should enter.

The diminutive dowager's drawing room was set up with tiny furniture to maximise her comfort and the discomfort of her guests. While this was not normally a hostess' intention, The Dowager Countess, Lady Pembroke, was acutely aware of the strategic value of such a power play. Manning indicated that Tuchinsky should take a seat on the low, narrow settee opposite the throne-like, higher, armchair that the dowager preferred, which allowed her to glare imperiously at her guests.

Tuchinsky was no stranger to power plays and immediately understood the rationale behind the room's setup; it only made her admire the dowager more.

The dowager had very strict notions about how long she should be kept waiting in other people's drawing rooms – preferably no time at all. However, she felt no qualms about keeping her guests waiting. Indeed, these concepts were two sides of the same coin in her mind; she deserved nothing less than to be waited on immediately, and other people deserved no such courtesy from her. Nevertheless, as soon as Manning had sent word to the dowager's boudoir that Tuchinsky was downstairs, the dowager, luckily already dressed for the day, made uncharacteristic haste to greet her guest. Miriam Tuchinsky fascinated the dowager countess as few people did. That the woman had carved out such a powerful position for herself amongst the male criminals of the East End, engendering fear and respect, was something that the dowager regarded with the highest approbation. There were very few people the dowager felt she could learn anything from, but Tuchinsky might just be one of the few.

Entering the drawing room ahead of Manning, the dowager saw Tuchinsky perched uncomfortably on the low, rather hard settee and immediately snapped, "Manning, why did you not bring a more comfortable chair for my guest? Please have Michael bring a more comfortable armchair immediately."

Having sent Manning off on his task, the dowager bustled into the room, going up to her guest with an outstretched hand. Again, this was not normally her inclination; particularly when dealing with the lower classes, the dowager was wont to insist on the formality of being curtseyed to. It was a mark of what an intellectual equal the dowager considered the woman before her that she brushed aside such social norms.

Whether or not Tuchinsky had any inkling of what a more comfortable chair and an outstretched hand signified was unclear. While Miriam Tuchinsky had dealt with all manner of grifters, petty thieves, cold-blooded killers, and crooked businessmen in her time, she had no experience of the aristocracy before meeting the dowager, Tabitha and Wolf. It had occurred to her that perhaps the threesome was not representative of the ruling classes, but again, she had nothing to compare them to.

Finally, seated in the far more comfortable armchair, a cup of tea in her hand and the social niceties of small talk about each other's families out of the way, the dowager asked, "So, what can I do for you, Tuchinsky?"

"You don't believe I've just come for a visit to see how the toffs live?" the other woman asked, laughing.

"I believe that you have a thriving business to run and no time to make social calls on a Wednesday afternoon that don't have a purpose," the dowager said in a matter-of-fact tone. As it happened, her more than-usual interest in Tuchinsky meant she would have been thrilled to receive a mere social call from the woman. However, she was astute enough to recognise someone on a mission when she saw them. Tuchinsky's impatience with the small talk had been evident; she had weightier issues she wished to discuss.

Putting down her teacup, Tuchinsky glanced away for a moment as she considered how she wished to phrase her request. Finally, deciding there was no better way to say it than bluntly, she answered, "Lady Pembroke, I want to hire you to find a murderer."

Whatever the dowager had been expecting, it was not that. In truth, ever since she had made the decision more than three months before to launch herself into the world as a private inquiry agent, she had been at somewhat of a loss for how to drum up business. Initially, she had tried milking her high society gossips, Ladies Hartley and Willis, for possible cases. She had thought that effort had surfaced a potential investigation. However, she had then been sidetracked when Mickey D, the Whitechapel Irish crime boss, had unexpectedly recommended her services to a madam. It was a matter of dispute between her and Tabitha and Wolf as to whether her subsequent adventures running a brothel in Villiers Street had been a reckless, ill-considered undertaking that had almost got her killed, or a brilliant and daring launch into the world of investigations. Whichever was closest to the truth, since then, she had been disappointed at the total want of subsequent potential clients beating their way to her door.

It had briefly occurred to the dowager to put an advertisement in one of the London newspapers. Indeed, she had considered how the title she had printed on her calling cards, *The Investigative Countess, Rapier Sharp Logic paired with Great Insight and Boldness, A Private Inquiry Agent*, might look in a broadsheet. However, on further reflection, that felt rather too akin to being in trade, and there was no greater horror as far as the dowager was concerned. Of course, if she had been pressed as to why setting herself up in business didn't feel like lowering herself to be no better than a solicitor or bank manager, but advertising the fact did, she might have momentarily been lost for words. Perhaps it didn't feel the same because she had never really considered the commercial aspects of her new chosen profession. She had no need for money and had set herself up as an inquiry agent solely to alleviate her boredom.

The dowager had considered how cases just seemed to crop up for Wolf and had hoped that she might be similarly blessed. Now, that actually seemed to be the case, and she was both delighted and, uncharacteristically, somewhat nervous. "A murderer you say? You want me to find a murderer?"

When Vicky Sharpe had engaged the dowager to find her twin sister, Margery, neither woman had expected that the sister had been murdered. Indeed, for all the dowager's time spent at Margery's brothel, it had been Tabitha and Wolf who had uncovered a body in the morgue matching the missing woman's description. The dowager, for her part, had never suspected Margery's killer, Lou, and had instead managed to get herself abducted by Lou and her brother. If Tabitha, Wolf, and Bear hadn't rescued her, that situation might have turned out very differently. While she might spin the yarn to make herself the heroine of the hour when happily relaying it to her society cronies, the dowager secretly harboured a little bit, a very little bit, of self-doubt.

"Who has been murdered?" the dowager asked. While she both admired and respected Miriam Tuchinsky, it was not lost on the dowager that the other woman was a criminal who had almost certainly punished Lou and her brother, Jason Bono, with gunshots to the temple. The dowager did not doubt that Tuchinsky had murdered many people besides those two, and that she had been lucky not to be added to that list. Was she about to be asked to get involved in some messy rivalry between East End gangs?

"A young Irish girl, a maid," Tuchinsky answered. "I'm worried that the Jews are going to be blamed again."

The dowager considered Tuchinsky's words, then speaking aloud her most immediate concern, she asked, "Why did you bring this to me and not to Lord Pembroke? After all, by this point you know his history as a thief-taker."

Tuchinsky chuckled, "My dear Lady Pembroke, do I strike you as someone who would choose a man over an eminently capable woman for a task? And my understanding is that it was you who Mickey D recommended to Mother Sharpe to help locate her sister, not Lord Pembroke."

That was true, and all made perfect sense to the dowager. Nevertheless, that annoying sliver of self-doubt insisted on poking through her otherwise impenetrable armour of hubris. "I would imagine that with your deep ties to the Jewish community and the high respect you are held in throughout the East End, you would be better placed to ferret out information."

Tuchinsky laughed again, "If 'respect' is a polite way to say I am feared, then you have your answer; people are too scared to talk to me. I need someone they will talk to without reserve who is able to sniff out the truth, or otherwise, in their statements."

The dowager wasn't sure whether to be offended at the idea that she did not strike fear into people's hearts immediately on introduction. However, she understood Tuchinsky's overall point: whatever fear the dowager might engender was related to her sharp tongue, not the possibility of an actual knife to the ribs. The other woman continued, "Of course, your investigation can benefit from my network of spies and associates, but I would suggest that we keep our affiliation known to as few people as possible."

While this suggestion made sense, it only fed the dowager's concerns about hunting a killer alone. "Would I be able to enlist Mr Doherty's assistance?" she asked. Without at least one of her Whitechapel contact's direct help, the dowager had no idea where she would even start investigating in a neighbourhood that was a world away from all she knew and understood in Mayfair.

"Mr Doherty? Oh, Mickey D," Tuchinsky said. She thought for a moment, then replied, "Mickey D and I keep our business activities at a discreet, and respectful distance from each other, wherever possible. There is not much overlap between our areas of interest, and Mickey and his gang keep away from Brick Lane and Spitalfields. But, if you really feel you'll need his help, then I guess it's alright."

For all her self-doubt, the dowager was almost beside herself with glee; this is what she had been waiting for, a real murder case of her very own. If ever there was a case worthy of *The Investigative Countess, Rapier Sharp*

Logic paired with Great Insight and Boldness, it was this one. Whatever her concerns and even fears, the dowager countess, Julia Chesterton, knew there was no way she could turn down this case. Or at least no way to turn it down and then be able to look at herself in the mirror, fully confident in her ability to excel in her new career.

Because what was the alternative? Hunting down lost baubles and philandering husbands? Being beholden to that shrew Lady Hartley for whatever morsels of gossip she managed to extract and then hoping that those crumbs would yield worthwhile investigations? No! She was the Dowager Countess of Pembroke, admired and feared throughout the society and the highest echelons of government. If she couldn't crack this case, who could?

"I would be delighted to take on this investigation, Tuchinsky," she announced.

Miriam Tuchinsky had brought a satchel with her and had put it next to her on the armchair. Now, she reached for it, pulling out a small tin and some papers. "These papers are all the information I was able to gather on the murder, including newspaper clippings. The contents of the tin are a gift from Bubbe, who sent you her best wishes."

Tuchinsky stood and brought the tin and papers over to the dowager, who removed the tin's lid. Inside, she saw some pretty little pastries that seemed to be dotted with raisins and smelled divine.

"These are Bubbe's ruggelach. Her recipe has a secret ingredient that she swears she will take to her grave. Whatever it is, I can say without prejudice that these are the best ruggelach you'll find in London. Perhaps anywhere."

"With nothing to compare them to, I will take your word for that," the dowager said teasingly, taking one of the pastries out and nibbling it. "My, my. These are absolutely delicious. Please give Bubbe my thanks and best wishes." Taking another bite, she continued, "I am assuming that this is a recipe Bubbe will not be willing to share with my cook?"

"I am sure she'll be willing to share the standard ruggelach recipe. And honestly, even ruggelach that aren't as good as Bubbe's are pretty wonderful. I'll have a copy of the recipe brought over."

A few more words of thanks on both sides and the East End criminal was gone, leaving the dowager to eat another of the ruggelach and contemplate what she had just agreed to. The question that consumed her was not whether she should have taken on the investigation; she did not doubt that she had done the right thing by saying yes. Rather, it was whether or not she should tell Tabitha and Wolf and ask for their assistance.

It took one more of the delectable pastries for the dowager to decide that she did not need help, at least for the time being. She could always approach Tabitha and Wolf if and when she needed help. Still, the further into the investigation she was able to get alone, the easier it would be for her to assert her dominance later. One thing she was glad of was that she had continued to employ Little Ian, the giant of a man originally on loan from Mickey D. The truth was that there hadn't been much for the man to do in the way of providing security since the end of the Villiers Street case. However, according to Manning, Little Ian seemed happy enough to live out in the carriage house with the groom and driver and help out with chores when needed.

Thinking about Little Ian made the dowager realise where she should begin this investigation: with Mickey D.

Chapter 2

Wolf found himself outside Langley House, reminiscing about the first time he had approached this door less than a year ago. Then, he had seen Maxwell Sandworth, the Earl of Langley, as a potential murder suspect. Their interaction had been tense and far from pleasant. The next time he had come here, it was because Lord Langley had abducted Melody, Tabitha's ward. Another less-than-ideal encounter. The reason for his visit that day, however, was a testament to the unexpected evolution of their relationship.

At Wolf's first rap on the knocker, the door was opened, as it had been on those previous visits, by Langley's butler, Talbot, first cousin to Chesterton House's own butler of the same name. However, unlike those first visits, Talbot was both expecting the new Lord Pembroke and welcoming. He relieved Wolf of his outer garments and then showed him through to Langley's study. Again, Wolf thought back to that initial visit and the extremely cold reception he had received. This visit could not have been more different; Langley rose on his entry and approached with a warm smile on his face.

"Pembroke, good to see you. I hope all is well." Langley indicated that they should each take one of the comfortable-looking leather armchairs in front of the fireplace.

The two men had only crossed paths a few times since their return from Wales in early January. Both had become caught up in their respective responsibilities: Wolf overseeing the changes and improvements he had initiated for the Pembroke Estate, and Langley, with his covert role in British Intelligence.

As they settled into their seats, Wolf reassured the older man, "Everyone is doing well, Langley." They engaged in small talk, Langley updating Wolf on Rat's progress and then discussing their mutual interest in Melody's well-being. The conversation, though brief, was a testament to their shared concerns and growing bond.

"I take it that you have come to see me with a purpose," Langley observed. "As it happens, I was intending on calling on you at some point this week."

Wolf nodded, "I have a request to make of you. Before I begin, I should say that Tabitha knows nothing of this, so far. I would appreciate your discretion until I am able to disclose it to her myself."

"I can assure you of my discretion, but I must admit to being quite curious after such an introduction."

Wolf smiled a little shyly, "It may not come as a surprise to you to learn of the tendre I hold for Tabitha, Lady Pembroke."

Langley chuckled, "No, that is not a surprise. I do not believe it would be a surprise to anyone who has been in the company of you both anytime in the last few months. In fact, I would go as far as to say that it seems to me that the two of you are very much in love."

Wolf blushed. He and Tabitha had believed that they had been quite discreet about their feelings for each other, but it seemed that their blossoming romance had been more obvious than they had hoped. Langley continued, "Indeed, I believe that the dowager countess has even observed it. She made a few comments over Christmas that indicated so."

Now, Wolf just grimaced; he didn't want to consider their friends and family making such observations behind their backs. However, it seemed likely that this was the case. Such a realisation only made him even more determined in his task that day.

"I hope to marry Tabitha and I have told her as such. However..." he paused, unsure how to phrase the issue. In truth, Wolf was uncertain just how much Langley knew about Tabitha's marriage to Jonathan and had no wish to betray any more of her confidence than was strictly necessary.

Luckily, Langley picked up the conversation and continued, "I suspect the trauma of her marriage to the late Lord Pembroke gives Tabitha pause about entering another such union, no matter how different a man you are from your cousin."

"Precisely. I know that this is not about Tabitha not trusting me. Rather, it is about her not trusting herself. She worries that she entered her marriage willingly, even enthusiastically, and that, even though it was more than three years ago now when she was little more than a child, that is an insufficient excuse for not realising the character of the man she was committing herself to."

Langley looked at the man in front of him, someone he had come to trust, respect and admire. Just as Wolf had on entering the house, Langley reflected on the almost unbelievable transformation of their relationship in a relatively brief period of time. Langley was an unsociable, taciturn man with few people he truly cared for. There was his one and only love, Cassandra, the Duchess of Somerset, who he hoped to marry once her mourning period for her deceased husband was over. Then, there was Cassandra's son, Anthony, the new Duke of Somerset, who was Langley's natural son. Besides these two, and Melody and her brother Rat, there was no one Maxwell Sandworth could say he had any true affection for, much less considered a friend. Until he met Wolf, that was. Their relationship was sometimes that of an older and younger brother, sometimes of mentor and mentee, often just two men who appreciated that neither gave their trust easily but had placed it in the other.

Speaking gently but with conviction, Langley answered, "Apart from her clear understanding of how different a man you are from Jonathan, she knows you in a way she did not know him before marriage. You share a home, care for a child, and have investigated multiple murders together. If there was any fault on her part, it was not of judgement but of having insufficient information on which to base the decision to wed. And in that, she is hardly alone in aristocratic circles."

Wolf acknowledged the wisdom of the other man's words but explained, "While all that is correct, and is what the rational, logical side of her brain is telling her, nevertheless, her emotions are preventing her from being able to embrace this truth fully. Which is why I have come to see you today."

Langley was intrigued; he couldn't imagine what role he might play in soothing these romantic rough waters. Wolf continued, "I have spoken to my solicitor about how to secure Tabitha's rights before we marry. As I am sure you know, The Married Women's Property Act did give women some degree of security in terms of owning and managing property in their own right and signing contracts. However, at least as explained to me by my solicitor, it primarily addressed property women might acquire during a marriage rather than assets they enter it with, which can still be subject to a husband's control. It also did not address a wife's financial dependence on her husband. More than all that, it is unclear how rigorous the enforcement of such a complex and controversial piece of legislation might be."

As Wolf spoke, Langley nodded. As an active member of the House of Lords, he had been involved in the passing of said legislation. At the time, he had advocated for it to go further than it eventually did. However, even the reform-minded Liberal Party under the leadership of Gladstone was disinclined to go any further with the already disruptive legislation. As it was, the Conservative Party under Robert Gascoyne-Cecil, the Marquess of Salisbury, with its deference to tradition and desire to maintain social stability, had managed to squeeze the original bill.

Seeing Langley's understanding of the situation, Wolf said, "I asked my solicitor whether I might draw up some kind of contract, prior to marriage, stating Tabitha's ownership and control of her fortune, but he said that, as her husband, I might be seen as within my rights to revoke any such agreement at will. However, he did suggest one mechanism that is likely to be the most airtight and immune to any future challenge I might make: a trust."

"What kind of trust?"

"Before marriage, Tabitha would put all her property and wealth into a trust, managed by someone, a man, she has absolute faith in. This man would ensure the good management of her fortune and, in the event of the dissolution of our marriage, or even a separation rather than a divorce, he would ensure that her money was at her disposal. In addition, he would provide her full access to her funds during the marriage to use however she sees fit."

"Are you asking me to manage such a trust?" Langley intuited.

"I am. My solicitor suggested that there be two trustees, both to ensure coverage in the event of of the death of one, but also to provide additional oversight. I intend to ask Bear. There are no two men I believe in more. And more to the point, who Tabitha's believes in."

Suddenly, Langley felt a lump in his throat; the enormity of faith involved in Wolf's request was overwhelming. Langley didn't know a lot about trusts, but he knew enough to understand that once Tabitha's fortune was placed in it, her financial future would be entirely in the hands of its trustees. Both she and Wolf would need absolute certainty about the characters of the men entrusted with such power.

Anticipating Langley's next question, Wolf said, "Tabitha knows nothing of this yet. I hope to present her with a plan that I am sure I can make good on before saying anything."

"So, she may object," Langley observed. He was an astute enough man to realise Tabitha's willingness to trust him after Melody's abduction had not progressed as quickly and thoroughly as Wolf's.

Wolf understood the man's concerns and assured him, "I know that Tabitha has been slower to come around, but I believe that she now feels almost as warmly towards you as I do." Seeing the look of scepticism on Langley's face, Wolf admitted, "Regardless of her feelings of warmth, I am sure that she has as much confidence in you as I do. She certainly trusts Bear. I believe that his addition as trustee will ensure her acceptance of the plan."

While he still wasn't entirely convinced of Tabitha's faith in him, that was for Wolf to manage. For his part, Langley was honoured to be asked to take on such a role and did not hesitate to accept. However, he felt obliged to add, "All I ask is that you ensure that Tabitha, Lady Pembroke, understands fully the magnitude of what she is agreeing to: in effect, handing over control of her entire fortune."

Wolf assured him that he would. He then continued, "I believe there is an additional incentive for her to agree to this plan: it will ensure that Melody will be taken care of, no matter what any heir of mine might choose to do. Whatever else Tabitha may feel about you, I believe she does not doubt your affection for the child. That you would do whatever you could to ensure Melody's continued well-being is beyond dispute. I intend to add to the trust on Melody's behalf to guarantee whatever she needs to be raised as a lady and to marry well or even enter an educational field if she chooses. There will be more than enough money included for a substantial dowry."

Happy to hear that provisions would be made for the little girl, Langley nevertheless had one more point he wanted to make, and he hesitated for a moment before adding, "You do realise that there is nothing that can be done to protect Tabitha's relationship with any children you might have together? Your full custody rights cannot be challenged under the current law."

Wolf sighed; he knew this was the fatal flaw in his plan and had hoped that Langley might be able to suggest a way around this problem. He had talked to his solicitor at length about what might be done and had realised that, while it was not sufficient, there was one thing. "It seems there is nothing I can do pre-emptively in case of separation or divorce. However, one safeguard I can ensure is in the case of my untimely death. As the solicitor pointed out, it is not unheard of for mothers to be kept from their children after divorce and for that situation to not be rectified after the father's death. He cited an example where some baron or other had separated from his wife and then died. On his death, the children had gone to live with the man's father who had continued to exclude the mother from her children's lives."

He considered the example he had just given, "Of course, I have no father or grandfather living and am not even sure who the next in line is if I don't have a son. Nevertheless, there is something I can do, and that is to establish guardians for any future babies. Again, I would like those guardians to be you and Bear."

This request might have been even more meaningful to Langley, and he answered without hesitation, "I would be honoured."

Wolf's relief at having his request so positively responded to was palpable. Langley stood and said, "Perhaps we should toast this agreement and then I might ask my favour of you."

CHAPTER 3

On arriving back at Chesterton House, Wolf went in search of Tabitha. As he expected, he found her in the comfy parlour they used when they didn't have guests. She was curled up in a large, comfortable armchair, re-reading her favourite book, *Pride and Prejudice.*

"Are you reading that book again?" he teased. "I thought you finished it over Christmas?"

Tabitha acknowledged the truth of his words, adding, "I have read it many times and will likely read it very many more over the course of my life. Each reading is as entertaining as the first time."

Wolf wasn't much of a reader, his talents and interests lying more towards mathematics. "How can it be as entertaining when you know what is going to happen?" he asked, genuinely bemused.

"From the moment one opens the book, there is no doubt how it is going to end; it is a romantic comedy of manners, after all. The pleasure is in the characters, the dialogue, the wit and charm of it all."

Wolf shook his head. This was not the first time they had engaged in such a conversation and yet he no more understood Tabitha's words than he ever had. Acknowledging that the constant reading of the same book might seem odd to many people, Tabitha set it down and cocked an eyebrow. "Were you looking for me?"

Tabitha had been aware that Wolf was going out that afternoon. While he was under no obligation to share his comings and goings with her, he usually let her know at breakfast his plans for the day. As far as she could tell, he hadn't been gone very long, and he seemed to have come to find her immediately on his return. More than that, there was something about his manner that made her suspect his expedition had something to do with her.

They hadn't talked of marriage since their return from Wales. Wolf had told her that he had a plan for how to mitigate her concern, and she trusted in him and hadn't questioned him during either of Mr Anderson, his solicitor's, recent visits to the house. Tabitha suspected that she and their proposed marriage had been the topic of conversation when Wolf was holed up with Mr Anderson. Still, he hadn't volunteered any information, and she had respected his privacy. She knew Wolf well enough to realise that he would want to have a proposal fully in place before putting it before her.

Wolf sat in his usual chair and told her the second part of his conversation with Langley. Tabitha was correct in her assumption that he did not wish to tell her about the guardianship or trust until he had smoothed out every wrinkle. He had decided to ask Langley before he asked Bear and so didn't wish to say anything to Tabitha until then. He thought it highly unlikely that his dearest friend would refuse to help, but Bear was always a voice of wise counsel and might raise an objection that Wolf hadn't considered.

Instead, Wolf said, "Langley wants to engage us, on behalf of British Intelligence, to work on an investigation."

Tabitha's eyebrows shot up, "He does? British Intelligence wants to hire you? And me? They know about the cases we've been involved in?"

"Apparently Langley has been keeping them abreast. After the case involving the German spies, it is hardly surprising. Beyond that, we asked for the Home Secretary's help getting a warrant when we were in Edinburgh. It was naive to think that questions would not be asked."

Tabitha acknowledged the truth of his words. "But why does British Intelligence need our help? Don't they have people? Spies? Policemen? I don't know what you call their men, but I assume they have plenty."

Wolf laughed wryly, "Indeed, they do. However, given the rather unusual nature of some of my professional relationships as a thief-taker, and moreover some of our more recent dealings in the East End, there seems to be a feeling that we might be in a peculiarly unique position to help."

Tabitha's eyebrows shot up even further, "Are you talking about Tuchinsky?"

"Well, Tuchinsky, Mickey D, even Bruiser. I am well known in Whitechapel and its environs. And I have no doubt that saving Bubbe's life has bought me a lot of goodwill amongst the Jewish community there."

"And what is this investigation then?" Tabitha asked, consumed by curiosity.

"The government is worried that Jack the Ripper has struck again. Or, at the very least, someone is trying to make it seem as if he has," Wolf explained.

"Jack the Ripper?" Tabitha asked incredulously. "Why, it must be almost ten years since his gruesome killing spree."

"His first victim, Mary Ann Nichols, was murdered in the summer of eighty-eight," Wolf confirmed. "As I'm sure you know, no one was ever arrested for the murders. There was a lot of speculation at the time as to Jack the Ripper's identity, with the newspapers spreading increasingly absurd rumours. There was even conjecture that he was a member of the Royal Family, for goodness sake. However, one of the more enduring bits of speculation was that he was a Jew from the East End of London."

"I was so young then and shielded from most of the news of the times," Tabitha admitted. "I have a very spotty understanding of the details. Why the Jews?"

"From what Langley told me, for the most part, it was a convergence of locality and general anti-Semitism mixed in with discontent, fomented by the labour unions at the manufacturing and other labouring jobs that recent immigrants, particularly Jews, were perceived to be taking from native-born Englishmen," Wolf tried to explain. He didn't remember much more of the sensational crimes a decade before than Tabitha did. Not much more than twenty at the time, he was far more interested in striking out on his own in the world than in the London news, however grisly.

"So, there was no reason to suspect a Jew?" Tabitha asked, genuinely curious.

Wolf gave a little half-shrug, "Apparently, there was some cause for suspicion, not the least of which was that there was a character who was running some kind of protection racket on the Whitechapel prostitutes. The rumours were that he was a Jew. But as I said, there was also a suspicion that Jack the Ripper was Prince Albert himself."

Wolf was still trying to process what Langley had told him and the investigation he had asked them to take on. He focused on the salient part of Langley's narrative, "What is key is that the killer was never identified for certain, Yet the anti-Semitism it caused at the time was so significant that the Jewish community banded together in volunteer groups to patrol Whitechapel and help find him. There was even a reward offered by the local Jewish Member of Parliament. All of this was because there was a deep-seated concern that this was a coordinated attempt to incriminate the Jewish community."

"And so the Government believes that the Ripper is still at large, or someone is trying to make it appear as if he is?" she asked, still not sure why this wasn't something that the Metropolitan Police could handle.

"Well, yes, but that's not all there is to this. I don't know if you remember when a French military officer, Alfred Dreyfus, was convicted of treason a few years ago." Tabitha shook her head. Before being thrown into investigations with Wolf, she had never given much thought to foreign or even domestic affairs. Like all young women of her class, she had been raised in the belief that such things were too complex and too ugly for the delicate flowers of the aristocracy to worry themselves about.

"Well, it seems that Dreyfus, who is a Jew, was convicted and sent to a penal colony. However, a little over a year ago, evidence came to light that made it clear that Dreyfus was innocent and that the culprit was a different French army officer, a man named Esterhazy. However, not only was Dreyfus not exonerated, but the new evidence was suppressed and forged documents appeared that enabled the French Government to double down and charge Dreyfus with additional crimes. Apparently, despite the French Government's best attempts, word of the evidence against Esterhazy began to spread and just last week, a prominent French writer published an open letter in a newspaper accusing his government of antisemitism and a cover-up."

"This is all terrible, but isn't this a French problem?" Tabitha asked in confusion.

"Well, it is a French problem, for now. But, apparently, there is a concern amongst Jews in the highest levels of politics, business and intellectual life that this latest outbreak of anti-Semitism could spread to Britain. Moreover, there is a belief that these latest so-called Ripper murders, could add fuel to the fire."

Tabitha was finally piecing it all together and replied, "So, the hope is that using our contacts in Whitechapel and the rest of the East End, we can do what the police have been unable to do and catch this killer, who is either Jack the Ripper or someone impersonating him, and in doing so, defuse the anti-Semitic tensions that are on the rise in London?"

"Essentially, yes."

There was one question that Tabitha still needed answered before she could consider the request, "What if we find the killer and he indeed turns out to be from the Jewish community?"

A similar thought had occurred to Wolf during his conversation with Langley. "Well, that will be dealt with if and when it happens. Langley's thought was that, if the killer is a Jew, then the newspapers will be fed a narrative of a community quick to turn in one of its own for the greater good of the people of London. Or something like that. He seems to feel that, even in such a circumstance, if the killer is caught quickly and the wound to the community cauterised, the damage can be kept to a minimum."

Such political machinations were not things that either Tabitha or Wolf had any taste for, and they decided that such eventualities could be left to Lord Langley if and when they happened. However, there was one concern that immediately came to mind for Tabitha, "If we take this case, and I assume you would like us to, what do we tell Mama?"

Wolf sighed, something he seemed to be doing a lot that day, "That was a question I put to Langley, in fact. We know that Lady Pembroke insists on inserting herself into investigations, regardless of good sense or efficacy. However, in the past, she has either been the one to request our help or has been travelling in our party when investigations have presented themselves. Neither is true in this instance. I see no reason to inform her of our activities."

Tabitha agreed, "More to the point, perhaps, many of our past investigations have benefited from Mama's encyclopaedic knowledge of the histories and peccadillos of aristocratic society. I cannot imagine how her unique talents might assist in this case." Wolf had thought much the same. Given that Langley had counselled against involving the dowager, this seemed to be the end of the matter.

Chapter 4

The first time the dowager had visited Mickey D, the notorious Whitechapel criminal, she had thought nothing of wearing her finery and taking her carriage. In fact, she had considered it a good thing if the trappings of aristocracy announced to the general populace of Whitechapel that they had someone very important in their midst. She had to admit that she had learned a few things since then. Previously, she had berated Wolf for wearing his old thief-taking clothes when visiting his old haunts. Now, she had some more understanding of why he might not have wanted to advertise his new status as an earl.

In her bedchamber, she rang the bell for her maid, Withers, and considered the persona she wished to adopt for her visit to Whitechapel. During her first solo investigation, she had pretended to be the Sharpe twins' cousin, Julia Phillips. Phillips had been her maiden name, which she had quite liked until she married a man called Philip, at which point everything about the name was abhorrent to her. Despite her desire never to hear the name again after her husband's welcome death, she had adopted the pseudonym because it was close enough to the truth and was easy to remember.

The dowager had constructed a backstory for Cousin Julia that had been, if not ironclad, at least plausible. Born into a solidly respectable, if poverty-stricken family, Cousin Julia had been thrown into further penury thanks to poor investment choices by her father. She had then taken work as the governess for the children of a wealthy mercer and had continued as such for multiple generations of the family until she could finally retire on her meagre savings a few years earlier.

At the time, the dowager had hoped this would explain her accent and poise sufficiently. As it happened, various characters at the Villiers Street brothel, particularly the eventual villain's brother, Jason Bono, had never fully bought into this backstory. However, at the time, Bono had concluded that it was even more implausible that an actual member of the aristocracy had chosen to lower herself to live and work amongst a bunch of prostitutes. The dowager was counting on similar logic working in her favour again.

At the conclusion of that investigation, the dowager hadn't bothered to specify what should be done with the workaday, brown serge dress that she had worn. The dowager had got the distinct feeling that Withers had been eyeing it for herself and, at the time, had not cared that her lady's maid snag herself a new gown, even if she hadn't understood the appeal in such an ugly, if practical, item of clothing.

Now, as Withers entered the room, she asked if she still owned the dress. On receiving a nervous affirmation, she demanded that the maid fetch it immediately. Twenty minutes later, the dowager found herself transformed once more into Cousin Julia. As she had before, the dowager decided that her simple, elegant chignon hairstyle was workable, but she removed all of her jewellery. While she had once relished Mickey D's promise that she might walk through Whitechapel in her finest diamonds unharmed, she had come to accept, albeit begrudgingly, that perhaps putting that to the test wasn't the wisest idea.

Looking at her transformation in the mirror, the dowager considered the task ahead of her. During her first investigation, she had immediately recognised that one of the strengths Tabitha and Wolf brought to their cases was their partnership. As much as she enjoyed ruffling Tabitha's feathers whenever possible, the dowager recognised the girl's intelligence and logical thinking. The dowager had seen for herself the power of collaboration and debate as they had wound twisted paths through various investigations, often hitting dead ends and dealing with false leads.

Previously, when considering the value of collaboration, the dowager had reflected on who she might use as her sounding board. She quickly dismissed the value of conferring with any of her cronies and realised that Lord Langley was too loyal to Wolf to be a trusted confidant for her. Finally, in what even she admitted was not her finest decision, the dowager had turned to Rat. While the lad was young and uncultured, the dowager admired his intellect and street savvy.

However, after their adventures over Christmas when the dowager's insistence on involving Rat yet again had almost led to his death, she had been warned in extremely serious tones by Tabitha, Wolf, and Langley that she was to never involve the boy again in her machinations. While, as a general rule, the dowager did not take kindly to being spoken to in such a manner, the implied threat was that if she did not comply, Rat's sister, Melody, would no longer regularly visit "Granny".

Her first choice of collaborator removed, the dowager thought back to an earlier idea: a servant. Previously, she had dismissed such an idea as ludicrous. She knew that what made Tabitha and Wolf such a successful team was that they didn't immediately agree with each other's suggestions and instead debated and weighed all ideas. The thought that she might give one of her servants leave to question her decisions was abhorrent to her.

However, she then considered the tall, thin, rather stern-looking woman buzzing around her bedchamber. She knew that Withers had a backbone and was able to assert her own opinion strongly on occasion. Just recently, when dressing her mistress for Lady Witherspoon's ball, Withers had expressed a very determined opinion about a wine silk dress over the dowager's preference for one that was green. In the end, Withers had made her case deferentially but intelligently and firmly and had won the day. Would her lady's maid be able to balance providing enough challenge to her mistress while never forgetting her place?

Deciding to put this question to the test subtly, rather than putting her servant on notice as to the role she was auditioning for, the dowager said in as casual a voice as she was able, "Withers, I will be wearing my plain black coat to go out this afternoon, and..." she paused, "you will be accompanying me to Whitechapel."

If the maid felt any surprise or even concern at such a command, she was wise enough not to let it show on her face. Instead, she curtsied, retrieved the requested coat from the wardrobe and then excused herself to get her outerwear.

As previously commanded, Little Ian was waiting in the vestibule and, after helping the dowager into the carriage, went to sit with the driver. As they sat in the cab on their way to Whitechapel, the dowager considered how much to reveal to Withers. She wasn't sure just how much the servants knew of her Villiers Street adventure, but between her disappearance at the time, reappearance wearing this same plain dress, apparent association with the Tuchinsky family, or at least Bubbe, and Little Ian's establishment in the household, she was sure that tongues had wagged.

Finally, a decision was made, and the dowager said, "Withers, as you likely know, I have become associated with a Jewish family in the East End of London." Her maid said nothing but nodded. The cook, Mrs Anderson, had regaled the entire servant body with her story of visiting the Brick Lane kosher butcher, being told how to select the best fowl and spending the afternoon in Bubbe's kitchen learning how to make the chicken soup and lokshen pudding that the dowager so enjoyed.

The dowager continued, "Bubbe's granddaughter, Miriam Tuchinsky, has asked me to take on an investigation." The dowager wasn't sure it was necessary to reveal Tuchinsky's status as a feared East End gang leader just yet. It was unclear what, if anything, of Tuchinsky's business Anderson had intuited from her visit with Bubbe. Still, the dowager thought it not relevant to the investigation before her and saw no reason to confide in Withers more than necessary. "We are on our way to visit Mr Doherty, who is in a similar line of work to Miss Tuchinsky and has proven himself to be a valuable resource." Any thoughts that Withers might have on Mickey D and his line of work were again kept to herself.

The dowager said her next words quite deliberately, watching her maid's face for any reaction, "I have brought you with me so that you might act as an assistant of sorts. In reading the novels of Sir Arthur Conan Doyle, it has become clear that even the most brilliant of minds might benefit from a partner by his side, however much of a dullard such a companion might be by comparison." If it occurred to the dowager that a not-so-subtle insult lay behind her words, she certainly never acknowledged it. "I believe that you might be sharp but also discreet enough to act as a Watson to my Sherlock Holmes."

As she said these words, it occurred to the dowager that Withers might have no idea of the fictional character to whom she referred. She was almost certain that her maid could read, but even after thirty years of loyal service, the dowager had absolutely no idea what Withers did with her spare time. If she read novels, were they penny dreadfuls? As it happened, the dowager secretly indulged in the tawdry but immensely popular fiction, but she did so in the knowledge that she might read Theodor Fontane's *Irrungen, Wirrungen* in the original German if she chose.

Whatever she had expected her maid to say, the dowager was a little surprised but relieved when the other woman answered, "It would be my honour to be Dr Watson to your Holmes, m'lady." Withers, her face its usual mask of calm servitude, had always been quite inscrutable, something the dowager had appreciated for the past thirty years; no one wanted an emotional lady's maid. However, now she began to wonder if that very supposed virtue would, in fact, be a hindrance. When Tabitha and Wolf disagreed with something, their feelings on the matter were evident on their faces no matter their words. If Withers couldn't break the habit of a lifetime of agreeing with her mistress' every word and her true feelings on the matter were undecipherable, what good was she as a sounding board?

The dowager considered this dilemma, then said cautiously, "Withers, as a retainer, you have been an exemplar of discretion with a reserved manner that I have long appreciated." Withers gave a slight nod in acknowledgement of having spent almost her entire adult life biting her tongue around a difficult mistress. The dowager continued, "However, I believe that the endeavour we are undertaking requires a minor and highly localised modification to our relationship. In order for your turn as Watson to be effective in spurring on my genius I will need you to disagree with me."

The maid raised her eyebrows slightly. The dowager held up her hand to forestall any panic, "Not vehemently of course, and only when it is warranted. Moreover, I assume it goes without saying that any such expression of disagreement will be limited to conversations about an investigation and that you will not use this license to take additional liberties."

"Of course, m'lady." This was said with such deference that it did cause the dowager to wonder whether the maid would be able to oscillate between total complaisant and occasional, very specific and targeted dissent. Any further discussion on the topic was forestalled by their arrival at Mickey D's home in Whitechapel.

Chapter 5

After helping the dowager and Withers out of the carriage, Little Ian went and knocked on the door. As it usually was, the door was opened by Angie, Mickey D's common-law wife. Plump and rosy-cheeked, Angie beamed when she saw the huge man at her door. It had been months since Mickey D had released Little Ian to work instead for the dowager, and the motherly Mrs Doherty was delighted to see the sweet-natured man again.

Little Ian moved aside just a little so Angie could see her illustrious guest. Dropping into a curtsey, Angie said, "Your ladyship, what an honour. How may I help you?"

The dowager was contemptuous of most people in her aristocratic circles, considering them crashing bores at best and degenerate, hedonistic wastrels at worst. When it came to the middle classes, she was even more disdainful, if that were possible. Yet, to the amazement of those closest to her, the dowager somehow seemed to feel very differently about London's lowest classes, or at least some of them. Mickey D and Angie were two of those individuals. During Tabitha and Wolf's second investigation, the dowager had hosted Mickey D and Angie for dinner and had become quite enamoured of the couple, calling them, "A breath of fresh air."

Normally one to insist on the rules of social etiquette being strictly adhered to, the dowager put out her hand to Angie, raising her up, saying, "Dear Mrs Doherty, there is no need for curtseying with such a dear friend."

Angie stood, "Are you here to see Mick, m'lady?"

"I am."

"I'm afraid he's not around. I'd send one of the lads for him, but he's gone to Brighton to help our Jeannie and Tommy out with a spot of bother." During their recent visit to Brighton, Tabitha, Wolf and the dowager had visited Mickey's brother, Paddy, who was married to Angie's sister, Jeanine, in the public house they ran. "I'm sorry you've come all this way for nothing. Can I offer you a cup of tea and some ginger biscuits? I've just made a fresh batch."

Angie's ginger biscuits were one of Wolf's favourite treats and the dowager had tried them multiple times. Accepting the offer, she followed Angie into the house, Little Ian and Withers not far behind.

Settled in the Doherty's simple but clean and comfortable parlour, a cup of tea in her hand, the dowager considered what she had wanted to ask the gang leader. "Mrs Doherty, I came seeking information about a case I have been asked to investigate, but it occurs to me that you might know almost as much as Mr Doherty."

Angie sat primly, hands in her lap, quite overawed by her illustrious visitor. This was not the first time that the dowager had been a guest in her house, but previously, Mickey D had hosted, and Angie had been able to escape to the kitchen. Now, she felt the full force of the dowager's eminence. While the dowager had never been anything less than gracious and charming towards the Dohertys, not usually behaviours associated with the old woman, nevertheless, Angie felt overawed in her company.

"If I can help in any way, m'lady," she assured the dowager.

The dowager considered how candid to be. Finally, decided that she would get nowhere by shilly-shallying, the dowager said, "I have been engaged by Miriam Tuchinsky. She is concerned that the recent murder of an Irish maid, so similar in technique to the style of the notorious Jack the Ripper, may spark new attacks against the Jewish community. She has asked me to discover who the killer is."

"Isn't that a job best left to the police?" Angie asked cautiously.

"One might conclude that," the dowager conceded. "However, the

Metropolitan Police were unable to apprehend a suspect in 1888, and five young women were brutally killed. I believe Tuchinsky has little faith that they will do better this time."

Then Angie voiced one of the dowager's own concerns, "And what if the killer turns out to be a Jew? I know that rumours flew around in eighty-eight, but some of them seemed to have legs."

"Indeed. I will face that hurdle if and when it presents itself. Meanwhile, is there anything you can tell me about this recent killing?"

"As it happens, I believe you've met the victim."

"I have?" the dowager exclaimed incredulously. She couldn't imagine how she might have come into contact with an Irish maid living in Whitechapel.

"Yes, the poor lass, Aoife, worked for Vicky Sharpe in Gunthorpe Street."

The dowager cast her mind back to her first attempt at a solo investigation in early November. She remembered her visit to Mrs Sharpe's brothel and her surprise at how ordinary-looking the maid was who answered the door. However, the dowager couldn't recall anything more about the girl; she wasn't given to considering servants too closely, except to notice when their service was anything less than exemplary.

Angie continued, "It was the girl's day off last Sunday. My understanding was that she had gone to church in the morning, as she always did, and then had met another maid in a local tavern for a spot of lunch. Afterwards, she went to visit her mammy up on Hanbury Street." Angie paused, unsure how much detail to go into. Finally, she decided that the dowager had come seeking information, so she should share all she knew. Angie continued, "Hanbury Street is where one of the killings was in 1888. Annie Chapman, God bless her soul. I had a passing acquaintance with the poor lass."

The dowager remembered little about the notorious Jack the Ripper killings. Almost a decade earlier, she had given little thought to and no care for the murder of prostitutes in the East End of London, a neighbourhood so seemingly far from her life and concerns that it might have been in the Far East. She could never have guessed that not only would she visit the area multiple times but that she would be well acquainted with multiple of its more colourful characters, including gang members and madams.

Perhaps reading the lack of knowledge of the murder on the dowager's face, Angie continued, "The papers liked to say that Annie, the victim, was a dollymop, but that wasn't the whole story now, was it? Was a time she was a respectable married woman with children. But the marriage had gone sour, and Annie had fallen on hard times. She tried to make ends meet by selling some crochet work and other bits and bobs, but it's not easy being a woman alone on the streets of Whitechapel. From what I remember, she did take a couple of regular johns, but she wasn't one of those women, hanging out on the street selling themselves to any Tom, Dick, and Harry."

While the dowager wasn't as convinced as Angie seemed to be that there was a meaningful shading of moral degradation within the activities of Ladies of the Night, she said nothing and let the other woman continue to tell her story. "Anyway, it was probably a week or so after that first gruesome killing of Mary Ann Nichols when poor Annie's body was found. Horribly mutilated, it was. I remember it well. I've known Cammy O'Brien, the mother of this new poor lass, Aoife, since I was a wee 'un. I remember all too well Cammy's shock at the murder ten years ago, and it happening two doors down from her. And now to think that it's been her own lass killed by that monster."

These words struck the dowager, who said, "So you believe that this young maid was killed by the same man who called himself Jack the Ripper ten years ago?"

"Stands to reason, doesn't it?" Angie claimed. "Same methods, same neighbourhood."

"However," the dowager felt compelled to point out, "from what I do remember of the murders, little as it is, all of the victims then were engaged in prostitution, to one extent or another, were they not?" Angie nodded in agreement. "Moreover, it has been ten years. Why did this Jack the Ripper stop after those five murders, and why suddenly start again? Is it not more likely that this is either an unfortunate coincidence or a diabolical imitator?"

It was evident that neither of these questions had crossed Angie's mind. She considered them and shrugged her shoulders. "I've not a mind to worry about the hows or whys. It's enough to know that someone is abroad killing young lasses again. I've told my girls to stay close to home and that, if they have to run errands, to take one of the lads with them."

Withers had been sitting in a chair in the corner of the room, silently shrinking into the shadows as befitted a servant. Angie had shot her a couple of curious glances but hadn't inquired who the stern-looking woman accompanying the dowager was.

Now, the woman seemed to sit up a little straighter, pulling herself out of the gloom of the corner she had been sitting so quietly in. The dowager noticed the change in her maid's posture and asked, "Withers, do you have something to add to the conversation?"

Such a question had never been asked before by the dowager of any servant and certainly was outside of Wither's long experience as the woman's lady's maid. However, the conversation she and the dowager had engaged in during the carriage ride had spurred her to break with her usual role as invisible companion. "I do, m'lady," Withers said hesitantly.

"Then out with it, woman."

"I followed the murders quite closely in eighty-eight," Withers explained. Given that the dowager hadn't been totally certain the woman could even read, the idea that she was a regular reader of newspapers and kept up to date with current affairs surprised her employer. "The general feeling at the time, after the fifth murder, was that the public's heightened awareness and the police's increased activity in Whitechapel had deterred the killer from continuing his spree. At the time, there were volunteer groups, many from the Jewish community, patrolling the area every evening, and there was even a reward offered for the Ripper's capture. Perhaps, with all this attention, he left London but has now returned," she theorised.

The dowager sniffed. It was unclear if this sniff was directed at her maid in response to the woman's unusual interjection into a conversation or a judgment on the likelihood of her theory. Whatever the reason, it was response enough to cause Withers to sink back into the shadows.

It soon became clear that Angie Doherty had little more to add. She hadn't seen Aoife O'Brien since she was a child and had lost touch with Cammy. She was happy to give the dowager the woman's address on Hanbury Street. After allowing herself one more of the delicious ginger biscuits, the dowager thanked Angie for her hospitality and left the Doherty residence.

Back in the carriage, Withers seemed as if she was expecting to be berated for her comments. Instead, the dowager said, "I believe that our next call will be to Mrs Sharpe in Gunthorpe Street. Narrowing her eyes a little as she looked at her lady's maid, the dowager said with uncharacteristic concern for someone else's sensitivities, "Withers, I must warn you that Mrs Sharpe runs a brothel. In the course of my recent investigation, I had cause to enter multiple such establishments and engage with their inhabitants. I understand that you may not have a spine made of iron, as mine is. If you would prefer to wait in the carriage, I will not hold that against you."

Withers wasn't sure what she was more surprised at, that her aristocratic mistress was no stranger to houses of ill repute or that she was considerate enough to offer her maid the option not to join her in a visit to one. Whichever it was, she replied, "Thank you, m'lady. I feel that it is my duty, both as your maid and as your Dr Watson, to attempt to replicate your fortitude and accompany you."

The dowager's slightly raised eyebrows revealed her thoughts on the likelihood of a servant, or indeed any mere mortal, managing to match her strength of character. Nevertheless, she inclined her head, accepting her maid's words.

Chapter 6

Over dinner, Tabitha and Wolf discussed how best to begin the investigation. They had asked Bear to join them; he was originally from Whitechapel and was even more familiar with the various factions in the neighbourhood than Wolf.

"I think that there's an obvious place to start," Bear observed.

"Bruiser?" Wolf guessed, referring to the Whitechapel detective inspector with a rather fluid sense of morality. Bear nodded. Bruiser had grown up in Whitechapel alongside the criminals he was now supposed to be arresting. He had earned his nickname, Bruiser, from the many street fights he'd won as a youth. While Bruiser was feared by the criminals and respected by the locals, he also wasn't above supplementing his income on occasion by working on the other side of the law. More than anyone, Bruiser had his ear to the ground and was likely to know what word was on the streets of Whitechapel about this latest murder.

"Then let us make our way to The Cock tomorrow morning." As Wolf said these words, Tabitha looked at him expectantly. Since inheriting the earldom, Wolf had made multiple visits back to his old stomping ground, the public house in the heart of Whitechapel that was popular with local working men and criminals. Whether it was to The Cock or elsewhere in Whitechapel, Wolf had refused to allow Tabitha to accompany him on most of his previous visits to the East End, bar one, a visit to see Mickey D. On that occasion, Tabitha had disguised herself as a young man. At the time, despite Wolf's feelings to the contrary, she had been sure that her disguise was successful. Since then, Tabitha had come to realise that she hadn't fooled Mickey D for a moment and accepted that perhaps her attempt to pass herself off as male hadn't been very convincing.

Wolf had always said that he both wished to shield Tabitha from the horrors of one of London's poorest and more disreputable neighbourhoods, as well as to attempt to shield his new status as Earl of Pembroke. When he had first inherited the title, Wolf had made a point of not alerting anyone from his old life as a thief-taker. Instead, he had done his best to ensure that word was spread by local gossip that he had merely left town for an extended period.

On his occasional visits back to Whitechapel, Wolf had donned his clothes from his thief-taking days and had done his best not to draw attention to himself. However, he was aware that driving up Brick Lane in the Pembroke carriage, as he had been forced to in order to rescue the dowager from Tuchinsky's clutches, had likely blown that story. While Brick Lane hadn't been one of his East End haunts, strictly speaking, the Whitechapel, Spitalfields, and Shoreditch neighbourhoods were not so large that news wouldn't have spread of the toffs who now associated with the Jewish gangsters.

Over time, Wolf had come to realise that his Earl of Pembroke persona probably helped more than it harmed in investigations; most people were in awe of the aristocracy and, particularly when he assumed the mannerisms, voice, and condescension reminiscent of his grandfather, it was amazing what people could be persuaded to do and say. So, perhaps it was more positive than negative that the acquaintances from his old life now knew of his change in fortune.

As for Wolf's attempts to shield Tabitha, she had impressed on him that she neither needed nor wanted to be protected from the harsher realities of life. He had accused her in the past of being naive when it came to the world outside of her gilded life in Mayfair, and she'd agreed and argued that she wanted to understand more but couldn't if he kept her wrapped in cotton wool. In fairness to Wolf, he had taken her comments to heart and had made a genuine effort to involve Tabitha in aspects of investigations from which he had formally shied away from exposing her. However, Tabitha was curious to see if this would extend to taking her to The Cock to meet Bruiser.

Tabitha had been correct in her thinking about Wolf's initial instincts; he had no intention of taking her with him. She was also correct that Wolf had been making a genuine effort to curb such instincts and to accept that he neither could nor should protect her from the world's harshness. He had fallen in love with Tabitha because of her compassion, her bravery, and her intelligence. The only way to demonstrate his genuine appreciation for these traits was not to forget about them situationally in order to make himself feel more comfortable when a potentially difficult set of circumstances arose.

Finally, addressing Tabitha and Bear, Wolf said, "Given that it is highly likely that my good fortune and new status is now known throughout the East End, I see no reason to pretend otherwise. While I see no reason to flaunt my wealth, we will take the Pembroke Carriage and not wear our old clothes." Then, turning to Tabitha, he continued, "I'm sure it goes without saying that you should not wear your best jewels – you are not the dowager countess, after all. However, I would suggest wearing one of your plainer gowns."

Tabitha beamed, "Thank you, Wolf. This means a lot."

Wolf made a noise in his throat that sounded suspiciously like one of the dowager's harrumphs. So like one, in fact, that both Bear and Tabitha had to try hard not to smirk. It was evident that, while Wolf had immediately accepted her accompanying them the following day, he was hardly reconciled to it.

Wolf knew from long experience that mid-morning was a likely time to find the detective inspector in The Cock enjoying a tankard of ale and a meat pie. His excuse, if ever he had been asked, was that sitting in The Cock for an hour or two each day, he found out everything he needed to know about what was happening on the streets of Whitechapel. Deals were made there, crimes were planned, and palms were greased. Of course, given the dual nature of Bruiser's professional life, using his badge and authority to intimidate criminals, making it clear that they would have to pay up if they wanted to operate in Whitechapel, and also turning a blind eye to the activities of the gang bosses who kept him on their payroll, it was also a very practical place to situate himself on a regular basis.

Tabitha, Wolf, and Bear had agreed to meet after breakfast and make their way to Whitechapel. The ride was not long, but it could have been a thousand miles for how dissimilar the two neighbourhoods were. Unlike the wide, well-maintained thoroughfares in Mayfair and its environs, the streets of Whitechapel were a tangle of narrow roads and bustling alleys. The streets teemed with people going about their business, legal or otherwise.

Rows of tightly packed, rundown tenement buildings shared the streets with shops and bustling market stalls selling everything from soap to live chickens. Cobblestone pavements echoed with the constant clatter of horse-drawn carriages and the chatter of pedestrians talking in various languages and accents, creating a lively, yet chaotic, atmosphere. An interesting mix of odours filled the air as smoke from nearby factories mingled with the smells of the food being sold by the street vendors. An energy pulsated through the neighbourhood, yet looking out of the window at the streets they were driving through, Tabitha could sense the underlying poverty and hardship felt by the people of Whitechapel who were struggling to survive and take care of their families.

Despite the desperation that lingered in the air, as strong as the pungent-spiced jellied eels and vinegar-scented pickled herring, Tabitha shivered with excitement. Apart from her visit to Whitechapel in disguise, she had been to Mickey D's and then to Brick Lane when they were in search of the dowager who had disappeared. However, neither of those times had the same sense of risk and attendant thrill as this visit to one of the most notorious public houses in the East End. Against Wolf's better judgement, she had visited public houses in Edinburgh and Brighton. On both those occasions, Wolf had made sure to rush her through to the somewhat more civilised saloon bar.

Tabitha knew that on this occasion, he would have to accept her presence in the public bar, and she could hardly wait. Reflecting on her eager anticipation of the adventure ahead, Tabitha did wonder a little guiltily if she were no better than the dowager, thinking only of the "fun" of an escapade. However, she shook herself out of such contemplation and considered what they might learn from Bruiser.

Wolf had similar thoughts running through his head. "How do you believe we should approach this interview?" he asked Bear.

His long-time friend and confidante, who knew Bruiser even better and for longer than Wolf had, considered the question. "I think we should begin by getting the facts, at least as far as the police know them. In what ways was this murder similar to the ones of eighty-eight? Do the police really believe that Jack the Ripper has struck again ten years later?"

Wolf agreed with these suggestions. It was one thing to hear Langley's opinion from the lofty perch of British Intelligence, but what did the bobbies on the street think?

Bear continued, "I remember that we had recently met when the murders began that August."

"Yes, I stormed out of my father's house and made my way to London in July."

Tabitha knew little about how Bear and Wolf had first met, and was hopeful that this would be an opportunity for the men to open up, but she was to be disappointed. Instead, Wolf said, "We had met but hadn't yet started to work together. I was still hoping to make my fortune through less disreputable means." Bear and Wolf both smiled at the memory. "I do remember vaguely this constant hum of accusation against the Jews that ran through the East End."

"I remember my mother commented on it," Bear said. "We used to have our knives sharpened by a Jew, and Ma had far more sympathy for the community than some of our neighbours did." Tabitha and Wolf knew Bear's mother, Mrs Caruthers, well, and both could imagine such a compassionate response from the woman.

While the streets of Mayfair were also cobblestoned, the constant bumping of the carriage indicated that these roads were in far greater disrepair. Tabitha hoped that they were almost at The Cock because she was starting to feel quite ill from the trip. Luckily, in less than five minutes, they had pulled up outside of the public house. The outside of the building looked as if it could do with a fresh coat of paint and the windows with a good cleaning. A large, hand-painted sign featuring a rooster was swinging in the wind next to the door. Every swing of the sign creaked, an almost painful sound to listen to. Tabitha was glad when Wolf moved them into the public house quickly.

Tabitha wasn't sure what she had expected The Cock to look like. In many ways, it was not unlike the taverns she had been in previously: dimly lit and smelling of stale beer and tobacco smoke. However, even next to the public houses in Edinburgh and Brighton, The Cock was filled with an unsavoury-looking bunch of characters, and that was saying something. The Cock's patrons were a rough crowd of mostly dockworkers, factory workers and criminals who spent their evenings drinking away their wages. At this time of the morning, the workers were mostly absent, and the criminals had the place to themselves.

The publican was a gruff and burly man named Bill, known to many as Old One-eye because of the empty eye socket, now sewn up. The man was surly, and quick to eject anyone causing trouble or refusing to pay. However, Wolf had reason to know that the man did not lack compassion; he had let Rat and Melody sleep in his cellar after their parents died. In addition, Wolf had done the man a favour many years ago which he had always remembered. Back in his thief-taking days, Wolf and Bear had used The Cock as something of an informal office; people always knew that they could either find them there or leave a message for them with Old One-eye.

Seeing the threesome enter the bar dressed as the toffs they were, even if they had dressed down, Old One-eye raised an eyebrow. Like many others in Whitechapel, word of Wolf's good fortune had reached the publican. Even more reason why he was surprised to see Wolf resurface in the East End.

Hitching his chin slightly, he indicated a free table over in the corner. As it happened, Bruiser was seated nearby. Wolf led the way over to the small, round table.

CHAPTER 7

Bruiser was busy eating one of his favourite meat pies. At first glance, Tabitha could see how he might have earned his nickname; even though clearly well into middle age, the man retained the look of a street fighter. He had a thick neck and a nose that looked as if it had been broken more than once. One of his earlobes was missing a chunk, and the hands that held a meat pie in the left and a tankard in the right looked as if they could do some real damage if they happened to collide with a man's face.

The detective inspector seemed as curious about Tabitha as she was about him. Bruiser put down his pie and ale, wiped some crumbs and foam off his greying moustache, and eyed her with interest. Then his glance turned to Wolf. As they had discussed the night before, while Wolf wasn't decked out in the finery that his valet Thompson most desired him to be seen in at all times, his clothes were well-tailored, and it was evident that they were made of the finest cloth.

"Decided to stop playacting Wolf the thief-taker and embrace your new status as a toff, Wolf? Or should I say, your lordship?" Bruiser asked sardonically. Given that this was exactly what Wolf had decided, he made no answer. Instead, Bruiser looked back at Tabitha and asked, "And who is your lovely companion?"

"Detective Inspector Christie, may I introduce the Countess of Pembroke."

Bruiser had remained seated up until this point, but now he stood and offered Tabitha a nod of the head that might have counted as a sort of half-bow. "Your late cousin's wife, from what I understand," Bruiser said, indicating that he'd kept up with Wolf's life since he had left Whitechapel. Wolf made no reply. Instead, he indicated that Tabitha should take a seat, and then he followed suit, settling into the chairs at the next table, which was so close to Bruiser's that they would be able to talk in relative privacy.

"I assume that you are not all decked out in your finery merely for the entertainment of slumming it at The Cock," Bruiser observed.

Wolf ignored the man's sarcastic tone and replied, "What can you tell me about the recent murder of the Irish maid? The one that bore a chilling resemblance to the Ripper's killings."

"Now, which of your high-born friends has an interest in the murder of an unimportant colleen?" Bruiser asked in a nasty voice, using the slang for an Irish girl.

"That's none of your business, Bruiser. Suffice it to say, there are concerns that either the Ripper is at work again, or someone wants to scare people into believing that."

Bruiser picked up his tankard and took another sip of his ale, "And the people with these concerns don't believe that the Metropolitan Police are capable of handling this matter and need the help of the likes of you and her?"

Wolf barked out an incredulous laugh, "Do you believe the police are capable of handling this? You never caught him in eighty-eight, after all."

Bruiser had the good grace to look a little chastened by this. "I was just a beat copper back then, but for the latest one, I was called to the scene. It wasn't a pretty sight, I can tell you." Glancing over at Tabitha with concern, he said, "Let's just say, if it's not Jack the Ripper, it was at least as gruesome."

"Detective Inspector Christie, there is no need to edit your speech on my account," Tabitha said firmly. "Say what you must."

"There was blood everywhere. The girl's throat had been slashed, her private areas stabbed multiple times, and her innards were falling out of a gaping hole in her abdomen. In all my time on the force, I've never seen anything like it." The man quickly explained, "I never saw the original victims, only heard about them. But nothing I heard prepared me to see it. Gruesome it was. I thought I'd seen some horrific things in my more than twenty years working these streets, but I've never seen anything like that."

Tabitha paled at the man's words but managed to keep her face immobile. "Detective Inspector, were the wounds considered similar enough to the original mutilations that a link between the killings was suspected immediately?" she asked.

"We brought in one of the bobbies who was working with Chief Inspector Abberline at the time; he's a sergeant these days with a cushy desk job. He took one look and just nodded his head. He couldn't even find the words. I hope I never see anything like it again," the man admitted.

When Langley had asked Wolf to take on the case, he had given him all the known details about the victim, Aoife O'Brien. Thinking back to that conversation, Wolf said, "From what I've been told, one of the salient differences between this killing and the ones ten years ago is that, back then, all the victims were involved in some sort of prostitution. There doesn't seem to be any evidence that this Irish maid was. Or is there something that the papers haven't reported?" Wolf doubted that there was anything that Bruiser knew about the victim that Langley and British Intelligence didn't, but he was curious to hear what the man had to say.

"Well, there was the fact that she was a maid for Mother Sharpe. So, even if she wasn't a dollymop, she worked for one. Perhaps the killer thought it was close enough."

Wolf considered the man's words; perhaps there was something to the sentiment of "close enough."

Tabitha seemed to be thinking along the same lines and said, "Perhaps the killer knew that Mrs Sharpe runs a brothel, saw Aoife leaving one day, not in her maid's outfit, and assumed that she was one of the ladies working there in a particular capacity. Is that possible?"

Bruiser chuckled, "Particular capacity? Is that what we're calling it? But, to answer your question, it's certainly possible. We know that Aoife O'Brien was killed on her day off, so she left the house wearing something other than her maid's uniform. If the killer wasn't a local, there would be no reason for him to be able to distinguish the dollymops from the other girls working there."

Wolf thought that Tabitha's observation was a very interesting one, but there were still things that didn't add up. "Yet, if he wanted to kill a streetwalker, there are certainly enough of those hanging around the streets of Whitechapel. Why wait around for this girl? Also, weren't all the original victims much older than this maid?"

"Of the ones we thought were murdered by the same killer, four were older, but the last, Mary Jane Kelly, was only twenty-five. Aoife O'Brien was about the same age. Also, not all the original victims were street-walkers in the strictest sense of the term. From what I remember, Annie Chapman really had two regulars. I'm sure that she supplemented what-ever she made with a bit of streetwalking when she had to though," he acknowledged.

Bear had gone to the bar to order some drinks. He knew that Wolf had a particular fondness for The Cock's meat pies, so he had ordered a couple. He wasn't sure what to get Tabitha to drink and finally settled on half a pint of small beer. At this point in the conversation, he returned to the table with the drinks and said the pies would be over shortly. Tabitha confirmed that she was not hungry and that the small beer would be acceptable.

"You look like you've gone up in the world, Bear," Bruiser observed, looking the giant man up and down and noticing that his suit, while not as obviously expensive as Wolf's, also bore the hallmarks of good tailoring. "Being friends with an earl pays well, it seems."

Bear ignored this slight; he didn't care what anyone in Whitechapel, particularly Bruiser, thought of his elevation in position with Wolf's change in fortunes. In the months since they had moved to Chesterton House, it had been important for Bear to feel that he had some purpose in the household and was not merely the new earl's friend who drank his wine and slept on his fine linens. After holding the nominal role of valet for a brief time, he was now established as Wolf's private secretary and was busy learning all he could about the Pembroke Estate and Wolf's business holdings. He was comfortable in the position he held and his value to Wolf as a secretary and as an associate in his investigations and felt no need to explain himself to anyone.

The food arrived. As wonderful as the food made by Mrs Smith, Wolf's cook, was, he still missed the pies at The Cock, washed down by its better-than-average ale. He took his first bite and sighed with pleasure. He wasn't sure it was even worth asking Mrs Smith to try to replicate the recipe. The likelihood was that she would insist on using the finest ingredients, and he suspected that these would somehow detract from what made these meat pies so good. Wolf was sure that his cook wouldn't appreciate the suggestion that she buy her meat and veg from a barrow on Petticoat Lane.

Finally, his initial hunger satiated, Wolf asked, "Do the police have any suspects at this point?"

"Well, we looked back at all the suspects from eighty-eight. Some are dead; one, Kosminski, who was one of the likeliest suspects at the time, has been in an asylum for the last decade. One emigrated to America. There's only one, at least one who was a serious contender back then, who we thought was still alive and living in Whitechapel: a John Pizer, who was known as 'Leather Apron.' We arrested him at the time, but he had alibis for each of the killings."

"Leather Apron?" Tabitha asked. "What kind of name is that?"

"Well, back then, there were rumours of a man wearing a leather apron, a Jew, who was harassing and even attacking the dollymops." Tabitha realised that this was the suspect that Wolf had told her about and nodded her head. Bruiser continued, "This John Pizer seemed to fit the description of the man. He had firm alibis but even after he was exonerated, the man had a hard time of it, never able to shake the stench of the accusation fully."

"Have you talked to Mr Pizer about this latest murder?" Bear asked.

"We went looking for him, and it turns out he'd died of gastroenteritis last July. So that was the end of that road. As far as we can tell, no one was a suspect before who is still alive and living in London," Bruiser admitted, shaking his head at how much harder this investigation was going to be than it might have been.

"All of which supports the theory that this is either totally unrelated and just coincidentally gruesome, or the work of someone imitating the infamous Jack the Ripper."

Thirty minutes later, they were back in the carriage. "I think we need to visit Vicky Sharpe and learn more about the victim," Wolf said.

Chapter 8

Whatever Tabitha and Wolf had expected on arriving at Gunthorpe Street, the very last thing they had imagined seeing was the dowager's carriage with its matching Pembroke insignia to their own conveyance.

"Blasted woman! What on earth is she doing here? How does she even know we're investigating the murder?" Wolf exclaimed a little more passionately than he intended.

Tabitha's reaction had not been dissimilar to Wolf's. Still, in an attempt to calm him, she suggested, "We do not know that Mama is inserting herself into this investigation. She continues to associate with the group of madams she refers to as the Ladies of KB. Perhaps she also has remained in touch with Mrs Sharpe." If the Dowager Countess of Pembroke could continue to fraternise with one group of women who ran brothels, why not maintain a friendship with others?

Tabitha's words did calm Wolf slightly. Nevertheless, he leapt out of the carriage and charged towards Mother Sharpe's establishment even before Tabitha had been helped out of the carriage by Bear. Such ungentlemanly behaviour was unheard of from Wolf, and Tabitha knew it spoke to his agitation. She and Bear followed him and reached the unassuming house with the blue front door just as he was rapping its knocker.

Tabitha noticed that the house did not have any of the traditional trappings of a house in mourning. Of course, it was not unusual for the death of a servant not to be accompanied by the closed curtains and black cloth draped over the front door customary when a family member died. She could also imagine that Mrs Sharpe would be unwilling to do anything that might scare off business.

It took a few minutes longer than expected for someone to answer the door, but the household was down a maid. Finally, the door was opened by Mrs Sharpe herself. Or at least that was who Tabitha assumed the petite old woman with silver hair and dark blue eyes was. When the dowager had first met Vicky Sharpe some months before, she had taken on a case investigating the woman's twin sister's disappearance. In service of this investigation, the dowager had pretended to be a cousin to the Sharpe sisters. Looking at the woman in the doorway, Tabitha could see how that might have been a believable ruse.

Vicky Sharpe looked extremely surprised, but not unhappy, to see Wolf and Bear on her doorstep. She glanced at Tabitha but did not comment. Instead, she said, "Wolf, Bear, what an unexpected pleasure. How can I help you?"

"May we come in, Vicky?" Wolf asked. "We have some questions for you."

Vicky Sharpe paused and seemed unsure how to answer. Wolf continued, "I believe that the dowager countess is also visiting you."

Vicky Sharpe nodded, then stepped aside to let them in. She led them down the hallway to her study at the back of the house. The room only had two armchairs, so she asked Bear if he would fetch additional chairs from the parlour.

Tabitha and Wolf entered the room behind Vicky Sharpe and saw the dowager comfortably ensconced in an armchair by the fire, enjoying a cup of tea and a slice of cake. She looked up at their entrance, seemingly as surprised to see them there as they were to see her. They also noticed Withers sitting quietly in the corner. It was unusual for the dowager to take her maid with her as a companion. Tabitha wondered what that was all about but was distracted from the thought by the dowager's belligerent greeting. "Tabitha, Jeremy, what on earth are you doing here?" she demanded.

The dowager's first thought had been that Tabitha and Wolf had somehow learned about her investigation and had chased her down to castigate her and insist that she desist. Her hackles immediately up, the dowager glared at them. Bear followed Tabitha and Wolf into the room with a chair in each hand and insisted that he would take himself off to the kitchen. Everyone quickly seated themselves, and the dowager repeated her question, "What are you doing here? Have you followed me?"

"Mama, we had no idea you would be here," Tabitha said with utter sincerity. "Nothing could have come as a greater surprise as we pulled up."

The dowager narrowed her eyes suspiciously, "Then what are you doing here? While I might believe that dear Jeremy is visiting an old friend, there is nothing you can say, Tabitha, that will persuade me that you accompanying him is benign."

Realising the truth of the dowager's words, Tabitha and Wolf knew there was nothing they could say that would be believable. Wolf glanced at Tabitha and then said truthfully, "We are investigating the murder of Mrs Sharpe's maid."

"No, you are not!" the dowager exclaimed so vehemently that she jolted her teacup and sloshed tea into the saucer. "I am investigating the murder!"

Tabitha and Wolf's amazement at this explanation was no less than the dowager's at theirs. "What do you mean you are investigating?" Wolf asked. "Did Langley ask you to look into it as well?" As soon as he said these words, Wolf realised how implausible they were and how foolish he was to have shown his hand in this way. He couldn't imagine anything less likely than that Lord Langley had chosen to speak to the dowager and had voluntarily asked her to involve herself in the investigation. He certainly couldn't imagine Langley doing so without warning him first.

Having tipped his hand so thoroughly, Wolf was not surprised that the dowager pounced on his explanation like a cat done playing with a mouse and now ready to inflict the final brutal end. "Langley? Langley has somehow inserted himself into my investigation, the one that Tuchinsky asked me, and only me, to take on? And as if that were not bad enough, he has pulled you in to interfere!"

Tabitha and Wolf looked at each other, thoroughly confused about what was happening. "Mama, Tuchinsky asked you to take on a case? This case? The murder of Aoife O'Brien? Why would she do that?"

The dowager put down her teacup and saucer and threw back her shoulders, "Because, and I quote, I am eminently capable. Furthermore, as she pointed out, when Mr Doherty wanted to recommend someone to help Mrs Sharpe, he turned to me and not to you and Jeremy."

While this was true, Wolf had always been suspicious of Mickey D's motives in doing so. He didn't mention this but instead asked, "Why does Tuchinsky care about the death of an Irish maid?"

Tabitha answered this question for him, suddenly understanding the Jewish gang leader's reason, "Because the killings in 1888 caused terrible prejudice and even violence against the Jews of the East End, and she is worried that fears that Jack the Ripper has resurfaced will do so again."

"Indeed, Tabitha," the dowager said, adopting a tone of one in the know. "As a leader in her community, Tuchinsky feels an obligation, an admirable obligation, to protect her fellow Jews from a resurgence of what they suffered last time." Privately, Tabitha wondered whether "leader in the community" was the appropriate moniker for a criminal who extorted her neighbours for protection. The dowager continued, "After making some inquiries, I determined it expeditious to speak to Mrs Sharpe about her maidservant."

"Indeed," Vicky Sharpe confirmed, "and I was happy to see her ladyship and answer her questions. After all she did to determine what happened to poor Margery, I was grateful to learn that she is now looking into poor Aoife's murder. I will never forget what she did to help uncover my sister's murderers."

Tabitha and Wolf exchanged looks. There seemed no point in disabusing Vicky Sharpe of the notion that the dowager had uncovered the truth about her twin's disappearance. While it was true that the dowager's meddling insistence on establishing herself in the Villiers Street brothel had eventually flushed the killers out, that was hardly the same thing as solving the case.

Vicky continued, "I have told her ladyship all I can about Aoife and what I know of that day; it isn't much."

It was evident from these words that Vicky Sharpe had no interest in retelling the story. However, there was one question which Wolf was doubtful the dowager would have asked already, "Vicky, did Aoife ever take on any clients of her own?" He gave a particular emphasis to the word 'clients' and was sure Vicky would understand his meaning.

The madam shook her head, "Aoife comes from a good Irish Catholic family. I know that her parents were horrified enough that she was even working for me as a maid. All that kept them from insisting that she stop was that I pay more than double what she might hope to make in most other jobs in Whitechapel. I even pay more than many of your fancy Mayfair neighbours do. And because I pay so well, she would have no reason to supplement her wages. My girls are those who would rather earn their money on their backs than on their knees scrubbing floors, but at least in my house, there's not much of a difference in earnings between the two kinds of work. "

Wolf acknowledged the woman's words but pressed further, "I understand that Aoife was not working for you in that capacity, but is it possible that she took on clients on her day off?"

"As I told her ladyship, to the best of my knowledge, on her days off, Aoife went to church, met her friend and then went to spend the rest of the day and evening by her family. I have no reason to believe that she did anything but that. She's my cook's niece and I think I would have heard if Aoife was getting herself into any trouble."

Tabitha doubted that a young woman would confide in an aunt if she decided to become a prostitute on the side, but she also couldn't imagine why Aoife would if she was making good coin as a maid. Unless they found evidence otherwise, the most plausible explanation was that if this new killer was targeting prostitutes, then he erroneously believed that his victim was one on seeing her leave Mother Sharpe's brothel.

It appeared that they had nothing more to learn from Vicky Sharpe. What Wolf wanted to do was to visit Aoife O'Brien's family and talk to them. However, he realised that there was no way that the dowager was going to agree to be excluded from the interview and they all needed to resolve their current standoff before taking the investigation any further.

Standing and thanking Vicky Sharpe for her time, he said to the dowager, "Lady Pembroke, might I suggest that we reconvene at Chesterton House and discuss our overlapping investigations?"

"Overlapping investigations, hah! Is that what we are calling your interference in my case? I will follow you to Chesterton House in order to discuss this matter but be assured that I will be continuing to investigate the matter that I have been asked to look into."

Wolf saw no reason to continue to debate this topic in front of Vicky Sharpe and suggested that they each take their carriage and make their way back to Chesterton House. The dowager agreed.

A few minutes later, alone in their Pembroke carriage, Tabitha asked, "What are we going to do? You know she will not be dissuaded. She clung like grim death to the investigation into Margery Sharpe's murder and, having been asked by Tuchinsky to do so again, I cannot imagine her being any less tenacious."

Wolf knew she was right but still couldn't help shaking his head in exasperation. "So, what is to be done? I cannot imagine Langley being happy to have her involved. This is an investigation on behalf of British Intelligence, for goodness' sake."

"Mama has proven to have her uses," Tabitha pointed out. "Many of our cases would have been far more difficult to resolve, one might even say would not have been resolved, without her help."

"Help? Is that what you call what she did in Wales?" Wolf demanded. "The woman got Rat involved again, and he almost died. She went weeks without telling us the truth about why she wanted to return to Pembrokeshire, and we still do not know the entire story. If that is the kind of help she is going to provide, I think we can do without it."

Tabitha sighed; she knew his anger and frustration were entirely justified. However, she also knew that they were stuck with the dowager whether they liked it or not, and replied, "Regardless, we both know that it will be easier, and likely safer, for all of us if we include her from the beginning." Tabitha paused, considered her words then continued, "I believe that the bigger question is not whether we are prepared to involve her, but rather if she is prepared to involve us. She believes that this is her investigation and may choose to go off, cocksure that she is more than capable alone."

"And I can only imagine how much more difficult that will make things for us," Wolf acknowledged.

"Exactly. We have already seen evidence of that today; we were unable to question Mrs Sharpe thoroughly because she felt she had already been interviewed sufficiently. However, not only do we not know what Mama may have failed to ask or follow up on, but we were unable to see Vicky Sharpe's facial expressions as she answered and so will only have Mama's opinion, at best, on her candour."

"Indeed. I know that you are right, Tabitha. I see that we have no choice but not only to invite her to join us but to plead with her to do so. I can only imagine how obsequious we will have to be in order to placate her."

Tabitha smiled, she had a good idea how much they would have to prostrate themselves, and it was going to be a hard pill to swallow.

CHAPTER 9

The roads were quite busy on the return journey to Chesterton House, and Tabitha and Wolf reached Mayfair before the dowager. During the drive, they had agreed that Lord Langley needed to be alerted to the new complication in their investigation. So, even before he had removed his outerwear, Wolf had Talbot put a telephone call through to Langley House. A telephone had been installed at Chesterton House by the dowager without Wolf's consent or even knowledge, and Langley's mother had installed one at her son's residence. Despite his initial irritation, both at the device and at the manner in which it had been forced on his household, Wolf now had to admit that it could be useful.

Wolf quickly apprised Tabitha of his brief conversation with Langley, "He is on his way. If we are lucky, he might even be here before Lady Pembroke arrives."

Tabitha had quickly thrown off her outerwear and had retired to the drawing room to prepare herself for the conversation ahead. As it happened, she had more sympathy for the dowager's insistence on involving herself in investigations than Wolf did. After all, hadn't she, herself, insisted that she be involved fully with Wolf's activities when he had tried to sideline and shield her? And hadn't she also been thrilled by the intellectual challenge and excitement that the investigations had injected into what had been a dull and monotonous life previously? How could she blame the other woman for her glee at having new, important challenges when she had spent most of her long life unable to utilise her intelligence and skills on anything more important than trivial manipulations of members of the upper class?

Nevertheless, she knew her erstwhile mother-in-law well enough to realise that the situation before them needed to be handled with great care. While they had dealt with killers before, this investigation was different; these murders were horrifically gruesome and seemingly random. This was far more dangerous than anything they had investigated previously, and she and Wolf were concerned that the dowager did not grasp the importance of not approaching this with her normal insouciance, as if no one would dare harm the Dowager Countess of Pembroke. It was likely they were dealing with a killer who neither knew nor cared about the old woman's pre-eminence in aristocratic circles and would not be cowed by gossip about how she had, on multiple occasions, even caused the Prince of Wales to wither.

They only had to wait a few minutes before Langley was shown into the room. While Langley House wasn't very far from their own, Tabitha and Wolf were surprised at the speed with which he had made the trip. Clearly, he was as anxious about the dowager's interference as they were.

Without even greeting them, Langley said breathlessly, "How did this happen?"

"Lord Langley, take a seat and compose yourself. Mama is not far behind us, and you are better off dealing with this situation with equanimity," Tabitha advised.

Recognising the wisdom of her words, Langley took a deep breath, then came and sat near her in an armchair. They had hoped to apprise him of the situation more fully before the dowager arrived, but that plan was scuttled when they heard the woman's strident voice as she entered the house, berating Talbot for his tardiness in taking her coat.

Finally, sweeping into the room, she noticed Langley harrumphed and said acidly, "It did not take you very long to tattle on me, did it, Jeremy?"

Standing at her entrance, Lord Langley bowed his head briefly and replied, "Lady Pembroke, it was entirely appropriate that Lord Pembroke alert me as to the situation. I asked him to investigate on behalf of the government. Not a request to be taken lightly."

If Langley had hoped to chasten the old woman, he was to be disappointed. Though having known her his entire life, he realised that it was probably too much to hope that his words would appropriately subdue her. Instead, she took a seat, stared him down, and said, "Maxwell, I cannot imagine why you believe that a request by this bumbling bunch of incompetents we are governed by is more important than the party on whose behalf I am investigating. Why, I remember Salisbury when he was a snot-nosed third son in short trousers. I never thought much of him then, and I still have my doubts."

No one had any desire to inspire the dowager to list her grievances with the policies of the Conservative government, particularly those around Irish land reform. While Salisbury's government could not be called anything other than cautious and minimalist when it came to its policies towards Ireland, the dowager still considered its incremental moves towards reform to be outrageous. She had told Lord Salisbury so more than once when the Prime Minister had been unfortunate enough to attend the same soirees as she had.

Instead, Langley tried another approach, "Lady Pembroke, dear Lady Pembroke, I am concerned for your safety."

"Ha! I am not sure when I last heard such poppycock, Maxwell. Do you really know me so little that you believe that I can be mollified with such transparent insincerity?" Tabitha shot Langley a look of exasperation; she also couldn't believe he was so naive.

The dowager continued, "And as for my safety, need I remind you of the many times during previous investigations where I have more than held my own against would-be attackers," she paused, narrowed her eyes, and said in an icy tone, "including when you made the outrageous decision to kidnap me at gunpoint?"

The unfortunate incident in question was still a cause of great shame to Langley, and he coloured appropriately at the memory. Deciding that this fruitless attempt to dissuade the dowager had gone on long enough, Wolf interjected, "Langley, Tabitha, and I have discussed the matter, and we believe that it is best all around if we invite Lady Pembroke to join us in investigating this murder."

Langley's eyebrows shot up. Wolf wished they had been afforded more time before the dowager had joined them so that he and Tabitha could explain their thinking to the man, but it now was what it was. If necessary, Wolf would return with him to Langley House and explain their predicament on the journey back. Luckily, despite his initial surprise, Langley quickly understood their quandary. It was obvious to him that once the dowager had not only caught wind of their investigation but had also been asked to look into it separately, she would be intractable in her insistence on participating. He had witnessed enough of her recent interference to come to the same realisation as Tabitha and Wolf had; all things being equal, it was better to agree to the dowager's involvement and retain some measure of control over her actions than to have her go off on her own and create who knew what trouble.

Reluctantly accepting the situation for what it was, Langley changed tack and asked, "What have you all discovered to date?"

Tabitha had requested that Talbot fetch their corkboard and some blank notecards, and he had returned with it while the dowager was in full-throated admonishment of Langley. Now, Tabitha took the stack of notecards and a pen and, as she and Wolf told Langley and the dowager what they had discovered, she wrote each fact and each open question up on its own notecards.

"So, you believe that whoever this killer is, whether it is the same man from eighty-eight or an imitator, might have believed that the victim was a lady of the night?" Langley asked.

"Well, it would seem to make some sense, given who she worked for," Tabitha explained. "It seems an unlikely coincidence that he chose a maid who just happened to work in a brothel."

"That is, of course assuming that this killer has a similar motive to Jack the Ripper," Langley pointed out.

"Indeed," Wolf agreed. "We spoke to a detective inspector I know in Whitehall who saw the body. While he had never seen any of the original victims, he confirmed with a colleague who had that the wounds inflicted were very similar, both in their location and horrific manner of infliction."

The dowager was eager to make her contribution and interrupted, "And I had a long conversation with the victim's employer, a Victoria Sharpe, one of the madams of my acquaintance." If Langley thought anything of this casual admission by the dowager countess that she had more than one woman in her social circle who ran brothels, he kept it to himself.

"Mrs Sharpe had nothing but laudatory things to say about the young woman who was killed. She had worked for her for almost a decade and was a hard worker and a good Catholic girl who went to church regularly and sent most of her money back to take care of her large, Irish family." The dowager's words might have been mistaken for approbation if everyone assembled didn't know all too well her views on Catholicism and the tendency of the working classes, particularly the Irish ones, towards extreme fecundity.

"It is clear that our next call must be on Aoife O'Brien's family. As much as I hate to disturb a family so freshly grieving, we must understand more about the victim's movements on the day of her death." As Wolf said this, he looked towards the dowager and said, "Tabitha and I will get you at eleven o'clock tomorrow morning, if that is acceptable."

Knowing how much the woman hated leaving her bedchamber before noon if she could help it, Wolf half-heartedly hoped that the suggested hour might dissuade her from joining them. However, it would take more than that to deter their new investigative partner, and she immediately accepted the suggestion.

Disappointed but not surprised, Wolf addressed Langley, "Have there been any developments within or against the Jewish community that we should be aware of?"

"I know that the Prime Minister is being kept informed of the sentiments in the community and their neighbours by Mr Samuel Montagu, the Jewish Member of Parliament for Whitechapel. It was Mr Montagu, in fact, who tried to offer a reward leading to the apprehension of Jack the Ripper in eighty-eight. At least from what I have heard, the East End Jews are very apprehensive, but at least so far there have been no direct actions taken against them. As I told you, the Prime Minister is very concerned about the situation in France at the moment bleeding over into Britain and fomenting similar anti-Jewish sentiment."

"Perhaps it is worth talking to Mr Montagu," Tabitha suggested.

"It may well be," Langley agreed.

"Is he by any chance a member of White's?" Wolf asked, referring to the preeminent club that he had inherited membership in, and that seemed to be where every man of wealth and power spent his evenings.

Langley laughed hollowly, "White's would never allow a man such as Montagu to join." Seeing the look of confusion on Wolf's face, he explained, "Remember, he is a Jew." He then continued, "However, I happen to know that he does belong to the National Liberal Club, an institution far more welcoming to a diverse membership."

"How do you know that?" Tabitha asked.

"Somerset is a member." This would have been an obscure answer if it were not for the fact that everyone in the room knew that Langley was Anthony Rowley, the Duke of Somerset's, natural father. In addition, the younger man was also involved in British Intelligence.

"The Duke of Somerset is a Liberal?" the dowager said in the horrified tones of someone who had been informed that an acquaintance was the greatest of degenerates.

"I have not inquired what Somerset's politics are, but for the purposes of some of the work that he and I do together, it is deemed necessary that we socialise in a wider social circle than a club such as White's affords. I will contact him immediately and ask if you and I can accompany him, perhaps even tonight."

Tabitha knew what this meant, and she hated it; however progressive the National Liberal Club was and however diverse it intended its membership to be, that did not extend to welcoming women as members. She might fight to be included in all aspects of an investigation and might even be able to persuade Wolf to take her to The Cock, but there was one place to which she would never be able to accompany him: a gentleman's club.

Langley promised to contact Anthony as soon as he returned to Langley House and then to telephone Wolf to make arrangements if they were able to meet up with him that evening.

CHAPTER 10

Langley was as good as his word, and within the hour, he had telephoned Chesterton House. After taking the call, Wolf returned to the parlour where he and Tabitha had retired to after their guests had left.

"So? What did he say?" Tabitha asked, rather more churlishly than she wished. She knew that it was not Wolf's fault that she was denied entry to the National Liberal Club. Yet she chafed at the restrictions imposed on her merely because of gender, and he was the nearest male she could take her frustrations out on.

Wolf understood what sat behind Tabitha's snappishness and sympathised. Answering her in a neutral tone, he said, "It seems we are in luck. The club has a speaker tonight talking on the plight of the working class of the East End and Mr Montagu is sponsoring him. Somerset said that if we meet him there at nine o'clock, we will be able to catch the end of the talk and ensure that Montagu is still there."

"You have no wish to go earlier and hear the speaker?" Tabitha asked sarcastically. She knew that despite Wolf's genuine compassion for the plight of London's indigent, he did not have the patience to listen to someone talk about it for an hour.

In answer, Wolf raised his eyebrows. "I believe that I can better benefit the poor by helping and giving rather than by listening to self-important do-gooders lecture me." Tabitha didn't disagree.

Dinner was a subdued affair; Tabitha still hadn't got over her pique at her exclusion that evening. Wolf, realising there was no way to rationalise her out of her warranted irritation, allowed her the space for her emotions. After dinner, he changed and then took the carriage to pick up Langley.

Despite Wolf's growing friendship with the other earl, he had never pressed Lord Langley on the state of his relationship with Anthony Rowley, the Duke of Somerset, or his mother, Cassandra. Many months ago, Langley had stated his intention to marry Cassandra, his first and only love, once her mourning period for her husband was over. Once he did so, he would be able to embrace openly a fatherly role towards his new stepson with no questions asked by society. What was their relationship in the interim? Wolf wondered.

As if guessing his companion's thoughts, Langley offered, "Since the old duke's death, Somerset and I have spent some time together. Our shared work for British Intelligence has helped provide us a reason to seek each other out. He is a fine man and one I am proud to call my son." Wolf nodded in agreement. During his first investigation with Tabitha, Wolf had come to know and admire the young duke. Anthony had been despised and tormented by the man who had raised him and who had long known that his heir was not a product of his loins. Wolf could imagine that he was happy to build a relationship with his real father.

"What, if anything, was he able to tell you about Mr Montagu?"

"He does not know him well, but what he does know is entirely praiseworthy. The man seems to be an exemplar of devotion to social causes and his community. He has worked hard to create opportunities for recent Jewish immigrants and those of a more entrepreneurial bent. He has advocated for fairer business practices towards Jews and has a more far-reaching concern for social reform, particularly regarding the under-privileged, no matter their background."

"The man sounds like someone I would like to meet regardless of the needs of the case," Wolf admitted. "And the club sounds like somewhere I might be more comfortable than White's."

It didn't take the carriage long to drive to the National Liberal Club, located on the north bank of the River Thames on Whitehall. The building, which had been completed just over ten years before, was a striking one, replete with turrets and a multitude of architectural details. Entering through its doors, Wolf was impressed by an interior as lavish and imposing as its exterior. High ceilings, beautiful stained-glass windows, walls covered in gilt, and a magnificent grand staircase all spoke to a membership of wealth and stature that struck Wolf as somewhat incongruous in the face of its stated egalitarian principles.

Approaching the clerk behind a large oak desk, Langley gave their names and titles and said that they were meeting the Duke of Somerset. The National Liberal Club was not White's, where dukes and earls were aplenty, and the clerk looked appropriately awed at the grand personages standing before him. He wrote their names in a large, leather-bound ledger and informed them that the duke was waiting for them in the smoking room. He gestured to a servant who had been standing silently and almost invisibly in the shadows and told the young man to escort the duke's guests to him.

The smoking room looked as if it could grace any aristocratic home; beautifully crafted tiled columns were dispersed around the sumptuously decorated room. Large, comfortable leather armchairs were scattered around the room, and bookcases separated the sides of the room into alcoves where members could speak privately. It seemed that this had been Anthony's plan as the servant led them to a secluded space where there was a leather sofa and two more armchairs, and Anthony Rowley, the Duke of Somerset, was sitting drinking a brandy and reading the newspaper.

Anthony looked up, and upon seeing them entering the alcove, a shy smile graced his features. While both he and Langley acknowledged their familial relationship, it was still new enough that they were cautious and respectful around each other. Their work for British Intelligence gave them a safe topic of conversation and a reason to spend time in each other's company that needed no explanation. Anthony was a slight, delicate young man, his frame slim and his entire being exuding a certain femininity. His facial features were almost ethereal, and long, fair lashes framed his striking blue eyes. Not much older than Tabitha, the new duke had not fully grown into his manhood yet, and Wolf couldn't help but think, not for the first time, that he looked remarkably young to be one of the highest-ranking Peers of the Realm, let alone a member of British Intelligence.

Wolf and Langley both ordered brandies and took seats close enough to Anthony that they could talk privately. "The talk is happening in one of the large meeting rooms," Anthony explained. "It started over an hour ago and so should be finished quite soon. Lord Langley explained that you wish to talk with Mr Montagu. Of course, I know what you have been asked to investigate, Pembroke. Why do you believe that Mr Montagu can provide any insights?"

Wolf gave a half-smile, "I have no particular reason except that he is somewhere to start. The man is obviously a stalwart of the Jewish community in the East End. He is both their MP and a significant philanthropist towards the people there. We know that he took an interest in the impact of the eighty-eight killings on the local Jews and I assume he is similarly concerned now. I am interested, well, Tabitha and I are interested in his thoughts on the matter and in who he might introduce us to."

Anthony nodded; there was not much new in Wolf's statement that he hadn't already surmised. "Then take your brandies," which had just been delivered, "and let us make our way into the meeting room, and I will introduce you."

The meeting room was not as impressive as the smoking room. Nevertheless, the opulence and grandeur were still on display. It seemed that the speaker had just finished taking questions, and the meeting was breaking up. Men stood waiting to talk to the guest of honour, while some seemed eager to make their way to the dining room or bar. Standing off to the side was a dignified-looking, somewhat portly man with an impressive, long, white beard. He was dressed quite austerely in a black jacket, trousers and waistcoat. The only nod to his wealth and status was a fine-looking gold pocket watch hanging from his waistcoat. His hooked nose and somewhat sunken dark eyes gave him a stern, quite serious appearance. Anthony nodded his head towards the man to let them know that this was Samuel Montagu.

Anthony led his guests towards the man they had come looking for. As they approached, Mr Montagu looked up, inclined his head, and said, "Your Grace, how good to see you."

"Montagu, might I have a word in private?" Anthony indicated to

Langley and Wolf and said, "I would like to introduce you to Maxwell Sandworth, the Earl of Langley and Jeremy Wolfson Chesterton, the Earl of Pembroke."

Montagu's raised eyebrows were the only evidence of any surprise at having his meeting graced by not one, but three, men of such eminence. "There is a small room off to the right here where we might speak privately," he said.

The men followed Samuel Montagu into a room with a long table surrounded by chairs. Montagu closed the door behind them, and each man took a chair.

"How can I help you, my lords?"

Wolf quickly explained that he was investigating the latest murder in Whitechapel. In the carriage, he and Langley had discussed what they would say when the question of why an earl was bothering with an East End murder was inevitably asked. "Before I ascended to the earldom, I worked as a private inquiry agent of sorts."

Of late, Wolf had taken to characterising his previous career using this somewhat gentler phrasing than the more controversial 'thief-taker'. "I have continued to involve myself in select investigations, and this has come to the notice of some in the British government. Because I have some connections within Whitechapel and its environs, I have been asked to look into this murder, discreetly." This was essentially the truth and merely left out the roles that Langley and Somerset had in British Intelligence.

"Of course, in my capacity as a member of parliament and the representative of the people of Whitechapel, I am fully aware of the Home Secretary's concerns about another eruption of ill will towards my community. I am not sure whether you know this, but I tried to offer a reward for the capture of Jack the Ripper ten years ago, for this very reason."

"I am aware," Wolf admitted. "This is one of the many reasons I wished to speak with you. To be honest, I have no idea where to start. I spoke, well, my investigative partner and I spoke, with the woman the victim worked for." He saw no need at this juncture to reveal that Aoife O'Brien worked in a brothel, even though it was possible that Samuel Montagu already knew.

Wolf continued, "We intend to visit Miss O'Brien's family tomorrow morning. It is our understanding that she always spent the afternoons of her days off visiting them." He didn't know how to phrase his next point diplomatically, and so, after a moment's consideration said, "It was never proven whether or not Jack the Ripper came from within the Jewish community, and so it is possible that this latest killer, whether or not he is the same man, is a Jew."

Samuel Montagu stroked his long beard and didn't answer for a few moments. Finally, he replied, "While a prohibition against murder is one of the ten commandments, I will not pretend that this rules out any Jew as the perpetrator of this atrocity. Jews are human, after all; some are good, and some are evil. Just as with any religion, some men use a twisted understanding of the rules of God to justify bad deeds. I said ten years ago, and I say again that if the killer turns out to be a Jew, then he turns out to be a Jew."

The man stopped stroking his beard and leaned forward slightly. Speaking with determination, he said, "However, until it is proven definitively that this butcher is a member of the Jewish community, I expect that the same presumption of innocence is granted as it is to any Englishman."

Wolf nodded his head in agreement. "Mr Montagu, can you think of anyone who might want to cast aspersions on the Jews and who might have committed this murder to reignite anti-Semitism in London?"

Mr Montagu laughed, a deep, belly laugh. "Reignite? Is that what you think? Anti-Semitism doesn't need to be reawakened; it is always here. Sometimes, it lurks in the shadows, and sometimes, those who would wipe my people off the face of the earth feel emboldened to speak their vile words out loud and to act on them. But no Jew is ever foolish enough to believe that it isn't something that casts a shadow over them every day of their lives."

He gestured around the lavishly appointed room, "I have done well for myself in business and am now a member of parliament. I might pretend to myself that this means that I am finally accepted. But any acceptance is merely skin deep if that."

Speaking directly to Wolf, he asked, "Lord Pembroke, I assume that you are a member of White's or Brooks' or one of those illustrious clubs?"

Wolf nodded, and the man continued, "Yet, I can never join. There is no amount of money, power, or even titles that I could accumulate that would give me entrée into one of those establishments. Do you know that Benjamin Disraeli himself, despite being Prime Minister and despite having been baptised into the Church of England as a child, was still not admitted to either of those clubs? The stench of his heritage followed him around, regardless of how he might try to shake it."

Finally, satisfied that he had made his point, Montagu sat back and said, "You may not know this, but I was a founding member of the Federation of Synagogues, which brought many of London's Jewish religious communities together under one umbrella organisation."

Neither Wolf nor Langley knew this and so said nothing as the man continued, "At this point, we have almost forty such communities as part of the Federation. We have monthly meetings of all the rabbis within the Federation and, as it happens, our monthly meeting is tomorrow morning at the Great Synagogue in Aldgate, which is where I pray during the week. I will ask the assembled group what they know and request that they keep an ear out for anything at all that might indicate a clue as to the identity of this killer."

"That is very kind of you, Mr Montagu," Wolf said.

Montagu acknowledged Wolf's words, then said, "Tomorrow night is the beginning of Shabbat, the eve of the Sabbath. Why don't you, Lord Langley, and your associate, join my family for dinner?" Evidently, seeing the scepticism on their faces, he explained, "It is a mitzvah, a blessing, to invite strangers to share a Shabbat meal. In Hebrew, we call it hachnasat orchim. There is no stipulation that those strangers need to be fellow Jews. Abraham himself invited guests for Shabbat meals, providing them with both physical and spiritual nourishment."

Wolf was touched by the invitation but immediately realised the challenge: the dowager. Having said they would cooperate with the woman, he had to inform her of the dinner. Despite her unexpected embrace of Miriam Tuchinsky and her family, he wasn't convinced that her liberality would extend to all members of the Jewish population.

Langley, intuiting Wolf's dilemma, said, "Mr Montagu, we should inform you that Lord Pembroke's investigative team includes the Dowager Countess of Pembroke, a woman known for stridently stating her strong opinions." Well, that was a polite way of saying it, but it essentially covered the basics of the dowager's personality.

Montagu laughed again, "Machloket, or debate, is deeply embedded in Jewish culture. In fact, it is at the heart of Talmudic study. I look forward to meeting this dowager countess and engaging in discussion with her."

Neither Wolf nor Langley thought that Samuel Montagu realised what he might be letting himself in for. Nevertheless, they gratefully accepted the invitation. He informed them that, given the time of year, Shabbat fell quite early. Given the need to walk to the synagogue over Shabbat, he attended services closer to his home in Kensington at the synagogue in Bayswater. They should plan to meet him at his home before sunset.

<h1 style="text-align:center">CHAPTER 11</h1>

The following morning, promptly at eleven o'clock, Tabitha and Wolf collected the dowager and proceeded to Whitechapel. Over breakfast, Wolf had told Tabitha about Samuel Montagu's invitation to dinner and her reaction had been much like his own. They had agreed to introduce the dinner invitation casually into the conversation; they knew that nothing would make the woman jump to accept it more than a suspicion that they wished her not to.

With the dowager settled and the drive underway, Wolf told her briefly of his meeting with Samuel Montagu, the man's offer to put the rabbis of the Federation on alert, and his extension of a dinner invitation.

As casual as he tried to make the telling, there was not getting much past the sharp-witted dowager, and she narrowed her eyes and said, "I hope you are not planning to exclude me from this dinner, Jeremy." She paused, then continued, "Or were you and Tabitha hoping that I would decline to join you because this Mr Montagu is a Jew?"

Neither Tabitha nor Wolf had an answer for that, and their silence was all the confirmation that the dowager needed. "Need I inform you both that I was the person engaged, on behalf of the Jewish community, to investigate this murder? Not you. You were merely engaged by British

Intelligence. Furthermore, need I remind you of my great affection and continued association with Mrs Tuchinsky?"

Tabitha wasn't sure she'd call the dowager sending her cook over to Bubbe's for a cooking lesson a continued association, but it wasn't the time to point this out. Instead, she tried to save the situation and replied, "Mama, I am sure that all Wolf meant was that you might have other plans at such short notice."

"Ha!" the dowager exclaimed. "Is that what Jeremy meant? Other plans? What other plans might I have? Another dreary evening of whist with Lady Willis, or perhaps an interminable dinner with the Prime Minister? If either you or Jeremy believes that I would give up the opportunity to dine at Mr Montagu's table in favour of any society event, then you do not know me very well."

Tabitha and Wolf glanced at each other, then Wolf said carefully, "Lady Pembroke, dear Lady Pembroke, I would be remiss if I did not point out that this is not merely an invitation to dinner; Friday night dinner is sacred to the Jewish people. There are many rituals and prayers surrounding it. My understanding is that they are not able even to light candles after sunset but instead must do any work before. While these customs might appear strange to us, we must respect them while in the man's house."

The dowager sniffed, then said in a terrifyingly cold voice, "Jeremy, I am not sure where you got the idea that I am an uncivilised barbarian, unable to control myself and without the basic understanding of social etiquette. I know very well how to behave as a guest in someone's home. And I challenge you to find someone with a greater respect and appreciation for the cultures of other people."

Tabitha almost choked; as it happened, she wasn't sure anyone had less respect and appreciation. Their recent visits to Scotland and Wales and the dowager's constant griping about the food, speech and traditions of those regions were only the latest examples. However, nothing would be gained by pointing this fact out, and so she and Wolf resigned themselves to the dowager being one of their party that evening.

There was a lot of traffic on the roads of London that Friday morning, and the drive to see Aoife O'Brien's family took longer than it usually would have. However, eventually, they came to a stop on Hanbury Street.

While they had spent enough time in Whitechapel to be used to its poverty, the squalor that met them shocked them all. The tenements were squeezed together, the smell of refuse filled the air, and the people walking the streets looked so hopeless that the scene might even have touched the dowager's heart.

The Pembroke carriages appearance in the East End was always an event, but in Hanbury Street, it seemed to be viewed as no less amazing than if the Queen herself had appeared. A crowd of scrawny children immediately gathered around the carriage door, begging for coins. It seemed that Wolf had anticipated this, and, descending from the carriage, he took out a purse of coins and distributed them into the greedily awaiting hands. Then, helping the dowager and Tabitha down, he approached the front door and knocked.

The door was opened by a woman who looked world-weary and tired. Her sickly pallor and sunken eyes made it hard to determine her age. She eyed the three toffs standing at her front door, trying to imagine what they could possibly want at 13 Hanbury Street. Debt collectors often turned up chasing one of the various occupants of the house, but these people looked far too fancy for that.

Wolf said, "We are looking for Mrs O'Brien."

The woman said nothing but pointed down the hallway to a door at the end. It was none of her business what these people wanted with Cammy O'Brien. Wolf, Tabitha, and the dowager continued down the hall to the door the woman had pointed towards. As much as the dowager had agitated to be allowed to join the outing, secretly, she was having second thoughts about her participation. None of her visits to the East End previously had exposed her to this level of poverty and squalor. Vicky Sharpe and Mickey D's houses were simple but quite respectable. The Tuchinsky residence, while not lavish, was clean and clearly a place no one went hungry if Bubbe had anything to do with it. However, this house, this street, the people they passed, and the woman who opened the door had such an air of desperation about them that this was a rare instance of the dowager second-guessing one of her decisions.

Before they even arrived at the door, they could hear the squalling of a baby and raised angry voices. Wolf knocked at the door, but it was at least a minute or two before the voices quieted, and someone came to open it.

The man standing before them looked mean. While Tabitha liked to think that she gave everyone the benefit of the doubt, she knew immediately that this man was violent and unpleasant. As if to reinforce her first impressions, he looked them up and down and snarled, "What do you want? We're not interested in whatever religion you're selling."

The man was about to slam the door in their face when Wolf, who wished they'd brought Bear with them, put his hand on it and asked, "Do I have the pleasure of speaking with Mr O'Brien?"

Freddy O'Brien was a man of many vices and few virtues. Whether it was drinking, gambling, or beating his wife, he thought of nothing but his appetites and his pleasure. He owed some money around town, but not to anyone he thought a big enough deal to send these toffs after him. So, who was this old lady who was looking at him as if he were a piece of rotten fish stinking up in front of her? Curiosity overcame his other instincts, and he replied, "You're talking to him. Who wants to know?"

Wolf didn't hold out his hand and didn't quite assume his grandfather's Earl of Pembroke persona, but he did say in a firm, dignified voice, "I am the Earl of Pembroke, and this is the Countess and Dowager Countess of Pembroke."

The man chuckled, "You expect me to believe that? That an earl and some countesses are roaming 'anbury Street and 'appened to come knocking on my door? What do you take me for?"

The man's reaction was understandable, and Wolf answered, "Mr O'Brien, perhaps we might come inside, and I can explain."

The other thing that Freddy O'Brien wasn't slow to see was a situation that might work to his advantage. Whatever these toffs wanted, they looked like they had a lot of coin to spare. Perhaps this was an opportunity for some of that coin to make its way into Ol' Freddy's pocket. He stood aside and let them in.

On entering the room, Tabitha had to work hard to control the gasp that was her immediate reaction. The dowager did not attempt to control her reaction and sniffed in disgust. The room was not large, but it was full of people. Full of children mostly, ranging from the baby that had been screaming through to a girl of maybe fourteen who was washing some clothes in a bucket in the corner. There was an unpleasant food odour that hung in the air and a definite smell of dampness and mould. There must have been ten children all told crowded into the room, and that didn't include Aoife and any others sent into service.

Tabitha's first investigation with Wolf had involved poor families in Whitechapel selling young girls into prostitution. Looking around her, Tabitha could well imagine this being the kind of family situation and Freddy O'Brien being the kind of father to participate in such a scheme. In fact, she immediately began mentally running over the names of the girls at the Dulwich House, trying to remember if any of them had the last name O'Brien.

Standing in the middle of the squalid room, Cammy O'Brien, a fresh bruise blooming on her cheek, stood trying to calm the baby. It was immediately evident that the bruise was not the only one on her body; her arms were covered in them, and her forehead sported a large, egg-shaped lump. Tabitha didn't have to guess how Cammy O'Brien had received her injuries. The only difference between the woman before her and Tabitha during her short but violent marriage to Jonathan was that Tabitha had a maid able to cover her bruises with makeup.

There was a small table in the corner of the room with three chairs, But Freddy O'Brien didn't bother to offer them to his guests. Instead, he barked, "So?"

"We wished to ask you about your daughter, Aoife."

At this, Cammy O'Brien's eyes filled with tears that began to run down her cheeks, though she didn't make a sound.

"What do you want to know, and why?" Mr O'Brien asked suspiciously.

"I, that is, we, are investigating her death on behalf of the government," Wolf explained.

Freddy O'Brien looked at them incredulously. "Why does the government care about what 'appened to someone as unimportant as our Aoife?"

It was a valid question, and Wolf struggled to find an answer that was both plausible and also suitably vague. "There is a concern that her murder might have broader implications," was all he said.

From the look on his face, it didn't seem as if Freddy O'Brien put much stock in that answer, but he also didn't care enough to argue. While Cammy might mourn the loss of a child, Aoife's father mourned the loss of her pay each week. He was already considering whether Vicky Sharpe could be persuaded to take on Aoife's younger sister, twelve-year-old Maggie. It was long past time for the girl to be out making money to support her family.

"What do you want to know?" Freddy asked.

"I understand that Aoife usually came to you after church on Sundays," Wolf began. "And that this Sunday was no exception. Is that correct?" Freddy nodded, and Wolf continued, "Was there anything that seemed different to you this Sunday?"

"No idea. I was down the pub that afternoon. By the time I got back, she was gone." He turned to his wife, whose tears were still evident though they had stopped streaming down her face, "What do you 'ave to say to the earl, Cam?"

Initially, it seemed that Cammy O'Brien might be too overcome by grief to answer. Tabitha came forward and gently touched the woman's arm, saying in a quiet, calming voice, "I cannot imagine the loss of a child, Mrs O'Brien. We merely want to help the police find out who did this awful thing to your daughter. If there is anything that you can tell us, however seemingly insignificant, we would be grateful."

Cammy O'Brien nodded and wiped her eyes. The baby started crying again, and she turned to the oldest girl, saying, "Maggie, come and take the baba while I talk to her ladyship."

Handing off the baby, she answered, "I didn't think much of it at the time, but she mentioned that a man had stopped 'er on the way 'ere and asked 'er for directions and that there was something odd about 'im and she thought she'd seen 'im before, maybe around Mrs Sharpe's 'ouse."

"Did she describe the man?" Wolf asked, his voice tinged with anticipation.

Cammy thought for a moment, "All she said was 'e didn't look or sound like 'e was from around these parts." In the melting pot of the East End, where countless immigrants blended, this was a vague clue at best. Cammy continued, "She didn't say nuffin else."

It was a puzzle piece, a small fragment of a larger picture. If the man's clothing and speech set him apart from the local inhabitants, it suggested that he wasn't from the Jewish community. Yet, even as Wolf thought this, it occurred to him that perhaps a young Irish girl from

Whitechapel hadn't had much exposure to her Jewish neighbours, no matter how close they lived. Nevertheless, this still suggested someone perhaps new to the East End, and that was more than they had known before.

"Did Aoife arrive and leave when she normally did?" Tabitha asked.

"Aye. She would go to church, meet some friend of 'er's in a tea 'ouse, and then come 'ere. She would stay the evening and 'elp me with the bairns, then go back to Gunthorpe Street for about eight o'clock. I usually have our Conor walk her 'ome. I don't like 'er out in the dark, alone. But 'e wasn't 'ome that night. I told 'er to leave earlier, but she said she would be fine and that I shouldn't worry." At this, Cammy started to cry all over again.

Freddy O'Brien looked irritated by her sobbing, and Tabitha knew he would have yelled at his wife, and maybe worse, if they hadn't been there.

Tabitha didn't think there was anything more they would get from Mrs O'Brien and looked at Wolf to indicate as much, when the dowager stepped forward and said, "Mrs O'Brien, was there any young man your daughter was stepping out with?"

This was a surprisingly astute question, and Tabitha and Wolf both couldn't believe that they hadn't thought to ask it and, more to the point, that the dowager had.

Cammy O'Brien nodded her head, "Aye, there's a lad, Finn O'Sullivan. 'E's been sweet on 'er a long time now. She didn't give 'im the time of day at first, but 'e's probably been coming 'ere with 'er on a Sunday for about a year now. 'E usually meets 'er at the tea house and walks 'er over. 'E 'as to leave early, which is why our Conor 'as to walk her 'ome. Finn works in a factory at night and 'as to be there at five o'clock, even on a Sunday."

"Did this boy accompany your daughter that Sunday?" Wolf asked.

"No. It seems they'd 'ad a spat. I'm not sure when it 'appened, but I suppose they got to see each other days other than Sundays sometimes."

"Can you tell us where Mr O'Sullivan lives?"

"Aye, that's easy enough. 'Is family live upstairs from us. It's 'ow they met. The O'Sullivans probably moved in about ten years ago now. Straight from Cork, they were." Looking at a shabby but sturdy clock on the wall, Mrs O'Brien continued, "You might be lucky. I know Finn gets in from the factory about ten in the morning, and 'e normally eats a meal before going to sleep. It's just one flight up, right above ours."

Tabitha would have liked to have pressed some coins into the woman's hand on leaving, but she had a strong suspicion Freddy O'Brien wouldn't have left them in her possession long enough to buy food for her children. When they had first learned of families knowingly selling their seven and eight-year-old daughters into prostitution, Tabitha had cursed the fathers who had accepted the money and the mothers who had allowed it. However, looking at the worn-down, battered, and hopeless Cammy O'Brien, Tabitha realised that she would have had no voice if her husband had made a similar choice for one of his children. While she stood by the decision that she and Anthony had made not to return the girls they had rescued to families that might turn around and sell them again, she made a promise to herself that she would investigate the families and see what might be done for the mothers and other children.

<h1 style="text-align:center">CHAPTER 12</h1>

They left the O'Brien home, such as it was, and made their way up the narrow, rickety stairs to the floor above. Again, Wolf took the lead and knocked at the door. A woman, no healthier or happier looking than Cammy O'Brien, answered the door. She was as surprised by the people standing before her as Freddy O'Brien had been. Again, Wolf gave his brief explanation as to their interest in Aoife's death and expressed a wish to speak to Finn. Mrs O'Sullivan seemed both as sceptical as Freddy O'Brien and as worn down as his wife. If she wondered what the real story was behind the toffs asking for her son, she was too tired to care to ask. Instead, she stood aside and let them in.

The room they were in was no larger than the O'Brien's, but it had fewer people in it, at least at that moment. A gangly young man sat at a table eating a bowl of what looked like porridge. Though what Tabitha could see, the thin, grey substance was as far from the creamy, hearty porridge they were served at Chesterton House as two things called by the same name could be.

As they entered the room, the young man looked up and stared at them quizzically. His mother went over and cuffed him around the ears, "Stand up, Finn. Can't you see we have guests?"

The young man reluctantly got to his feet. His watery blue eyes looked weary, and his scruffy, dark-blonde hair kept falling in his eyes. He would push it out, only for it to fall back almost immediately. Tabitha decided that if he were healthier and cleaner, he might have been considered quite good-looking. As it was, his skin was grey, and his eyes dull and lifeless. Of course, the young man had recently lost the girl he loved. It wasn't surprising if he seemed unhappy.

Wolf quickly explained who they were and what they wanted, even though it was hard to believe that Finn hadn't heard them at the door. When he answered, his voice was monotone, "She's gone. Wot does it matter why or 'ow?"

"Mr O'Sullivan, surely you don't mean that," Tabitha exclaimed. "You must want to know who did this to Aoife."

The young man shrugged, "Will knowing bring 'er back?"

Tabitha acknowledged that it wouldn't, but continued, "However, it might prevent the killer doing this to another young woman."

"Another young woman won't be the girl I love, will she?" Finn said in the same ennui-filled tone.

Reminding herself that the man was grieving deeply, Tabitha tried to ignore the utter lack of concern in his voice and asked, "Mrs O'Brien told us that you normally accompany Aoife on a Sunday." Finn nodded. "Is there anything you can tell us that was unusual about that Sunday?"

The young man thought for a moment and then shook his head. "Nuffin."

Wolf picked up the questioning, "Mrs O'Brien said that a man stopped Aoife to ask for directions. Were you with her at the time? She said that he didn't look or sound like a local."

"Aye, I was with 'er. Well, I was close by. We had stopped so I could talk to a bloke I know. While we chatted, Aoife had wandered off a way to look in the window of a bakery. She 'ad a terrible sweet tooth, she did. If she 'adn't promised her mam all her wages, she would have likely bought 'erself an iced bun. Anyway, she was standing there, and I looked over, and saw some geezer talking to her. I saw 'er answering 'im and pointing down the street. By the time I got over, 'e 'ad gone."

Well, this was progress, Tabitha thought. "Can you tell us anything about the man? How old was he? What did he look like?"

"I didn't take much notice, but if I 'ad to guess, I'd say 'e was in his forties maybe. 'E was short, shorter than Aoife, though she was quite tall for a lass. 'E was dressed like a farmer rather than like someone from round these parts. 'Ad a strong Irish accent, like 'e'd just got off the boat. Aoife thought that maybe she'd seen 'im before, but she wasn't sure. 'Ere's something that was odd, though I didn't think much of it at the time: 'e was carrying a black carpetbag. You don't normally see blokes walking around with those."

Tabitha didn't want to point out that if the man was the killer, then he might have been carrying the tools he used to butcher Aoife O'Brien in the bag. Instead, she asked, "Is there anything else you can tell us about this man? Did he have facial hair? What was his colouring?"

"As I said, I didn't take much notice, but from what I remember, 'e had ginger hair and a ginger beard. That's all I can remember. Now, I need to finish my grub so I can sleep." With that, Finn turned, sat back down, and continued to eat his unappetising-looking meal.

It was clear they would get nothing more from the young man, and the group thanked Mrs O'Sullivan and left the room and then the building, all glad to put the depressing squalor behind them.

Back in the carriage, the dowager said, "Well, was that helpful at all?"

Wolf considered the question, "I believe so. While we can't be sure, there does seem to be some indication that perhaps the man who had asked Aoife for directions had not done so randomly. Given that, it is possible that he was her killer. If so, we know more about him than we did an hour ago."

"Perhaps," the dowager conceded. "However, there are a lot of short, ginger-haired men in London. How on earth do we go about finding this one?"

It was a reasonable question, and no one had a good answer. With no immediate plans for the rest of the day, they intended to return to Chesterton House for lunch after dropping the dowager at home. They had been driving for a short while and were passing the British Museum when the calls of a newsboy on a street corner caught Tabitha's attention, "Extra, extra! Read all about it! Ripper strikes again."

Wolf heard the cries and rapped on the roof of the carriage for it to stop. He leapt out and purchased the first newspaper he saw. Melodramatic headlines covered the front page. He took the newspaper and got back into the carriage. Before it began to move, he scanned the headlines and then read them out loud. It appeared that the killer had taken another victim the night before. Again, it was a young Irish girl. The newspaper didn't say what her profession was, but it strongly implied that she might be a prostitute.

Leaning out of the window, Wolf yelled to Madison, the driver, to turn around and go back to Whitechapel. Pausing to consider where exactly to head, he then told him to go to The Cock.

"The Cock? Is that where Bruiser will be at this time of the day?" Tabitha asked.

"Who is this Bruiser?" the dowager asked.

Wolf sighed; this was not how he'd hoped that morning would go. "He is a detective inspector with the Metropolitan Police. His beat is Whitechapel. He is an old..." he paused; how best to put this? "An old professional acquaintance of mine."

The dowager had a loose sense of what Wolf and Bear had done professionally before coming to Chesterton House, but Wolf had hoped not to have to explain some of the seedier aspects of their life any more than had already been necessary.

Hoping that by answering Tabitha's question, he could forestall any more explanations to the dowager, Wolf said, "I cannot imagine much is to be gained by turning up in this carriage at the Leman Street Police Station and throwing my weight around. While I do not doubt that Bruiser's unusual assortment of associates is not unknown amongst his colleagues, at least to some extent, I see no reason to draw attention to our relationship. I suspect that a connection to an earl might be held against him more than one with a criminal." Wolf said the last sentence wryly. However, he also suspected it was true.

"Having already met Bruiser in The Cock yesterday, it is hard to imagine that doing so again today can make the situation any worse. I will send someone to fetch him." Wolf chewed his lip, considering his next words and knowing that there was no good outcome possible. "Lady Pembroke, dear Lady Pembroke." Tabitha had to hold back a smile; whenever Wolf began a sentence like that, it was certain he was trying to placate the old woman in some way. This ploy rarely fooled her.

Wolf continued, "I realise that you are made of stern stuff and may have even enjoyed our visit to the public house in Brighton. However..."

The dowager cut him off, "If you are going to suggest that I wait in the carriage, save your breath to cool your porridge." Turning to Tabitha, she asked, "Have you been in this Cock public house?"

Tabitha nodded reluctantly. "Then, dear Jeremy," and this was said with heavy sarcasm, "I will be accompanying you today."

It had been unlikely that she would be dissuaded and so Wolf reluctantly accepted the situation.

Settling back for the return journey to Whitechapel, Wolf continued to peruse the newspaper. It wasn't one of the more respected dailies like The Times. Instead, it was The Star, one of the more disreputable newspapers. When he had first purchased it, Wolf had focused on the biggest headline, announcing the second murder. Now, he read some of the smaller ones, also on the front page. "There are already grumblings about the Jews," he said.

As Wolf read, his brow furrowed further. "What is it, Jeremy? Do not keep us in such suspense. The last person to keep me waiting for this long for the rest of a story was Lady Willis droning on about her bad feet. One would think it was impossible to make a story about bunions any more boring. Somehow, she managed."

Wolf looked up from the newspaper. "This is an interesting piece of writing."

"How so?" Tabitha inquired.

"It manages to subtly, very subtly, weave in all sorts of anti-Semitic tropes, many of which fuelled the antagonism towards the Jewish community in 1888, from what I know from then. There are these undertones to the reporting. It is quite explicit in reminding readers about the various Jews questioned by the police after the original crimes. However, it fails to mention anything about the exoneration of those men and that none of them are alive and living in Whitechapel now."

"What do you find so surprising, Jeremy? From what I know, The Star is a muck-raking rag, and so is merely doing what it always does. Personally, I do not trust anything written in the newspapers. However, if I deign to lower myself to glance at one, I will only read The Times." As it happened, Tabitha and Wolf knew that this wasn't always the case and that the dowager secretly read the more sensational dailies on occasion.

The woman did have a point, Wolf thought. Was this nothing more than the usual slithering around in the mud that such a newspaper was wont to do? Perhaps. And yet, there was a tone to the piece that didn't sit easily with him and didn't bode well for public sentiment if this killer wasn't stopped soon.

CHAPTER 13

As the carriage pulled up outside of The Cock, the dowager could barely contain her glee. She had thoroughly enjoyed their visit to the public house in Brighton run by Mickey D's brother and his wife, Angie's sister. She had a feeling that this far lower-brow establishment would be even more of an adventure. Suddenly, realising how hungry she was, the dowager asked, "Jeremy, are we able to find sustenance in this establishment?"

Wolf wasn't sure if the dowager countess would consider The Cock's meat pie appropriate "sustenance", but he nodded his head. He was also hungry and was already salivating at the thought of having another one of the pies and a pint of ale. Resigning himself to the likely dramatics of their visit, he helped the two women down from the carriage and then led the way into The Cock.

If Wolf had hoped that his visit there, just the day before, with Tabitha, might have inured the tavern's patrons to the appearance of toffs amongst them, he was to be disappointed. Every head looked up, and silence fell over the place at their entrance.

Old One-eye was delivering a pie to a table near the door and looked over at them, saying mockingly, "Two visits in as many days from your lordship. To what do we owe such an honour? And you've brought another fancy friend with you," he noted, looking at the dowager.

Wolf was about to answer when the dowager moved towards Old One-eye and said imperiously, "Are you the owner of this establishment?"

Old One-eye laughed, "This is an establishment now, is it? But to answer your question, this is my place. How can I help you, duchess?"

The man's sarcasm was entirely lost on the dowager, who answered, "While I can certainly see how one might mistake me for a duchess, in fact, I am a countess, the Dowager Countess of Pembroke, to be more precise. While you would address a duchess as Your Grace, you may call me your ladyship."

Old One-eye wasn't normally one to be taken aback by anyone's behaviour; he thought he'd seen and dealt with it all in his many years running The Cock. However, the diminutive but rather terrifying-looking little old toff was something entirely different, and the man was momentarily lost for words. Finally, gathering his wits, Old One-eye made a half bow that seemed quite sincere and said, "Welcome to The Cock, your ladyship. How can I help you today?"

Wolf had been acquainted with Old One-eye as long as with Bear. He'd never known the man to be caught on the back foot with anyone. He'd seen him stand up to hardened criminals many times, yet faced with the dowager, Old One-eye was reduced to a puddle of subservience.

"Please point us to a table, my good man. Preferably one with a modicum of privacy. Then, you may send over three of those delicious-looking pies, two small beers, and whatever Lord Pembroke normally drinks when he is here," the dowager commanded.

The publican obediently led them to the same table that Wolf and Tabitha had sat at the day before, acknowledged the food and drink order, and then turned and left. The other patrons, deciding the show was over for now, went back to their drinks and conversation.

As Wolf had suspected, Bruiser was nowhere to be seen. Standing and going over to the bar, he had a quiet word with Old One-eye, who nodded his head. When Wolf returned to the table, Tabitha asked, "What did you ask?"

"I asked him to send someone to get Bruiser," Wolf answered.

"Are you sure he will come?" Tabitha asked.

"I am," Wolf answered, saying no more about whatever he had whispered to Old One-eye to be conveyed to the detective inspector.

The pies and drinks arrived before the policeman did, and Tabitha had to admit that they smelled delicious. As a rule, she might have been cautious about what exactly was used to fill such a pie in a place like The Cock, but she had heard Wolf speak rapturously on more than one occasion about its meat pies and so decided to throw caution to the wind and tuck in.

The dowager had been introduced to small beer in Brighton and had surprised everyone by how she had taken to the working-class beverage. Savouring her first sip, she lowered her tankard she said to Wolf, "Jeremy, I recall that you had promised to see my household amply supplied with a sufficient supply of this small beer."

As it happened, Wolf had promised no such thing. In Brighton, the dowager had made the outrageous demand that the Earl of Pembroke be personally responsible for ensuring the delivery of her chosen libation. However, in the turmoil of their recent investigations and travel, it seemed she had forgotten her dictate. Certainly, he had forgotten. He ignored the comment, and she sniffed but said nothing more.

The dowager tucked into her simple but hearty meat pie, served on chipped crockery and mismatched cutlery, with a gusto that Tabitha might not have believed if she hadn't witnessed it for herself. She had personally heard the woman complain on multiple occasions that the china used at the houses of various members of the aristocracy was not up to her standards. Yet, here she was, using a rather bent and tarnished fork, eagerly eating off a plate that, under usual circumstances, she wouldn't even consider fit for her servants. The woman was a bundle of contradictions, to say the least.

"Jeremy, call the publican over. I must convey how delicious this pie is," she commanded.

Wolf would like to have limited Old One-eye's further exposure to the dowager, but he realised that to resist was futile. Catching the man's eye, he indicated that he should join them.

"Everything all right?" Old One-eye asked cautiously. The last thing he wanted was a further dressing down from this little toff.

"Publican, I must commend you on your comestible," the dowager uttered in the same tone she might use when complimenting a Marchioness on the quality of her caviar.

Old One-eye looked to Wolf for a translation. "She likes the pie," Wolf said.

"Ah. Well, I'm chuffed it's up to snuff," the publican answered, with just a hint of sarcasm in his voice.

Wolf translated, "He is happy that it is up to your standards."

Wolf wondered how long this particularly absurd charade would go on for. Luckily, it was at this moment that Bruiser entered The Cock. He walked up to their table, his face a picture of irritation.

"You may be all high and mighty now, Wolf," he said with no preamble. "But I'm not sure what makes you think you can summon me like I'm your errand boy. We've had another murder, and all hell has broken out down at the station. The chief inspector himself was there earlier and said heads will roll if the killer isn't found. I've got enough on my plate without a bunch of nobs wanting a chat."

"Sit down, Bruiser, and have a drink," Wolf answered calmly, pushing the extra tankard he'd ordered towards the man.

Bruiser wasn't placated, but he did sit and take a long sip.

Wolf continued, "I asked you to meet us here precisely because it would be less conspicuous than a group such as ours," at this, he gestured to Tabitha and the dowager, "descending on the police station. I thought that might cause too many questions to be asked of you."

Bruiser made a sound that could have been exasperation or agreement; it was hard to tell. "Fine! Then what was so important?"

"There has been a second murder."

"Yes. So what?"

"We believe that we may have some information."

"What information do you have, Wolf?" Bruiser said impatiently. Now that he was there, he did wonder whether he might not just order another pie and eyed the remains of the dowager's greedily.

Wolf continued, "We talked to the first victim, Aoife O'Brien's mother and her young man. It seems that on her way to her family that Sunday, she had an interaction with a somewhat short man with ginger hair."

If Wolf expected Bruiser to dismiss this information, he was surprised by the evident interest on the man's face. "What is it?" he asked.

"There was a witness this time. Or at least there might have been," Bruiser admitted in a hushed voice. "We managed to keep this from the rags; don't want to put her in danger."

"What did this witness say?" Tabitha asked, already guessing what the answer would be.

"She talked about a man with ginger hair."

"Who was the victim?" Wolf asked.

"That's what's interesting. This time it was a young girl, named Molly Shipman. She worked in a shop, lived on one of the more respectable streets in Whitechapel. Nothing to do with the dollymops at all. She had worked late last night, finishing up an order with some other girls and must have been attacked on her way home, sometime after eight o'clock. The witness knew the victim and saw her hurrying home. They passed each other and said their greetings, then a short way up the road, our witness noticed a ginger-haired man walking behind Molly. She said that, at the time, she didn't think much of it. He looked respectable enough. But based on the time we know that Molly left the shop, this witness must have seen her just before she was attacked. It seemed a slim lead at the time, but based on what you've told me, I think that our witness might have seen the killer."

"Do you think that this witness could describe the man more fully?" Wolf asked.

"No idea. She was pretty shaken up when she came by this morning. Said she heard the news about Molly and wanted to tell us what she saw. We're keeping her identity as secret as we can."

Wolf nodded; he had no wish to put the young woman in harm's way. However, he had an idea. "Bruiser, I would like to send Bear to talk with this witness."

"Bear? Why on earth do you want to do that?"

Tabitha knew immediately what Wolf was thinking. "Because he is an excellent artist and has helped us catch a suspect in the past by capturing their likeness. No one would have to know why he was there, and he could talk to the witness and try to work up a picture of this supposed killer," she explained.

Bruiser looked sceptical, but he also couldn't see what harm it would do. He told them the girl's name and address, then polished off his ale and left, saying as he stood, "And Wolf, don't make a habit of ordering me to wait on you."

Wolf would have happily left The Cock as soon as Bruiser had left, but the dowager seemed in no hurry to be gone. Happily sipping on her small beer, she looked around the room, fascinated by the other patrons. "Jeremy dear, do you know some of these people?" she asked in a voice that was just a little too loud.

Answering in a much quieter voice, Wolf said, "I have a passing acquaintance with some of them, yes."

"Would you introduce me?"

Wolf had just taken another sip of his ale and almost choked on it at her question. "Lady Pembroke, these men are not quaint characters in a book; many of them are hardened criminals. Why do you want to be introduced?"

Taking umbrage at his tone, the dowager sniffed and said, "I am not sure what kind of naive fool you take me for."

Sighing, as he so often seemed to around this woman, Wolf tried to use a more measured tone when he replied, "I apologise if my reply implied such a thing. Of course, that is the last thing I believe. However, my question stands: why do you want to be introduced?"

"Because so many of them look to be fascinating characters."

Wolf looked around the busy public house. He had spent ten years living and working amongst its patrons. Would he consider them fascinating? Some were working men, others petty thieves. He saw a couple of Mickey D's boys standing by the bar, talking to a dollymop. Men were eating, drinking, arguing, and, in the case of an old, wizened man with only one arm, sitting in the back corner, sleeping. He compared the people milling about The Cock to the members of White's. The latter were better dressed and cleaner, though, after almost seven months living amongst them, he wasn't sure they were any more honest or reputable.

As Wolf looked around, he saw a few men he knew. Catching one man's eye, Wolf inclined his head slightly in greeting. The man raised an eyebrow, then put his tankard down and wandered over.

Wolf considered the invitation he had just offered; if he had to introduce the dowager to anyone in that public house, it was likely safe enough for that person to be Johnny Do Good. The man's real name was Johnny Dugger, and he had once been a man of God, or so he liked to say. Probably in his mid-fifties, he had earned his nickname from the attempts he had made when he first moved to Whitechapel to save the souls of the local prostitutes. Johnny Do Good had long since given up such a futile undertaking and now divided his time between running errands for Mickey D and drinking away his earnings in The Cock.

As Johnny Do Good reached the table, Wolf said, "Lady Pembroke, I would like to introduce you to Johnny Do Good. You and he have an associate in common."

Johnny now raised both eyebrows. Wolf wasn't sure whether the man's surprise was being introduced to someone of the dowager's rank or the idea that they knew anyone in common. Wolf continued, "Lady Pembroke, Johnny works for Mickey D."

The dowager smiled, "It is very nice to meet you, Mr Do Good. Any friend of Mr Doherty's is a friend of mine." Wolf tried not to roll his eyes. What had his life come to when the Dowager Countess of Pembroke could make such a statement?

Wolf glanced at Johnny Do Good. What did this man think of the likelihood of the notorious gang leader being on friendly terms or even knowing a Mayfair aristocrat? The man's face gave little away, probably a useful skill to have acquired over years of doing Mickey's bidding.

"Do join us, Mr Do Good," the dowager offered. Tabitha looked over at Wolf. However, he seemed as nonplussed by the old woman's intentions as she was. It was one thing to be introduced to one of The Cock's patrons, but planning on conversing with him for some time as if this was the drawing room at Chesterton House was quite another. Unfortunately, or perhaps fortunately, depending on how the conversation might have gone, Johnny Do Good had to decline the offer. He was already late for a little job Mickey D had asked him to do, and he didn't need to draw attention to his tardiness by loitering to chat with toffs.

Finally, persuaded that they all needed to return home to prepare for their early dinner, the dowager reluctantly left The Cock, saying as they were finally seated back in the Pembroke Carriage, "I will expect you to accompany me on a return visit to that establishment, Jeremy." Wolf was seated next to the dowager and so did roll his eyes this time at Tabitha, sitting opposite, who tried not to grin in response.

CHAPTER 14

Tabitha had thought long and hard about what dress to wear that evening. She and Ginny then discussed it further. "My understanding is that Orthodox Jewish women are very conservative in their dress," Tabitha explained. "While I am sure they would not expect others to follow their customs, I do not wish to give offence in any way."

After Jonathan's death, Tabitha had instructed Ginny to dispose of most of the ugly and unflattering dresses she had been forced to wear during their marriage. They had kept back just a few in anticipation of their possible uses during investigations. Now, Tabitha was glad to have had such foresight. There was a dark green silk evening dress somewhere in the back of her wardrobe that she believed might be suitable. While Jonathan had insisted on austerity in her clothing, he also wished his wife to reflect his wealth and power. Because of this, all her clothing had been in the finest fabrics and of the highest quality tailoring, even if they hadn't been particularly attractive. Since Tabitha had come out of mourning, Ginny had altered any clothes they had decided Tabitha should keep, so that all the dresses, while still quite severe, at least were more stylish and flattering.

If Wolf had any thoughts about Tabitha's choice of dress, he kept them to himself. The carriage ride to collect the dowager was a short one, but they used it to consider what they might ask Samuel Montagu that evening. "I understand why the government is worried about anti-Semitic sentiments being stirred up again with these killings, but is there a reason that someone might want to start such trouble now?" Tabitha pondered aloud.

"What do you mean?" Wolf asked, not following her train of thinking for once.

"Well, why now? Let us make the assumption that, regardless of who Jack the Ripper was, this killer is not the same man."

"I am not sure we have any reason to make such an assumption," Wolf interrupted.

Tabitha acknowledged his words but continued, "Well, most of the original suspects are either dead or overseas, and ten years is an awfully long time to suddenly begin killing again." Wolf wasn't sure that it really was, but he let her have the point. "If we do make this assumption, then our killer is a different man. Possibly the man with ginger hair. Is this just a sick-minded imitator or is someone hoping to stir up anti-Semitic sentiments, similar to those back in 1888? And, if the latter theory is correct, then why now?"

Wolf shook his head, "I confess, I do not know enough about the affairs of the Jews of London to have an answer for that."

"But I am assuming that Samuel Montagu does," Tabitha concluded.

Finally, following her logic, Wolf agreed with what they wanted to glean from their host that evening just as the carriage pulled up outside of the dowager's home. A few minutes later, the carriage door opened, and a footman helped the diminutive old woman into the vehicle. The dowager was wrapped in a fur-trimmed cloak, so Tabitha couldn't see what she was wearing, but she could see that the infuriating woman had decided to wear her most lavish diamonds. They weren't really appropriate for even a society evening, let alone the dinner they were headed to. They were the kind of diamonds most commonly worn at state dinners or grand balls.

Tabitha knew immediately why these diamonds were being worn that evening: the dowager was hoping to make her superior status quite clear. While the woman might tolerate, even enjoy the company of Bubbe and Tuchinsky, they were working-class Jews. They knew their place. Who knew what this banker and his wife might think of where they fit into the social hierarchy? The dowager intended to make very sure that they were left in no doubt that, wherever they might imagine they had clawed their way to on that ladder, she was far, far higher up. Tabitha reflected that this hardly boded well for the rest of the evening.

They arrived at the Montagu's Kensington home at almost the same time as Langley. As Wolf handed her down from the carriage, Tabitha looked up at the large, elegant townhouse. While nowhere near as grand as Chesterton House, the Montagu's residence was a picture of understated elegant prosperity. This impression was extended to the woman who answered the door. There seemed no doubt that the stylish woman answering the door was Mrs Montagu. She was perhaps in her late forties, maybe a little older, with dark hair that had just a little silver at the temples. She was not a beautiful woman, but she was handsome, with intelligent brown eyes and a face filled with kindness. Her dress was not unlike Tabitha's own: conservative, elegant, expensive simplicity.

Standing just behind her were two young women who bore enough of a resemblance to the woman at the door that Tabitha assumed they were her daughters. What was striking about all three women was that nothing about their appearances or dress would have caused anyone to guess they were Jews. In fact, the two young women had lighter hair than their mother and blue eyes.

As if seeing her guests surprise that she opened her own front door, Ellen Montagu said, "My dear Lord Pembroke, both Lady Pembroke's and Lord Langley, please excuse us, but in Judaism, the sabbath is holy whether you are of our people or not. We call this shvitat Shabbat. While some use perceived loopholes in the Talmudic rulings to continue to have servants work, Samuel feels very strongly that, as leaders in the community, we should not do so." As she spoke, Mrs Montagu and the two young women standing next to her helped their guests off with their outerwear, entirely at ease with doing the work of a butler or maid, and then led the way down the hallway into a large dining room.

"Samuel has just returned from shul, and the sun will be setting soon, and we must light the candles at least eighteen minutes before it does."

During their welcome into the house and the explanation about the lack of servants, Tabitha had tried hard not to look at the dowager, worried what evidence of horror she might see writ large on the woman's face. She was grateful that the dowager, normally such a stickler for the maintenance of social norms, at least by other people, had not so far said anything that might offend their hostess. Now, her hopes sunk as she heard the dowager ask, "And why must it be eighteen minutes, Mrs Montagu?"

As she asked this question, they entered the dining room where Samuel Montagu and two young men, presumably his sons, were waiting. Mr Montagu answered for his wife, "That you ask that question, Lady Pembroke, is evidence of what a wonderful Talmudic scholar you would have made if you had been born a Jew. To be always questioning and challenging is a vital part of our religious heritage."

Tabitha finally glanced at the dowager, unsure what the woman would make of such a statement, even if it were meant as a compliment. To her surprise, the dowager beamed at Samuel Montagu's words and replied, "Well, is that not so much more sensible than the Church of England, which seems intent on pushing its strictures down our throats, no matter how absurd, no questions asked. The next time I see the Archbishop of Canterbury, I will inform him of how much more rational the Jews seem to be about such things."

The dowager claimed to keep a running list of things that she intended to inform the Archbishop about the next time she saw him. Given that neither the existence of such a list nor the dowager's willingness to corner the man was likely hyperbole, Tabitha could only imagine the efforts the man went to in order to ensure their paths rarely crossed.

"Before I answer your question, and any others you may have, Lady Pembroke, let us prepare to welcome Shabbat. Once we are seated, I will explain our traditions to you," Samuel Montagu suggested. The dowager was a guest in the man's house, and simple good manners dictated that she accede to his suggestion.

Mrs Montagu and her daughters had placed laced coverings on their heads and approached a pair of expensive-looking but simply decorated silver candlesticks. Lighting the candles, they bowed their heads and began to intone what sounded like a prayer in a language Tabitha did not recognise. From the little she had learned from Bubbe while staying in the Tuchinsky household during Wolf's recovery a few months before, she believed the prayer was in Hebrew.

Following the candle lighting, Mr Montagu then poured wine into a highly decorative glass and said another prayer. He then poured the wine from the larger glass into enough small glasses that everyone at the table, including their guests, could drink. The small glasses were passed around the table. Again, Tabitha was concerned about what the dowager might say and glanced over at Wolf. He gave a brief shake of his head, though what he was trying to communicate, she wasn't sure. Luckily, and rather surprisingly, the dowager said nothing and took a sip of her wine when everyone else did. Actually, if the look on her face was anything to go by, she was quite fascinated by the rituals.

When everyone had sipped their wine, Samuel Montagu went over to a large wash basin standing on a table off to the side of the room. He removed his jacket, rolled his shirt sleeves up, said another prayer and then used a porcelain cup by the side of the basin to first pour water over one hand, and then the other. All the Montagues followed Samuel's lead and similarly washed their hands. No one suggested that their guests follow suit, and Tabitha reflected that this was probably for the best – it might have been a bridge too far for the dowager.

The final ritual was a prayer over a delicious-looking, shiny, braided loaf of bread that Mrs Montagu informed them was called challah. After the prayer, slices were cut, and chunks of bread were given out to everyone at the table. This seemed to signify the start of the meal. Food had been laid out on burners on a sideboard, and one of the two Montagu girls began ladling out what smelled like chicken soup into bowls while the other daughter handed the bowls out.

Ellen Montagu explained the soup served: "Chicken soup is a very traditional start to a Shabbat meal."

Before she could get any further, the dowager piped up, "One of my favourites, I can assure you. I particularly enjoy the kneidlach and lokshen."

Whatever the Montagu's had expected the Dowager Countess of Pembroke's reaction to their traditional food to be, that wasn't it. The old woman looked on, delighted at the surprise writ clear on their faces. There was perhaps nothing she enjoyed more than subverting people's expectations of her. She continued, "My dear friend, Mrs Tuchinsky of Brick Lane, taught my cook how to make the soup and stressed the vital importance of using a kosher, what did she call it now? Yes, a kosher boiler."

The look on Ellen Montagu's face really was priceless. Finally, she managed to compose herself and said, "I do not know Mrs Tuchinsky, but she is entirely correct. My cook makes a twice-a-week pilgrimage to a kosher butcher in Whitechapel."

As they ate the soup, Samuel Montagu explained the various rituals and traditions of the Jewish Sabbath, Shabbat. This included answering the dowager's question about why they lit the candles eighteen minutes before sunset, explaining that, while there were multiple reasons given in the Talmud, the simplest was to ensure that the "work" of lighting the candles was done before Shabbat had begun. Not normally one for ecclesiastical musings of any sort, the dowager nevertheless seemed quite riveted by Mr Montagu's explanations of the various Talmudic explanations and dictates. The man was a born teacher and managed to make his explanations both accessible and interesting.

The soup course gave way to roast chicken with tzimmes, a delicious stew of carrots, sweet potatoes, prunes, and raisins. There was also a very hearty and tasty noodle pudding called kugel. The food wasn't fancy, but it was tasty and comforting on that cold Friday night.

Samuel Montagu's stories and explanations continued through most of the main course, and Wolf was beginning to worry that they might never get to discuss the real purpose of their visit. Finally, putting his knife and fork down and wiping his mouth, Samuel said, "I am sure you are impatient to hear what the gathering of rabbis had to say this morning."

No one contradicted the man, and so he continued, "As you can imagine, the entire community is very concerned, both that there is a killer on the loose again in Whitechapel, but also that blame will once again fall on the Jews. Already, the whispering has started." The man paused, shook his head sadly, then continued, "There has already been at least once incident."

"What kind of incident?" Lord Langley asked.

"A message painted on a wall in Shoreditch that is eerily reminiscent of an identical message ten years ago, 'The Jews are the men that will not be blamed for nothing.' As well as similarly bad grammar as the original message, just as then, Jews was spelled incorrectly as 'Juews'.

Either this is the same perpetrator as 1888, or someone has a long memory."

Lilian Montagu spoke up, "There has been more. I heard that a group of men, Irish it seemed, attacked a young man today in Whitechapel, the son of the local kosher butcher. They left him unconscious and bleeding."

Samuel's wife picked up the narrative, "This is how it always goes for the Jews; first we get blamed, then shamed, then the attacks begin." Addressing the dowager, she said, "Ask your friend, Mrs Tuchinsky, how it was for the Jews in Poland when the pogroms began. Britain was supposed to be a safe harbour, but if five thousand years of persecution has taught us anything, it is that there is no such thing." The bitterness in the woman's voice was unmistakable.

Tabitha looked at this seemingly very anglicised woman and her daughters, all of whom could have passed as British and Christian as Tabitha herself. It was hard to believe that they nevertheless felt as much the unwelcomed strangers as the poorest, most recent immigrants landing in Britain from faraway lands.

"My parents are German," Mrs Montagu explained. My grandfather was a well-respected goldsmith in Hamburg. He believed they were established in their broader community, perhaps even integrated in with their German neighbours. Then, the Hep-Hep riots began in 1819. While they did not start in Hamburg, they quickly spread there. A mob vandalised my grandfather's business and then attacked him. People he had known all his life were part of those riots. He recovered physically, but he was never the same man. My father and grandparents moved to England not long after. They believed things would be different here, better. But these murders prove that you scratch the surface just a little, and anti-Semitism is here, just as it was in Germany."

No one wanted to interrupt the woman and minimise her experiences or feelings. However, they needed to bring the conversation back to more immediate concerns. Luckily, before any of their guests had to interrupt her, one of the young women, Lilian, put a hand on her mother's arm and gently said, "Mama, do not upset yourself so. Let us return to why our guests have joined us."

Ellen Montagu blinked away unshed tears and said, "Of course, my dear. You are entirely correct. Please, everyone, excuse my maudlin ways."

Wolf had arrived with a leather folio which he had placed by his chair. Now, he reached down for it then opened it and drew out a few pieces of paper. As soon as she saw the top one, Tabitha realised that, in the time since they had returned from The Cock, Wolf had found Bear and sent him off to talk to the witness who had seen the ginger-haired man. The drawing Wolf held in his hand was the result of that conversation. Yet again, Tabitha marvelled at Bear's artistic talent. The charcoal sketch was quite simple, but with a few strokes, Bear had captured the essence of a man. She did not doubt that someone who knew their suspect would immediately recognise him from this.

Handing the drawing over to Samuel Montagu, Wolf explained, "There was a witness who saw a ginger-haired man to whom the police wish to speak. My private secretary went and spoke to the witness and created this likeness. He has drawn several copies, which he is even now distributing to the Whitechapel police and within the community. Can I ask you to take these copies and share them with your rabbis?"

Mr Montagu immediately agreed to do all he could to disseminate information about this suspect. As Lilian and her sister began to clear the plates and then bring in a dessert of various fruits and ruggelach, Lord Langley thought to give them a change of subject, "Mr Montagu, I heard talk about the land you are hoping to develop in Edmonton."

"Indeed, twenty-five acres, just south of Salmon's Brook, Edmonton. I hope to construct 700 houses to house well over 3,000 people. As I'm sure you know, the conditions in the East End are terrible. The poverty, terribly cramped conditions, and ensuing disease are unacceptable. The plan is that each house will have its own small garden, low rents and that the Jewish residents of Whitechapel will have priority."

Mr Montagu gestured to the well-appointed room, "I have been very lucky. My grandfather was a merchant and a banker and my father founded the banking house that later became the prestigious and successful banking institution that I now run. Among my fellow Jews, I have done unusually well. My family were Sephardic Jews who fled persecution during the Spanish Inquisition. They ended up in Holland and then made their way to England in the middle of the last century. They had tsuris, misery along the way, but also good fortune. However, so many of the Jews in London were peasants, poor farmers in the shtetls of

Eastern Europe. They fled here with not much more than the clothes on their backs, trading extreme poverty in one country for another."

"And so you feel it is your responsibility to help them make better lives here?" Tabitha asked.

"The Talmud tells us that 'Whoever saves one life saves the world entire'. If I can help more than 3000 souls to escape the filth and sickness of the tenements of the East End, it will be the greatest mitzvah of my life."

Wolf listened to his host intently, increasingly admiring of the man. Montagu certainly wasn't the first or only rich man to engage in philanthropy. However, Wolf rarely heard those efforts described with the heartfelt compassion and humility of Samuel Montagu, explaining what he hoped to achieve for the less fortunate of his Jewish brethren.

"The Edmonton City Council will be voting on my plan this month," Montagu continued. "I have been told that there is agreement within the council that my plan is solid and that its approval will not face any dissent. I hope to break ground by the late spring." The man paused, made a face that was somewhere between disgust and resignation, and continued, "As you can imagine, I have had to do some favours here and there to ensure that I can bring my vision to life. However, that is the way of business, is it not?"

Chapter 15

A s the group left the Montagu home sometime later, they decided that, given the still early hour, they would reconvene at Chesterton House to write notecards and discuss the evening's findings.

In the carriage for the ride home, the dowager was positively gushing about Samuel and Ellen Montagu. "What an absolutely delightful couple." Tabitha wasn't sure she'd ever heard her erstwhile mother-in-law describe anyone as 'absolutely delightful.' The woman carried on in a similar vein, "And I just find the Jewish traditions utterly fascinating, to say nothing of how delicious the food is. I wonder if Mrs Montagu could be persuaded to share the recipe for that challah bread."

"I am sure that Bubbe could also share a recipe," Tabitha pointed out. She was just relieved that the dowager had behaved herself all evening and had engaged quite enthusiastically with the Jewish Shabbat rituals. She could certainly imagine how the evening might have gone very differently.

Arriving back at Chesterton House, Talbot opened the door, and by the look on his face, Tabitha knew that something was amiss. Her first reaction was to worry that something was wrong with Melody. Talbot quickly put her mind at ease, at least about the little girl, and said, "Milord, you have a visitor, a Mr Doherty. Given that you received him in the parlour previously, I took the liberty of putting him in there again. I believe he is on his second glass of brandy."

If Tabitha's first reaction was relief that Melody was safe and well, her second was a suspicion as to why the Whitechapel gang leader had chosen to visit. As Talbot pointed out, the man had visited in the past. However, Wolf had hardly made him feel like a welcome guest who had an open invitation to visit whenever he wanted.

Whatever qualms Tabitha and Wolf might have about their surprise nocturnal visitor, the dowager was nothing other than thrilled. Thrusting her cloak at Talbot, she made her way quickly to the parlour door, trilling breezily as she entered, "Mr Doherty, what a delightful surprise."

Wolf and Tabitha followed behind her. On entering his parlour, Wolf found Mickey D making himself as comfortable as he always did on his visits. Ensconced in the most comfortable armchair in front of the fireplace, he had a glass of brandy in one hand and was reading the copy of *Pride and Prejudice* that Tabitha had left open on the side table.

Looking up as the three of them entered the parlour, he held up the book and said, "She's quite a character, this Mrs Bennet, isn't she? I think my Ange might enjoy this story."

Wolf was used to Mickey D making himself quite at home and didn't bother to comment on the fact. Tabitha answered, "That is my favourite edition of the book that my father gave to me, but I believe I have another copy in the library if you would like to take it for Mrs Doherty."

"I'm sure she'd love that." As the dowager came towards him, Mickey D stood and performed a neat little bow, "Lady P, always grand to see you."

"To what do we owe the pleasure, Mr Doherty?" she asked, seating herself in the chair opposite. They already had the corkboard set up in the parlour, and Tabitha walked over, picked up some blank notecards and a pen, and then took a seat. Wolf went to pour brandies,

As he poured himself an extra-large brandy, sure he was going to need it before the evening was out, Wolf asked, "As the dowager countess asked, what brings you to Mayfair, Mickey?"

"Perhaps I just want to check in on my dear friend, his lordship, the great and good Wolf," the man answered sarcastically. Wolf knew better than to rise to the bait. Ever since Wolf had ascended to the earldom, Mickey D took great delight in tweaking his nose.

Wolf refused to take the bait and instead seated himself, crossing his legs and sipping on his brandy in as relaxed a manner as he could assume. Finally, seeing that he would have no more fun at Wolf's expense, Mickey D explained, "I might have had a sighting of your ginger-haired man."

At this, everyone sat up a little straighter, eager for news. Mickey D continued, "Our Sean, Ange's nephew, works in the Spitalfields market, helping his da out on his stall. Anyway, he belongs to a Working Men's Club down that way."

"What is a Working Men's Club?" the dowager asked.

"Well, I don't belong to one myself, Lady P, but from what I can tell, it's much like one of your high and mighty Gentleman's clubs that I'm sure his lordship here has membership of now." He jerked his head towards Wolf, who refused to acknowledge the jab. "When this one was started, maybe ten years ago now, there was a hope that it would keep the men out of the pubs and cut down on their booze. Instead, this club was somewhere to gather, play some cards, form some kind of brotherhood that could come together to help the community, that sort of thing. Anyway, from what I've heard from Sean, that all went downhill pretty quick like, and now it's a place for cheaper beer, some occasional rabble rousing, that kind of thing."

"And Sean has seen our man in this Working Men's Club?" Tabitha asked

"Aye, or he thinks he has."

Curious about something that Mickey D had said, Wolf said, "Tell me more about this rabble rousing."

"It's no big deal. Just the usual stuff, from what I've heard: workers' rights, the usual Labour Party stuff. There's the occasional Fenian sympathiser, just a load of grumblers as far as I can tell." Mickey paused, "But there have been some words said lately about the Jews and these killings," he admitted. "There's a lot of Irish in this club and they don't take kindly to the notion that someone might be targeting their lasses."

"Is Sean there now?" Wolf asked.

"He should be. I showed one of the picture Bear drew to all the lads over dinner and Sean happened to be by. He said he was going to the club to play some darts later."

Thinking about the protocols at White's, Langley asked, "Do you have to be a member to enter this club? And if so, can your nephew take us in as guests?"

"That he can. In fact, that's what I've come to suggest. If you ask at the door, they'll fetch Sean, and he can vouch for you. I know the man who works the door, Jack Geraghty. His older brother is one of my lads. Tell him I sent you to talk to Sean, and he won't give you any trouble. Of course, there's no guarantee the man will be there."

Looking Wolf up and down, Mickey D added, "And you might want to change your clothes. Also, just a suggestion: take Bear and only Bear. There's no women allowed, and this one," he gestured towards Langley, "well, I reckon you can't find an outfit that will disguise what a toff he is. Wolf couldn't really argue with that observation. Unlike Wolf, Langley had never known anything but wealth and privilege and didn't have the ability that Wolf had honed over his ten years as a thief-taker to slip into the guise of a less educated and cultured persona.

Tabitha was frustrated that, yet again, she was to be excluded from a part of the investigation. However, as with Wolf and Langley's outing to the National Liberal Club, that she was not welcome in the Spitalfields Working Men's Club was the fault of a male-dominated society rather than these specific men.

As if sensing Tabitha's irritation and likely sharing it, the dowager said, "Well, Tabitha and I have an outing of our own tomorrow." Tabitha looked over, her eyes narrowed suspiciously; what was the old woman up to? It was unlike her to volunteer to share Tabitha's company. Her curiosity was quickly satiated, "Tomorrow is the monthly luncheon for the Ladies of KB, and I am hosting this one. Tabitha, I suggest that you join us. The Ladies encounter a wide range of characters due to their line of work." As she said this, the dowager opened her eyes wide and raised her eyebrows, apparently hoping to stress just how varied a clientele the madams' various brothels catered to. "It is very possible that they know something or might recognise the picture of our suspect."

Tabitha was less surprised that the dowager continued to meet regularly with her flamboyant friends and more so that she was extending an invitation for Tabitha to join her. Anticipating this question, the dowager continued, "If we are to be partners in this investigation, then it only makes sense for you to join, Tabitha." This still didn't really explain the woman's sudden magnanimity, but Tabitha knew better than to question her too deeply. For now, she would have to be grateful that the invitation had been extended, whatever the true motivation was.

Wolf downed the last of his brandy and then stood. "If I am to change and get over to Spitalfields by hackney cab, I best get going. Let us hope that Bear is at home tonight. When he handed me the drawings, he did not indicate that he had any plans for the evening, so hopefully I can track him down quickly."

"Wolf, you go and change, and I will look for Bear," Tabitha offered. "It is likely that Talbot has some sense of where he might be." This made perfect sense, and so Wolf took his leave of the dowager and Langley, then nodded at Mickey D, saying, "Thank you, Mickey, for coming to tell us this."

Sensing that he was being dismissed, the East End gang leader gulped down the rest of his brandy, then stood and said, "Trouble in the East End with the Jews is bad for business. I want this killer found as much as anyone."

Twenty minutes later, Wolf was in his old thief-taking clothes and shoes, looking as little like a member of the aristocracy as it was going to be possible for him to look. He had removed the signet ring that he had inherited with the earldom and that had once belonged to his grandfather. As he'd done so, Thompson, his valet had commented on his hands.

"Your nails, m'lord, they're too well-kept."

"Well, whose fault is that?" Wolf said in an accusing tone. When Thompson had joined the household as Wolf's valet, taking over from Bear who had held the position in name only, the fastidious man had insisted on buffing and shaping Wolf's fingernails regularly.

"I take full responsibility, m'lord," Thompson said in a tone that indicated no actual remorse. "However, I stand by my statement that clean, groomed, well-polished nails set an earl apart from a street sweeper. However, that statement's accuracy works against us now; you will never pass for a working man with nails like that."

Wolf looked down at his hands and tried to remember how they had used to look in his thief-taking days. "What do you suggest I do?"

"Well, I do think that perhaps going out to the garden and running your hands through the soil would help. Perhaps even smear some dirt on your cheek for good measure."

Despite his valet's imperiousness in matters of grooming, Wolf knew the man's true value was that he didn't bat an eyelash when called upon to help his master with some disguise or other. This suggestion was only the most recent evidence of Thompson's worth. Nodding, Wolf picked up the battered hat that he had worn for many years in his prior life and set out for the garden.

The rest of the Chesterton House servants had become somewhat accustomed to their new master's occasional outings in old, dirty clothes, and they were too well-trained ever to question his actions. Even so, there was enough gossip below stairs that it was generally understood that the master and mistress sometimes solved crimes. Whether this acceptance of his eccentricities would extend to seeing the new Earl of Pembroke scrabbling in the dirt and intentionally wiping it on his face would remain to be seen.

By the time he reached the kitchen, Bear was already changed into his old clothes and was sitting at the kitchen table, sipping a cup of coffee. Wolf told him Thompson's suggestion, and Bear agreed that it was a sensible suggestion that he might also take up. Together, they exited the kitchen door, found the nearest flower bed, knelt on the path – some dirt on their knees would only add to the overall disguise – and rubbed their hands through the soil.

Pulling his hands out after a few seconds, Wolf shook the loose earth off and looked at his hands. Luckily, he had been due for Thompson to cut and clean his nails, so they were long enough that dirt could get stuck in them. Once he brushed all the loose dirt off, his hands were left an ugly brown colour. He then wiped them on his trousers. By the time he was done, his trousers looked as if he'd been hard at work outside all day, and his hands were a fright. For good measure, he ran his hands over his jaw.

Looking over at Bear, who had been similarly engaged, Wolf laughed. "Do I look as bad as you do?"

Bear chuckled, "Well, if the aim was to disguise the fact that you're one of the wealthiest and most powerful men in Britain, I think you've succeeded. I can only imagine what the dowager countess would say if she could see you now."

"Then I would say job done. I am not sure what we will be walking into tonight. Do you think we should get some backup?" Wolf asked.

Bear considered the question. "I think that we want to be careful not to draw too much attention to ourselves. We could get Little Ian to join us, and between the two of us it would certainly ensure that no one tries to jump you. But at what cost?"

"Yes, I believe you have a point. You are conspicuous enough. At least when it is just us two, people are used to seeing us together in the East end, or at least they used to be. Are we ready? I think it is late enough that we should be on our way." Bear nodded his agreement and the two men slipped out through the back gate to try their luck hailing a hackney cab.

Chapter 16

The Spitalfields Working Men's Club was opposite the main entrance to Spitalfields Market on Fournier Street. It was a plain, unassuming, red brick building, far different from White's or even the National Liberal Club. A steady stream of working-class men came in and out. Wolf and Bear walked up the steps to the simple black front door where a large, rather thuggish-looking man stood guard. His intimidating appearance came not only from his size but also from a nose that looked as if it had been broken multiple times and a particularly ugly cauliflower ear. Hoping that this was Jack Geraghty, Wolf approached the man who looked suspiciously at the two strangers.

"Wot d'you want? You're no members," the man growled.

Speaking in a low voice, Wolf said, "Mickey D said you could help us. We're looking for his nephew Sean who is going to show us around tonight."

It seemed that Mickey D was the magic phrase; Jack Geraghty smiled broadly and said in a far friendlier tone, "Aye, Sean's inside. Hang on a minute and I'll go fetch him. I'd let you just go in if it were up to me, but there's rules."

"That's perfectly fine," Wolf told him. "We'll just wait here."

Wolf and Bear only had to cool their heels for a couple of minutes before Jack Geraghty returned with a man Wolf assumed was Angie's nephew, Sean. The young man had something of her smile and the twinkle she always had in her eyes. Sean didn't say anything to them by way of greeting; he merely hitched his chin slightly and said, "Uncle Mick told you the deal?"

Wolf wasn't entirely sure what "the deal" was and hoped that all Sean meant was that they had been told that he thought he had spotted their ginger-haired man. Jack Geraghty opened the door for them, and Sean led the way into the club.

Inside, the Working Men's club continued its divergence from the gentlemen's clubs of Mayfair, which tended to be all gilt, marble and highly polished woods. Instead, the inside of this club had more of the feel of a comfortable working-class living room. The entrance hall had simple wooden floorboards covered with the occasional rather threadbare rug. Scattered here and there were chairs and sofas, all of which looked as if they had seen better days.

Sean led them into a small room off the main hallway that looked as if it functioned as a library. There were a couple of bookshelves with books arranged rather haphazardly and tables, many with newspapers strewn over them. White's had a large staff dedicated to the welfare and comfort of its members, which included ensuring that the grand establishment never had a ring mark on a table or a chair out of place. It seemed that this club did not benefit from similar services.

Closing the door to the library, Sean indicated that they should each sit in one of the uncomfortable-looking armchairs arranged in a semi-circle by the fireplace. Then he asked, "Did Uncle Mick tell you I thought I recognised your man?"

Given that there could be no other reason that Wolf and Bear would have made their way to the Spitalfields Working Men's Club, they merely nodded their heads. Sean continued, "He's not a member, but he came in recently with a group who are. I don't have much to do with them, but I've got the sense over time that they're the kind who are always ready for a dust-up."

Wolf knew exactly the kind of men Sean was describing; he'd had run-ins with their sort on multiple occasions during his thief-taking days. Some had real principles and constrained their bullyboy activities to supporting the increasingly active workers' unions and even the Independent Labour Party. However, there were certainly men who were for hire to the highest bidder and might be as likely to be bashing in the heads of striking workers as they were to be intimidating factory owners. Given what Mickey D had mentioned about political agitators and even Fenians in the club, Wolf wondered where on the spectrum of thugs-for-hire the men Sean was describing sat.

Sean seemed as if he wanted to say something but was not sure how best to phrase it. Guessing a possible source of the young man's discomfort, Wolf assured him, "Our only interest in this club is the man we are searching for. Whatever else I may see or hear goes no further, I swear." Sean visibly relaxed at these words and Wolf did wonder just how much the man was himself involved in such activities. He had heard Mickey D rail against the Fenian cause more than once, but that did not mean that his extended family held similar sentiments. Having encountered Fenian sympathisers during his second investigation with Tabitha, Wolf understood how deeply and passionately those ideals were held.

"Is our man here tonight?" Bear asked.

Sean shook his head, "No, but his friends are. And they seem particularly riled up, like something is going on. Sometimes stuff gets started here; men work each other up, then they have a few drinks and the next thing you know, a gang of them is itching for a fight, and they usually find it somewhere." Wolf could well imagine. There had been multiple incidents reported in the newspapers recently that he could imagine began in the way Sean described, in an establishment such as this one.

"What are you planning to do?" Sean asked. It was a good question and one that Wolf didn't have a good answer to. What was he planning to do?

"We would like to observe these men for a while. Perhaps their ginger-haired friend will even join them." When he said these words out loud, Wolf realised what a loose plan this was. Still, they had no better idea how to begin tracking this ginger-haired man who might only be a coincidental bystander to the murders. With such a plan in place, the group rose and left the room. As they followed Sean further down the corridor, Wolf could hear loud, raucous voices and laughter that suggested they were nearing a bar. Indeed, their guide quickly turned into a large room that had a bar at one end and a billiard table at the other. Unlike White's, where the favoured tipples ran more to a fine claret or cognac, it seemed that the only tipple on offer was beer. All around the room, men were drinking from large tankards, which suggested that any origins the club might have had in the temperance movement were long past.

The mood in the room seemed as jovial as any public house might be by that point in an evening. In one corner, a very red-faced, loud man was telling a story that at least he found highly amusing if his constant guffaws during its telling were anything to go on. Leaning on the bar on the other side of the room were a group of men. It seemed as if a very intense debate was taking place. Sean led the way towards this group, stopping just close enough that they could eavesdrop on the conversation but far enough away that they would not get pulled into it.

The men ordered themselves drinks, then tried hard to listen to the neighbouring conversation without being too obviously doing so. At first, Wolf had a hard time distinguishing what was being said; too much alcohol was fuelling what sounded more like an argument than a rational debate. Men talked and sometimes yelled over each other. Finally, Wolf began to discern who the two main debaters were and their opposing arguments. There was a short, dark-haired man with a very large, bulbous nose who seemed very intense and perhaps more sober than his friends. He seemed to be arguing that Jews should be excluded from trade unions. Standing almost nose to nose with him was a pock-marked, dirty-blonde-haired man who was maybe in his early forties.

"Workers are workers," Pockmark argued. "You're Irish; did the English want us taking their jobs? No, they didn't. Now, we're turning around and doing the same to another group of immigrants. Allowing the Jews in will increase our numbers and strengthen our cause overall."

Bulbous Nose stuck his forefinger in the other man's face and, almost spitting in rage, exclaimed, "Don't compare the Irish to those dirty Christ-killing Jews. They come here, take our jobs, drive down our wages, and now they're killing our lasses again."

The argument didn't get much more elaborate than those two points of view. Still, the debaters went around and around anyway, with the others in the crowd periodically throwing fuel on the fire, sometimes seemingly just for the fun of riling the two men up even more. If Wolf had to guess where the overall sentiment of the room lay, he would have said it was far more on the side of Bulbous Nose. There were very few genuine words of support for Pockmark's position. Whatever case could be made for unity between the various immigrant communities and the benefits of inclusivity within the unions and the broader workers' rights community, it didn't feel or sound like there were many willing to rally to Pockmark's cause in that room.

In the guise of telling Wolf a joke, Sean leaned in and said in a low voice, "The man with the nose, he's the ringleader of that group. He's a nasty piece of work and gathers some equally nasty characters around him. Like he's saying now, he seems to really hate the Jews. He's pretty new to the club as far as I know but he's managed to rile the men up in the short time he's been coming. The rest, well, as I said, I think they're mostly troublemakers who don't care much about how or why they cause trouble."

Wolf thought about the story of the attack of the young Jewish man Lilian Montagu had described over dinner and wondered whether the group of men next to him had been responsible. If they hadn't been, it sounded as if they were at least of guilty of similar mischief.

While Sean had been whispering, Wolf had somewhat lost the thread of the argument down the bar, but now it seemed to have escalated, and the voices were raised louder than ever. Certainly, at this point, there was no reason to pretend they weren't paying attention because everyone else in the room was as well. All heads were turned to the increasingly belligerent men. It seemed as if Bulbous Nose had now been joined by a young, fair-haired man who couldn't have been more than nineteen or twenty. The young man would have been quite handsome if it wasn't for a vicious scowl that marred his otherwise regular, pleasant features.

Now Bulbous Nose and Vicious Scowl were standing shoulder to shoulder, the latter looking as if he'd like nothing more than to hit someone, preferably Pockmark. Wolf thought about the rules and etiquette of White's and asked, "Are they allowed to continue like this here?"

Sean chuckled, "Not what you're used to in your clubs?" he guessed. "We've a higher tolerance for men speaking their minds bluntly at the Spitalfields Working Men's Club. You see that they haven't actually laid a hand on each other. They might want to, but that's where the line is drawn, and if it's crossed, Jack at the door will come and throw them all out and ban them for a month. More likely, they'll eventually choose to take this outside. Maybe even more likely is that the one with the nose and his friend there will ambush the other on his way home."

Most of the argument seemed to be nothing more than pugnacious posturing of the kind that Wolf had witnessed many times in The Cock after one too many tankards of ale. Suddenly, one phrase rang clear through the room, "Perhaps we ought to give those filthy Yids a taste of their own medicine. Maybe show one of their women what a real man with a foreskin is like. Who is with me?" Vicious Scowl said in a nasty tone that caused Wolf to believe this was more than a drunk man's bluster.

At the man's words, there seemed to be a change in atmosphere in the bar. Throughout the argument so far, Wolf had felt that most of the men, even the ones sympathetic to Bulbous Nose's words, had been viewing the altercation as a carnival sideshow and part of their evening's entertainment. However, suddenly, it was as if Vicious Scowl's words had awoken something within the men, and a bloodlust had overtaken them. Wolf could hear muttered words and phrases. He and Bear exchanged looks; they were both alert and tensed, ready for action. Suddenly, Wolf was very sorry that they hadn't brought Little Ian with them. For all of Bear's size, even he was no match for a large, angry mob.

It seemed that Vicious Scowl had also sensed the emotions his words had stirred, "To spit in the eye of us good Catholics, them Jews have their sabbath tonight and tomorrow. What better time than the day of the week when they most flaunt their dirty, heathen ways to teach them a lesson? Join with me, brothers. Tonight, we'll take back the East End."

At this rousing call to arms, Vicious Scowl slammed his tankard on the bar and pumped his fist into the air. He began to move towards the door with a few of the men in his wake. Despite their full-throated endorsement of the plan for violence, most of the crowd were working men who had families and jobs and no real appetite to get caught up in criminal activities. Many of them looked guiltily at each other as they failed to move, clearly relieved to see a similar unwillingness to put actions to their words on the faces of their fellow club members.

Turning back at the door, Viscous Scowl saw how few of the men, including Bulbous Nose, were actually with him and yelled back at the group, "Don't matter, you lily-livered, chicken-hearted bastards. Me and the boys here will do your work for you." With that, Viscous Scowl stormed out of the room.

Wolf said to Sean, "We will follow them. Can you get word to Mickey D that there may be trouble tonight?"

"I'll come with you," Sean said nervously, his tone suggesting that he thought he ought to offer rather than wanted to.

Wolf put a hand on the younger man's shoulder and replied, "Thank you for the offer, but you will be more help alerting Mickey D. He has no desire to have these tensions spiral into a war between the Jewish and Irish gangs and I have a feeling that these hot-heads could be the flint that sparks the tinder."

CHAPTER 17

Wolf and Bear had followed many suspects in their time; few were as easy as following Vicious Scowl and his friends. They were drunk, belligerent, and garrulous. Wolf and Bear could have been far less careful than they were being, and still, the group of working men, bruising for a fight, wouldn't have known they were being shadowed.

Wolf didn't know much about Judaism, but he'd learned a few things while recuperating from injuries in the Tuchinsky household and then over their dinner at the Montagu's that evening. He realised that Vicious Scowl had chosen the wrong night to go hunting for Jews to attack. While observant Jews might go back to the synagogue after their Shabbat dinner, and indeed, that was what Samuel Montagu had said he was going to do, those prayers would be long over, and everyone would be safe in their beds by now. Or at least Wolf hoped they would be.

It seemed that the lack of Jews out quickly dawned on Vicious Scowl and his band of thugs. After walking the streets somewhat randomly for about fifteen minutes, there seemed to be less enthusiasm for their expedition. It was getting late, and most of the men had work early the next morning. The cold evening air had taken enough of the edge off their drunkenness that they were starting to wonder why they were wandering the dark streets rather than heading to their warm beds. Vicious Scowl's group had not numbered more than a handful of men to begin with. Now Wolf noticed as one man, followed by another, silently abandoned the group, slinking off into the shadows. At least now the odds were far more even; only four men, and then quickly three remained. Wolf did not doubt that he and Bear were more than capable of taking on those odds.

The group had been walking down Artillery Lane, but now they turned onto Sandy's Row. With a sinking heart, Wolf realised that Vicious Scowl had not been walking aimlessly but instead had a plan. He glanced at Bear, who nodded. It was clear he'd just had the same realisation: the men were headed to Sandy's Row Synagogue. Considering things from Vicious Scowl's point of view, the decision made some sense; if they couldn't find a Jew to attack, they'd do the next best thing: attack a Jewish house of worship.

The men turned onto Sandy's Row. Watching the reduced group approach the synagogue, it did occur to Wolf that they might be considering setting it alight. He very much hoped they would realise how foolish that was, and how unlikely a blaze was to be contained just to the one building. The men were drunk, but Wolf hoped not so drunk that they couldn't come to a similar conclusion.

Arriving at the plain brick synagogue, Vicious Scowl came to a stop. Watching him from a safe distance, Wolf thought it seemed as if the wind had even gone out of the ringleader's sails somewhat. The man looked around, then turned and looked some more. The street was deserted, but he had led his men into battle, and they couldn't retreat now without even having raised their weapons. Finally, the man bent down, picked something up, and hurled it at the synagogue's window. Whatever he'd thrown merely bounced off the glass. Suddenly, Wolf and Bear could sense a new energy and purpose in the reduced group.

Wolf considered how much to intervene. With Bear at his side, he would easily put the odds in their favour against a group of drunks. However, he didn't want to resort to a street brawl if he didn't have to. It was one thing to fight in order to prevent Vicious Scowl and his thugs from attacking someone, another if all they were going to do was throw a few stones through windows.

Vicious Scowl, apparently frustrated by his first attempt, seemed to have found a stray brick and now he hurled that at the window. This time, it smashed a pane of glass. The other two men cheered but didn't seem inclined to join in. The noise of breaking glass had attracted the attention of neighbours and voices could be heard calling out. It seemed to occur to the men that they might also draw the attention of a passing policeman. Suddenly, the energy drained from the group and the rest of Vicious Scowl's companions melted away into the dark, and he was left alone. Wolf wondered if he would also give up and go home. At least for a few moments, that seemed like it would be the case. However, the man then went to wherever he had found the first brick and found another. He hurled that through a second, large window, and now the noise of breaking glass disturbed even more neighbours. Lights went on in houses, and front doors were opened. Now, finally, Vicious Scowl followed his companions into the anonymity of the night.

Wolf considered their next move; there was no doubt that he could report the window breaking to Bruiser the following morning. However, he had no desire for the publicity that would likely follow and the questions that might be asked about why the Earl of Pembroke was hanging around the streets of Whitechapel on a Friday night and just happened to witness the act of vandalism. He thought a better course of action would be to alert Mickey D and let him deal with his fellow Irishmen.

Turning to Bear, Wolf said, "Let us return home. I do not believe there is any more for us to do tonight." Bear agreed, and they began to walk back down Sandy's Row in the hope of hailing down a hackney cab at some point. Suddenly, they heard a woman scream. The noise came from an alleyway, Artillery Passage, just off Artillery Lane. Running to where they thought the noise had come from, they ran up the narrow lane that ran between a butcher's shop on one side and a bakery on the other. The lane led to a small courtyard where they immediately saw a woman lying on the ground.

Bear was the first to reach the woman, but one glance told him that she was already dead. Quickly scanning the courtyard, he saw that there was another point of egress and caught sight of something, maybe the red lining of a cloak. Torn between following and staying to help Wolf, Bear hesitated.

Seeing his friend's attention drawn to the other end of the alleyway, Wolf said, "There's nothing more we can do for her. If you think you saw something, go. I will wait here with the body." Bear didn't need to hear any more and was on his feet, chasing what may or may not have been their killer.

Left alone, Wolf observed the body as well as he could. Luckily, the moon was out, and there was some light in the courtyard. Wolf usually carried a candle and a matchbox in the jacket of his thief-taking outfit. Glad for that foresight, he struck a match and lit the candle. From what he could see, the victim was another young woman. Her clothes suggested that she was in service; certainly, she wasn't a prostitute. From the bruises already beginning to bloom on her neck, it seemed she had been strangled. However, that was where the resemblance to the previous murders ended. This body had not been mutilated. At least it hadn't been mutilated yet.

As Wolf observed the scene, he saw a knife lying beside the body. The killer must have heard their approach and dropped it as he fled. The knife had a medium-length, simple, single-edged blade with what seemed to be a bone handle with an intricate design carved into it. Wolf considered leaving the knife for the police to find with the body, then dismissed the thought and picked it up. He stood, wondering how Bear was faring. A few minutes more gave him his answer when his friend returned to the courtyard empty-handed.

"He got away," Bear said flatly. "The streets are dark and I had no idea who I was looking for. In fact, I don't even know I was chasing anyone. I thought I saw the swish of a cape with a flash of something red, but perhaps I didn't."

"I think you did," Wolf replied. Holding up the knife, explaining, "I believe we interrupted our killer before he had a chance to perform his usual macabre acts upon the body." Looking over at the victim, Wolf continued with a weary sadness in his voice, "There is nothing more we can do for this poor soul. Let us find the nearest constable and report the murder, then continue home. One thing we do know, whoever our killer is, it isn't any of the men we followed tonight; they all disappeared in the other direction."

Bear agreed with this assumption. Of course, it would have been too simple for Vicious Scowl to have also turned out to be their murderer and perhaps too obvious. Whoever was killing these women seemed to have a cunning and intentionality that didn't match the hot-headedness they had seen on display that evening from Vicious Scowl and his friends.

After walking north for a few minutes, they came across a police constable on patrol. Wolf and Bear gave the details of the body, casually dropped Bruiser's name to persuade the young PC that they had some clout in the local precinct and gave the address where they might be found for further questioning. If the young policeman wondered why these scruffy men wandering the streets of Whitechapel had a fancy Mayfair address, he was far too overwhelmed by the prospect of being the first on the scene at a gruesome murder to say anything.

Finally, after walking for another twenty minutes, they were in a hackney cab and on their way back to Mayfair. The two men didn't speak much during the drive back. Bear noticed the knife that Wolf was holding but didn't ask any questions. This was one of Bear's characteristics that Wolf most appreciated, after the man's honesty and loyalty: he was not a big talker and had no problem sitting in silence, allowing each to contemplate the evening.

It was past midnight when they arrived back at Chesterton House. It seemed that Tabitha hadn't waited up for them, for which Wolf was grateful. He was not ready to discuss their evening yet. Finding the latest victim had shaken him profoundly. For all of the investigations he had been involved in recently, none of them had involved him stumbling across an actual dead body. He had always been brought into a case some time after a body had been discovered. He had seen dead bodies in his time, but never one so fresh that it was still warm to the touch. And never someone as young as the one in the courtyard that evening.

Entering the house and telling Talbot to lock up and then retire for the evening, Wolf headed for his study, Bear in tow. Bear went and poured them both large brandies while Wolf took one of the armchairs in front of the fire. Holding the knife on his lap, he stared at the blade. Had this knife been used to mutilate the other girls? The idea that he was holding such a weapon sent chills through his body.

Bear handed Wolf a glass of brandy, then settled in the other armchair. Still, the man didn't ask any questions. Finally, Wolf looked up from the blade and said, "This is the knife I found. I believe we disturbed the killer before he was able to perform his usual gruesome ritual."

"Can I take a look," Bear asked. Wolf handed the knife over. Bear inspected it for a few moments. "Interesting choice of weapon," he observed.

"What makes you say that?"

"Well, for a start, it's not the kind of easy-to-carry pocketknife that we have on us usually. The blade is quite long. While I suspect that the killer escaped with the sheath still on his belt, nevertheless, it doesn't seem like the most convenient thing to walk around London with."

"He was not merely walking through London though, was he? The man had a purpose."

"Even so, it wouldn't have been my first choice. There are far more convenient knives he might have used."

Bear's point was well-taken. However, acknowledging its truth didn't move them any further forward.

"I know a man who is very knowledgeable about weaponry. You might almost say he's a little obsessed," Bear said thoughtfully. "He's a quirky fellow, but if anyone will know something about a knife like this, it's him."

"How have I never met this associate in all the time I've known you?" Wolf asked, half jestingly, half seriously. He and Bear had lived and worked together almost continuously over the past ten years, and it was hard to believe that there was much they didn't know about each other.

Bear chuckled, acknowledging the sentiment that sat behind Wolf's question, "He's married to my Cousin, Phyllis."

"You have a Cousin Phyllis?"

"I do. She's the daughter of Pa's brother. Like me, she wanted nothing to do with the family business." Bear's father, Donny Caruthers, had been the self-proclaimed best forger in all of England. Despite Donny's efforts to pass his trade to his eldest son, Bear had made quite clear his lack of interest in the family business, and it now appeared that he was not the only family member to have done so.

"Phyllis and her husband, Victor, live in Fitzrovia. He's a bit eccentric, to say the least. Invents things. Some of his inventions are crazy, and others he's sold the patents for. He's not very good with money, so they seem to swing between reasonable middle-class prosperity and imminent eviction. Last I heard from Ma, Victor was on an upswing, and they'd bought themselves a little house. I haven't seen Phyllis in a while, but she's a good sort. We always got along, and she was one of the few family members, besides Ma that is, who understood why I didn't want to follow in Pa's and Uncle Simon's footsteps. We lost touch when she married Victor and moved away, but her mother still lives in Whitechapel, and it won't be hard to get her address. I probably owe Auntie Jean a visit anyway. I'll head over tomorrow morning and then we can go and visit my eccentric cousin-in-law, Victor Grund."

CHAPTER 18

The following morning, Tabitha was up early and had already breakfasted by the time Wolf finally surfaced. He and Bear had sat up late, neither feeling the lure of slumber after stumbling upon a new murder victim. Despite the late hour, Wolf wasn't hungry and instead of making for the breakfast room, asked Talbot where he might find her ladyship.

"She is in the drawing room with Lord Langley, milord."

Langley? At ten o'clock on a Saturday morning? That didn't bode well. Wolf made his way to the drawing room. As he approached, he could hear Langley's patrician baritone, occasionally punctuated by Tabitha's sweet voice.

He paused at the slightly ajar door. "Why would they write such terrible things?" Tabitha asked.

Wolf pushed the door open further and entered the room, asking, "What terrible things?"

"Ah, Pembroke. Good timing," Langley said, standing and putting out his hand to shake Wolf's in greeting. In his other hand, he was holding a newspaper. Based on the excessive illustrations he could see on its front page, Wolf assumed it was the usually melodramatic and overly sensational Illustrated Police News. The paper had first gained its reputation for outrageous muck-slinging in 1888 during Jack the Ripper's reign of terror, carrying lurid descriptions and illustrations of the murders. Much of the xenophobia and anti-Semitism that had been fomented during the prior murders could be traced to the weekly newspaper. If Langley's presence that morning was any indication, the newspaper was back at it.

Confirming Wolf's suspicions, Langley held the newspaper up. "This is nasty stuff, Pembroke. Perhaps even nastier than a decade ago. It's an ugly brew, containing some of the sentiments we've been seeing stirred up in France, some of the things the unions have been saying about Jewish workers, and just some of the usual vitriol lobbed at the Jewish community. And sentiments have already been stirred. Early this morning, there were two separate incidents where Jewish men were attacked on their way to their sabbath prayers. One just outside of the Sandy's Row, which also had windows broken last night, and another on the way to the Bevis Marks Synagogue."

Wolf noticed that Langley's normally imperturbable demeanour seemed to have deserted him. One answer why became clear, "I had a message from the Prime Minister at eight o'clock this morning. He is not happy and wants to know what progress we have made. He fears that this is only the beginning of the repercussions against the Jewish community."

"We have not even been working on the case for four days," Tabitha protested.

Langley held up his hands in mock surrender, "You do not have to convince me. However, it seems there was yet another murder last night."

"I know. Bear and I found the body," Wolf said, surprising Tabitha and Langley.

"How on earth did that happen?" Langley asked. Wolf gave a summary of their previous evening at the Spitalfields Working Men's Club and then how they followed Vicious Scowl.

"So, you do not believe that the men you were following could have committed the murder?"

Wolf shook his head. "They were a riled-up, drunken mob. These killings are premeditated. Even if the men had not dispersed in the opposite direction, there was nothing about their actions that suggested anything other than spur-of-the-moment violent impulses."

Langley nodded, acknowledging Wolf's logic. "What can I report back to the Prime Minister? Because I must report something back, however minuscule the progress."

"Wait here," Wolf said, rising and leaving the room. He returned a few moments later holding the knife. "We came upon the killer before our killer was done with the more ritualistic parts of the murders. In his hurry to escape, he dropped this knife."

Langley and Tabitha both approached, eager to see the first real piece of evidence that had been gathered. "I take it you did not tell the police about this," Langley said in a tone that suggested he wasn't unhappy about the judgment call.

"We did not. Bear says he has a man who might be able to tell us something about this kind of knife. I believe that we are better placed to make use of this evidence than the Metropolitan Police."

"I agree and will relay as much to the Prime Minister. He is eager for any crack in the case. While we have no reason to believe that this case could become as politically divisive as the Dreyfus affair has been in France, nevertheless, Salisbury is concerned. I believe he is under a lot of pressure from Baron Rothschild. That is not a family one wishes to cross if one cares about the financial stability of the country."

"Indeed," Wolf concurred. He considered what he wanted to say next, finally deciding that Langley knew him well enough to hear the unvarnished truth. "Please caution the Prime Minister that, while this may turn out to be a useful clue, it may also turn out to be a dead end. For all we know, knives like this are two a penny. However, one thing you might mention, though again, with a caveat: this knife has a Celtic design on it. It seems unlikely to be something a Jew in London would carry."

Langley acknowledged the warning and, shortly after, took his leave. Tabitha and Wolf continued sitting companionably in the drawing room. "So, who is this mystery man who may know something about this knife?" she asked. When given the answer, Tabitha looked surprised and said, "And you did not know of this Cousin Phyllis?"

Wolf laughed. "I once heard that the secret to a good marriage is to be always surprising each other. Perhaps the same is true of a good friendship. No, I had never heard of Cousin Phyllis and her eccentric inventor husband, Victor, until last night. Bear has gone to visit his aunt to get

Phyllis' address and then we will make our way over there. What time is your luncheon?"

Tabitha looked at the clock on the mantel, "At half past eleven. Apparently, they always start quite early because everyone has to get back to running their businesses." Tabitha said this with slightly raised eyebrows; she still wasn't quite sure what to make of the upcoming visit by the Ladies of KB.

The last few months working on investigations with Wolf had helped Tabitha to move out of the gilded cage she had lived in, first with her parents and then her husband, and she had come to understand the myriad of dire situations that might force a woman into prostitution. Nevertheless, her old prejudices were hard to shake, and she still couldn't quite believe that this colourful group of brothel owners was now part of the regular social set for the Dowager Countess of Pembroke. As she had this thought, she chastised herself. After all, wasn't the real wonder that the dowager was so willing to engage in an ongoing friendship with these women? And did Tabitha really want to be more closed-minded than the dowager? Even as she had this thought, she could imagine the tone in which the dowager would mock her preconceived notions.

Suddenly realising that she had just a little more than an hour, Tabitha said, "I must go and change if I am to be on time. I do not believe that luncheon will be long. Or at least if it seems like it might be, I could excuse myself. I would like to visit Cousin Phyllis with you." Given that Bear hadn't even returned, Wolf saw no reason not to agree to the request.

Forty-five minutes later, Tabitha was in the carriage, wearing one of her smarter new dresses. In truth, she hadn't been sure what the dress code for such a group might be, but the dowager had described the women as a colourful and stylish bunch, and so Tabitha intended to look her best.

The drive to the dowager's home was not a long one, and a few minutes later, the Pembroke carriage came to a stop. Another carriage pulled up at the same time, and just as the footman was helping Tabitha down, she noticed a tall, striking-looking woman descending from the other carriage. The woman was perhaps in her early sixties and was tall and willowy. Perhaps most extraordinary was what she was wearing: a flowing dress of a soft-looking fabric that didn't seem to benefit from a corset. The entire ensemble looked far less restrictive than was fashionable. While

Tabitha was a little shocked and couldn't imagine wearing such a dress herself, she also thought that the woman looked quite comfortable while also rather stylish. To top off her ensemble, the intriguing woman was wearing a turban with a peacock feather in it.

It quickly became evident that this woman and Tabitha were both visiting the same house, so Tabitha turned, offered her hand, and said, "I am Tabitha Chesterton, Lady Pembroke."

"Ah yes," the woman said knowingly. "We have heard all about you."

Tabitha was nervous as to what that statement might mean. Given what the dowager said to her face, she could only imagine what she said behind her back.

The woman flashed a friendly smile and said, "I am Madame Zsa Zsa. We are so glad you can join our little gathering today."

Tabitha was unsure what the dowager may have already told her friends about the investigation, and she certainly did not wish to repeat the same story multiple times. So, instead, she acknowledged the sentiment.

Manning answered the door almost immediately. If the always inscrutable butler had any feelings about the group gathering for luncheon at the home of the doyenne of aristocratic circles, Tabitha certainly couldn't discern it in his face or manner. He greeted Madam Zsa Zsa as he might the Duchess of Somerset or the Queen herself.

The two women were shown into the drawing room, where they were met by the most fascinating collection of women Tabitha had ever seen. Without a word being spoken, Tabitha could already see why the dowager might find these women's company more entertaining than her usual cronies in polite society.

The first thing Tabitha noticed about the women was their diversity. She thought Madam Zsa Zsa was probably the oldest and that the youngest was perhaps twenty years younger. However, their range of ages was hardly the most notable thing about this group. Instead, it was the variety of skin tones and ethnicities that was the most fascinating. Prior to their trip to Brighton, Tabitha's exposure to people of different races had been almost non-existent. Of course, she had read about other countries and the people who populated them. She had particularly enjoyed *The Jungle Book* by Rudyard Kipling. Tabitha had certainly known that

London was populated by people of all sorts of backgrounds and skin tones. However, her exposure to them had been almost negligible until she met Lady Arlene Archibald during their recent investigation.

Looking around the room, Tabitha saw a small, dark-skinned woman who she thought was from the Indian subcontinent. She was talking to a blonde woman whose arm was covered in the kind of colourful illustrations that Tabitha had only thought were sported by sailors and pirates. There was an oriental-looking woman who was dressed particularly stylishly and carried a reticule that Tabitha immediately coveted. This woman was sitting next to a petite, very pretty woman. In that same grouping was a woman with very curly hair, cut to just below her ears, wearing a man's suit. This might have shocked Tabitha more before her acquaintance with Tuchinsky.

Finally, standing, admiring a painting on the wall, was a tall, slim woman of indeterminate origin and another slim, pretty young woman.

"Ah, Tabitha, fashionably late, I see," the dowager pronounced. As it happened, Tabitha was on time, and the other women were early. The dowager stood and greeted Madame Zsa Zsa warmly, far more warmly than she ever greeted Ladies Hartley and Willis. "I see that you and Tabitha, Lady Pembroke, have already met. Let me introduce the rest of you to my late son's wife."

The dowager then went around the room, introducing all the women, many of whom had names almost as exotic and colourful as they were. Tabitha knew she'd never remember them all. There was Half-blind Kim, the tall woman looking at the painting. As far as Tabitha could tell, the woman could see perfectly well. The woman she had been standing with was Madame Tammy. The mannish-looking woman was, ironically, Girly Lizzy. The petite woman was Spanish Gemma and the woman with the painted arm was Russian Alexandra, though she insisted on being called Alexa. The Indian woman was introduced as Sameera, but it seemed that everyone called her Spicy. Tabitha wasn't sure she was willing to call a stranger, or indeed anyone, by that name. Finally, the dowager came to the stylish, oriental-looking woman who was introduced as Pretty Pearl.

Even though it was barely past noon, the women were drinking wine. This was not the done thing for aristocratic women. However, when the dowager nonchalantly passed Tabitha a glass, she accepted it and wondered for a moment why it was acceptable for men to drink at all hours of the day but not women. As she sipped on her wine, she observed how comfortable the women were with each other. While strictly speaking, Tabitha supposed they were business rivals, there was nothing competitive in the way each woman, by turn, teased, advised and encouraged the others.

Now she was amongst them, Tabitha could see why the dowager found the group so appealing. The dowager was often heard lamenting what crashing bores the supposed great and good of English society were. Honestly, Tabitha couldn't really disagree with the woman's judgement. Between the petty sniping at each other, continuous attempts at one-upmanship and endless gossiping, upper-crust society was not something Tabitha had missed when it turned its back on her. This group of women couldn't have been more different.

It wasn't until after luncheon, when everyone was gathered back in the drawing room for tea and coffee, that the dowager raised the topic of their investigation. She had a copy of the drawing Bear had created, and she passed it around the room. All of the madams looked at it closely but shook their heads when asked if they recognised the man. That was until the drawing reached Half-blind Kim.

"I think I recognise this man," she said uncertainly. "I haven't seen him for a while and he was never a regular, but I'm sure I know the face."

When the dowager had first been introduced to the madams, they explained the variety of tastes each of their brothels catered to. While the dowager had, of course, known about brothels, she had assumed that they all did no more than cater to men such as her husband in fulfilling needs that their wives no longer desired to satiate. She had been quite astonished to hear that Madam Tammy catered to men who preferred other men and that Spicy's clientele enjoyed recreating their days in the nursery. Perhaps the most astonishing to her was that Girly Lizzy catered to women who enjoyed the company of other women.

As shocking as these revelations had been, it seemed that Half-blind Kim's establishment catered to such deviant desires that she had demurred when her turn for explanation had come. Hearing that their ginger-haired suspect may have been one of Half-blind Kim's customers, the dowager was more intrigued than ever to discover what predilections were catered to in that house of ill repute. However, it seemed that the madam was going to reveal no more that afternoon than that she recognised the man.

"Can I take this drawing to show to my girls? They may remember more about him than I do." She thought for a moment, then added, "If he is the man I think he is, I can tell you that he's Irish."

That was certainly useful information, and Tabitha thanked the madam and asked her to send word to Chesterton House if her girls remembered anything else.

Chapter 19

Tabitha had pondered whether or not to tell the dowager about the proposed visit to Bear's cousin later that day. Finally, she realised that keeping information from the dowager about investigations in the past had only led to her going off on her own, and nothing good had ever come from that. They had agreed to work on this case as a team, so that was what they needed to do.

Once the Ladies of KB had all departed, Tabitha filled the dowager in on the details of Wolf and Bear's activities the previous evening and the knife they had found next to the latest victim.

"So, the plan is to go and visit Bear's cousin, Phyllis, in the hope that her husband can tell us more about this weapon?" the dowager asked.

"That is the plan," Tabitha confirmed.

"Well, that does not sound particularly exciting, but instead, one of the more workaday aspects of an investigation that does not benefit from my particular skillsets."

Tabitha held her breath; did this mean that the dowager didn't mean to join them? If she had known it would be that easy to dissuade her, Tabitha might have tried making other aspects of investigating sound more mundane. However, she also realised that she had to be careful; any indication from Tabitha that the older woman was not welcome would be sure to pique her interest in joining the expedition. Instead, Tabitha tried to affect as dispassionate tone as possible, saying, "Mama, the choice is entirely yours. It goes without saying that your participation would be most welcome."

"Ha! It goes without saying, does it? No matter, I believe I will return with you to Chesterton House and then decide."

During the brief carriage ride from one grand house to another, the dowager asked coyly, "So, how did you find my Ladies of KB?"

Tabitha considered the question, then answered, "I will confess that when you first announced that you would continue your association with these women even after the investigation was resolved, I did question the wisdom of such a decision." While the dowager said nothing, the look on her face spoke volumes about her feelings about anyone questioning any decision of hers, let alone Tabitha. Ignoring the woman's reaction, Tabitha continued, "However, having met your ladies, I can truly see why you wished to continue the friendship; they are delightful. They are an interesting, fun, and friendly group."

The dowager's smile on hearing this was less one of pleasure and more one of satisfaction at being acknowledged to be right.

Talbot was usually as imperturbable as Manning. However, when he opened the door to Chesterton House, there was a tightness to his smile and a terseness in his voice that indicated something had happened. Ever since Melody had been abducted, Tabitha had always been inclined to suspect the worst immediately. Seeing the look of panic immediately wash over her face, Talbot said hurriedly, "Nothing is amiss, milady. It is merely, well, that is to say..." the butler stuttered.

"Spit it out, man. I cannot stand all this shillyshallying," the dowager scolded.

Suddenly, from the direction of the drawing room, a loud, shrill voice rang out, "Tabitha, is that you?"

Tabitha suddenly felt lightheaded. It couldn't be, could it? What on earth was her mother doing here?

That question was about to be answered as Lady Jameson, the Marchioness of Cambridgeshire, came into view. Even well into middle age, Lady Jameson was a very handsome woman. Tabitha favoured her mother more than any of her sisters did. From her mother Tabitha had inherited her thick, rich, chestnut hair, though Lady Jameson's was flecked with grey now. Like Tabitha, Lady Jameson was quite tall, and her figure was as trim as any debutante's. The women shared similar features, though unlike her daughter, Lady Jameson's eyes were a brilliant blue. Tabitha's eyes radiated kindness and compassion, but her mother's were cold and hard.

"Mother, what are you doing here?" Tabitha stammered, trying to get a hold of her emotions.

"Well, that is not what I would call a warm welcome," her mother said with a sniff.

"It is just a surprise," Tabitha said, grasping for any excuse for her reaction.

"Yes, well, that was the plan: to surprise you. Though I had hoped it might be a more pleasant surprise."

Finally, regaining her composure somewhat, Tabitha stared at her mother, unsure how to answer that statement. Lady Jameson had always considered her youngest daughter her problem child and had been eager to marry her off. Whatever she might or might not have known or guessed about Jonathan's nature was not sufficient for her to caution Tabitha when Jonathan offered for her. Instead, she almost pushed her naive young daughter into the arms of a violent and abusive husband.

Once she was safely married off, Tabitha barely heard from her mother, who did not care for London. A year into Tabitha's marriage, her father had died, and then her mother had retreated permanently to the country estate for her mourning period. When Jonathan had died, and Tabitha had briefly been under suspicion for his death, she had heard nothing from her mother except a terse letter explaining that Lady Jameson was still far too overcome by her own grief to attend the funeral of her son-in-law. That was the last communication the mother and daughter had exchanged in over a year.

While Tabitha had been quite relieved not to have to deal with her mother's criticism and harsh judgements during her mourning period, she nevertheless had felt the absence of a warm, supportive maternal embrace during the most difficult, loneliest periods of her life. The idea that her mother would be offended that Tabitha didn't consider her unexpected appearance after all that time to be a pleasant surprise was beyond belief.

Tabitha didn't know what to say in answer. Luckily, and shockingly, she was saved from replying. "Lady Jameson, perhaps your daughter's surprise may be attributed to a suspicion that you had forgotten the location of Chesterton House, such has been the length of time since you graced it with your presence," the dowager said in a tone dripping with sarcasm.

"I will confess to having been surprised to learn that my daughter was still in residence here, living with the new earl, who I understand is a young, unmarried man. Perhaps surprised is not the correct word, and I should say appalled," Lady Jameson parried then thrust.

As amazed as Tabitha was that the dowager would come to her defence, she also felt the impropriety of conducting this conversation by the front door in front of the servants. Walking towards the drawing room, she indicated that the two older women should follow her.

It seemed that Talbot had ensured that Lady Jameson was well supplied with tea and cake, though Tabitha felt like she could do with something stronger than tea. Moving to the decanters on the sideboard, she poured herself a sherry and then offered something to the other women.

"Sherry in the early afternoon? Is this how you are conducting yourself these days, Tabitha?"

"I would love a sherry, my dear," the dowager answered. Tabitha couldn't believe what she'd just heard. Had her mother-in-law just used a term of endearment? She had known the woman for more than three years and had never been addressed so warmly. To be fair, she had never heard the dowager refer to anyone by a term of endearment except for "Dear Jeremy" and Melody. From the way the two other women were eyeing each other, Tabitha had the feeling that battle lines were being drawn and that the dowager had decided that the enemy of her enemy was her friend and had firmly aligned herself with Tabitha.

Finally, sherry in hand, Tabitha took a seat and asked, "So, what brings you to London, Mother?"

"Is it so incredible that I might come solely to visit my youngest daughter?"

Given that the answer was yes, it was incredible to imagine such a thing, Tabitha didn't bother to answer.

"Fine, I will tell you why I have come. Some scandalous news has reached my ears. As you may know, I have been in Matlock with Petra and Xander, helping your sister through her confinement for some months."

Tabitha didn't know this. Her mother continued, "Being so far out of society for some time, I was slow to receive all the London gossip. However, I dined one night at a neighbouring estate, and they had visitors from London, a Lord and Lady Hartley." Tabitha inwardly groaned. Lady Hartley was a notorious gossip. What terrible luck that she and her mother had met. Tabitha could only imagine what scandalous concoctions Lady Hartley had been eager to dispense.

"Lady Hartley? You came here because of something that gossiping harpy told you?" the dowager said derisively. "That woman makes up more than she knows. She would be better off using her breath to cool her porridge."

"So, it is not true that you are engaged to your husband's cousin?" Lady Jameson said with all the glee of someone who had just placed a winning hand in cards.

Tabitha gasped. How on earth did Lady Hartley get hold of that information, and what was she thinking of repeating it? Moreover, how should she answer? Tabitha and Wolf were not officially betrothed, but there was no doubt they had an understanding. If her mother's point was that Tabitha was now living in the same house as a man she had promised herself to, then the technicality of a formal engagement was likely not material to the inevitable scandal once society got wind of the situation.

As she pondered how to reply, she was again saved from answering by the dowager, who replied in a calm yet authoritative tone, "I can assure you that Tabitha is not engaged to Lord Pembroke."

Looking as if she were sucking a lemon, Lady Jameson shot back, "You can assure me of that, can you, Lady Pembroke? How can you claim to be so sure?"

"Because if they were engaged, I would know. I am very close to dear Tabitha and Jeremy; one might even say I am a confidante to them both." Tabitha tried hard not to snort with laughter at this statement. "As the closest thing to a mother Tabitha has had by her side during the trying times of her mourning and then over the months since, I am privy to all her secrets."

The absurdity of this entire statement almost had Tabitha rolling her eyes. However, she was aware that, in her own way, the dowager was defending her and so kept tight control over her reactions.

Lady Jameson did not seem impressed by any of the dowager's claims and instead addressed Tabitha directly: "If this is true, am I to believe then that there will be no engagement in the future?"

Tabitha couldn't help glancing over at the dowager. "Ha!" her mother said victoriously. "I knew there was something to this gossip. You are living in a state of sin so scandalous that without quick and forceful interference, it will taint us all." And there it was, the real reason her mother had deigned to visit. It was not from concern for Tabitha but rather fear about how any brewing scandal would affect her. Truthfully, Tabitha was relieved to understand her mother's true motivation finally; it put the world back to rights to realise that this visit was nothing more than pure self-interest.

"I see that I have arrived in the nick of time to prevent a complete disaster. You must move out immediately and return with me to Cambridgeshire," Lady Jameson ordered with the absolute certainty of being obeyed.

"I will do no such thing," Tabitha said more forcefully than she had ever talked to her mother. Whether or not she could continue to live in the same house as Wolf once their engagement was announced, the very last place she would go was back home to live with her mother.

"Do not use that tone of voice with me, young woman," Lady Jameson said in horror at the filial insolence. "I am your mother, and you will do as I say."

"I am no longer a young, unmarried woman living in your home and under your power," Tabitha said, feeling more confident as she spoke. "I am a widow with an independent income. I will do as I choose."

"Indeed," the dowager chimed in. "When it is appropriate, Tabitha will remove herself to my home for the duration of the engagement."

She would? Tabitha thought with horror. The idea of living under the same roof as the dowager did not feel like an infinitely better choice than returning home with her mother. However, now was hardly the time to say that. Instead, she answered, "Whatever I choose to do, I will choose it, not you, Mother. I am sorry that you feel that my living situation somehow negatively reflects on you. However, that is not a sufficiently good reason for me to move from my home."

Lady Jameson audibly gasped at her daughter's audacity. "You were always the most difficult and wilful of my children, and I see that you remain so as an adult. I had hoped that your husband would curb your tongue and rein in your recalcitrant behaviour. Indeed, from what I had heard, he used an appropriately firm hand and had tempered the worst of it. It is unfortunate that he died before his reformation of your character was more firmly in place."

Tabitha couldn't believe what she was hearing; her mother had known of Jonathan's treatment of her and had approved. Glancing over at the dowager, Tabitha saw the woman's face suffused with an emotion she had never witnessed there before: pity. Having spent time with the dowager and one of her daughters, Jane, Tabitha would hardly call the woman an exemplar of maternal virtues. Nevertheless, she had never heard even the dowager say anything quite as heartless and lacking in all parental concern as the words that had just come out of her own mother's mouth. And that was saying something!

Just when Tabitha thought that she couldn't be more appalled by her mother's words and more amazed by those of the dowager, the latter showed, yet again, that her behaviour should never be assumed. "Lady Jameson," the dowager said in a tone that conveyed both sadness but also certainty at her words, "my son was a brute. There is no other word for it. The world is a better place for his death, and Tabitha is certainly safer and happier with him gone from her life. To suggest that my son's indiscriminate use of his wife as his personal punching bag had any salutary effects is nothing other than vicious."

When Jonathan first died, the dowager blamed Tabitha, claiming that if she had been a sufficiently docile wife, he wouldn't have committed the violence that ultimately ended up leading to his death. Since then, there had been some softening of the old woman's words as she admitted that her husband was also violent towards her. Still, there had been no indication, in word or deed, over the last six months that the dowager had such genuine sympathy for what horrors Tabitha had endured during her marriage. To hear the woman say so now, even if it might have been merely to score points against an enemy, was nevertheless extraordinarily gratifying.

For her part, Lady Jameson seemed struck dumb, at least momentarily, by the dowager's words. The two women had jostled for power during the planning for their children's wedding and had then retreated to their corners in mutual dislike. Luckily, the preference of one for London and the other for the country had ensured that they rarely encountered each other. However, if they had, Lady Jameson would have expected deference to her higher rank. If nothing else, she would have anticipated that she and her nemesis maintain the dance of manners and insincere politeness that characterised even the most deep-seated loathing within aristocratic circles. That the other woman had broken from this norm and spoken so candidly was almost as incredible as the actual insults she had hurled.

Lady Jameson considered herself a paragon of social proprietary and, as such, would not lower herself to muck-slinging no matter how much she might be taunted. Instead, she stood, her spine ramrod straight, and said in the coldest of voices, "I see that neither my presence nor my advice is desired, and, as such, I will leave."

If Lady Jameson had expected her daughter would stop her and apologise, then she was to be sorely disappointed. Tabitha replied cooly, "I believe that is for the best, Mother." Lady Jameson could not have looked more shocked if Tabitha had actually struck her. Without a further word, she left the room, and moments later, they heard the front door shut behind her. Tabitha neither knew nor cared where her mother was planning to go; she was merely relieved to have her gone.

Tabitha turned to the dowager and said simply, "Thank you, Mama."

Sniffing, the dowager may have looked somewhat self-conscious and answered, "Thank you for what? I have no idea what you are talking about, Tabitha."

Chapter 20

While Bear had been in Whitechapel visiting his Auntie Jean, Wolf had been holed up in his study working on estate business. When Lady Jameson had appeared at Chesterton House, she hadn't asked for Lord Pembroke, and Talbot had wisely not volunteered the information that his master was at home. Thanks to his butler's quick thinking, Wolf had missed the entirety of Tabitha's mother's visit, and when he walked into the drawing room a mere ten minutes after her departure, he had no idea of his near miss.

Tabitha might have saved him the knowledge of her mother's visit and its purpose, but the dowager had no such qualms. "Jeremy, have you been here the entire time?" she demanded.

"What entire time?" he asked, thoroughly confused.

"The entire time that termagant was here berating dear Tabitha."

Now Wolf was more confused than ever. Since when had the dowager referred to her erstwhile daughter-in-law as "Dear Tabitha?" he glanced at the recipient of this endearment, who quickly shook her head and tried to communicate that she'd explain more later.

The dowager rarely needed another active participant in a conversation, and this one was no exception, "The sheer nerve of that woman. I know she is your mother, Tabitha." At this, Wolf's eyebrows shot up, "Still, she really is beyond the pale. Of course, society is littered with similarly appalling wives and mothers." It was evident to Tabitha and Wolf that the dowager did not include herself in this group.

Hoping to forestall a replay of the scene with her mother, Tabitha pivoted the conversation and asked, "Has Bear returned yet?"

"Yes. Bear has his cousin's address and her mother's assurance that even if Phyllis is not at home, Victor is bound to be. According to his mother-in-law, the eccentric inventor rarely leaves his workroom. We were merely waiting for you to return before heading out." Wolf paused, realising the implication of the dowager's presence and then amended his statement, "For you both to return." The dowager acknowledged his words, clearly having changed her mind about joining the expedition.

Twenty minutes later, they were all in the carriage and on the way to Fitzrovia. The streets were busy, and the ride took over thirty minutes. Fitzrovia was a part of London Tabitha was unfamiliar with, and she was fascinated by the eclectic neighbourhood with its narrow streets of modest brick homes, stores and lively public houses. Bear explained that it was considered quite a bohemian neighbourhood, and Tabitha felt there was a vibrant energy to the locale, notwithstanding its still quite gritty urban nature. There were people everywhere, sitting at pavement cafes, spilling out of taverns, hawking their wares on street corners. There was no doubt that the area didn't have the air of desperation that seemed to hover over Whitechapel and its environs. These were artists, tradesmen, and solidly middle-class families.

Cousin Phyllis and her husband, Victor, lived on Charlotte Street in the heart of Fitzrovia. Their narrow, brick-fronted three-storey house was indistinguishable from the many others in the neighbourhood. They had a red front door with a charming brass knocker in the shape of a downward-facing hand. Bear used the knocker to rap on the door. After a brief wait, a woman in her mid-thirties, who, both in size and visage, looked exactly like a female version of Bear, answered the door. Tabitha concluded this was Cousin Phyllis. Tabitha was very familiar with Bear's mother, Mrs Caruthers, and so already had a good idea of what the women in his family looked like.

On seeing her cousin, Phyllis' face lit up with the same warm smile that Tabitha had seen so often on Mrs Caruthers' face, "Albert! What on earth are you doing here?"

"Phyllis! I told you not to call me by that name! Why on earth can you and my mother not remember that simple request?"

Cousin Phyllis chuckled and pulled Bear towards her into an embrace. Then, holding him at arm's length, she scolded, "Do you know how long it's been since I last saw you? You've been neglecting your favourite cousin. And now I hear you've gone up in the world and are working for a duke."

"Actually, I'm an earl," Wolf interjected.

Cousin Phyllis suddenly noticed Bear's entourage and turned beet red. "Albert, you could have given me some warning that you were coming and with some fancy friends."

Wolf stepped forward and, in his most gracious Earl of Pembroke voice, said, "Mrs Grund, the fault is entirely mine. I do apologise for imposing it on you without notice."

Now Cousin Phyllis was all aflutter. Blushing even more deeply, she said, "Oh, m'lord, tis nothing. It's just that I would have put a fresh fruit loaf in the oven if I'd known, and as it is, I only have some ginger biscuits left over from yesterday."

Wolf took her hand, brought it to his lips, and then said, "Then I am the lucky one; ginger biscuits are one of my favourite treats."

"Then you better all come in," Cousin Phyllis said, suddenly realising that they were still standing on her doorstep. She led the way into her front parlour which was clean and neat as a pin, even if the fabric of the furniture and curtains was a little faded and the wood rather scratched up.

As if seeing her home with fresh eyes, Cousin Phyllis said apologetically, "I'm so sorry, m'lord and m'ladies. If I'd known you were coming, I'd have put some new curtains up."

"My dear Mrs Grund, there is no need to apologise. We are the ones bothering you," Wolf said graciously. He only hoped that Cousin Phyllis had not noticed the look on the dowager's face, which might lead her to believe that at least one of her guests was judging her curtains.

When they were all seated, and Cousin Phyllis had brought in a tray of tea things and the promised ginger biscuits, Bear said, "Is Victor home?"

"Victor?" Phyllis asked. "You came to see Victor?"

There was a hurt look in his cousin's eyes that made Bear feel as guilty as he knew he ought. He had neglected Phyllis, and it was shameful that he had only rectified that when he needed something. "His lordship needs to speak to your husband, but you're right; I should have come to see you a long time ago. Please forgive me, Phyllis. I promise I will not be so neglectful again."

Phyllis Grund was a big-hearted, generous woman, and it wasn't in her nature to hold grudges. She gave her favourite cousin Albert a big smile that told him all was forgiven. "Let me go and call Victor. He's busy with one of his contraptions." With that, Phyllis left the room.

Despite his lower-class background, the dowager liked Bear. She enjoyed the fear that his presence caused in her neighbours, and she'd grown to appreciate his gentle and kind nature. While she might have commented on the Grund curtains if he hadn't been in the room, she was not so ungracious as to do so in front of him. Instead, she merely observed, "I see quite a family resemblance."

Bear chuckled, "Poor Phyllis. When we were younger, she was told she looked like me in a wig. Not something any lass wants to hear. It's a good thing she met Victor, who appreciates her for the wonderful woman she is and who needs taking care of."

If anyone wondered what Bear meant by this last statement, it quickly became clear when Victor Grund entered the room. The man had a distracted air about him that made it quite believable that he needed a competent woman, like Phyllis, to ensure that he ate three times a day and remembered to go to bed at night. He wasn't a large man and might have been significantly smaller than many women. Next to Cousin Phyllis, there was something almost comical in the juxtaposition of their sizes.

Despite his Germanic-sounding last name, as soon as Victor spoke, it was clear that he was born and bred in England. He had some kind of regional accent, though it was hard to pinpoint exactly where it was from. The man's eyes were bright and sparkled with a never-satiated curiosity about the world. Victor and Phyllis had met quite by chance, and she had immediately realised that she had found a man who would always need her care and would never notice how she looked.

For his part, Victor's mother had recently died, and he had quickly realised that while he had no trouble understanding how the internal combustion engine worked, he had no idea how to use his stove. By the time he met Phyllis, he had been subsisting on bread and cheese for three months. He needed all the nurture and care she was longing to give; they were a perfect match.

On entering the room, Victor Grund seemed confused to find so many strangers in his front parlour. Looking back at his wife for an explanation, she said gently, "Victor, I just told you that Cousin Albert had brought friends with him who need to speak with you."

"Yes, yes. So you did, my dear. Excuse me," Victor said to Wolf, Tabitha and the dowager. "I have been so caught up with my latest invention. When my attention gets dragged away from my work, it often takes me a few minutes to clear my head."

Bear walked towards the man and took his hand, "Cousin Victor, it is so good to see you again."

Victor looked at Bear, confused. Given how much Bear looked like the man's wife, it was astounding that he was in any doubt as to who he was talking to. Nevertheless, Phyllis said, in the same gentle, calm tone, "Victor, you remember my cousin, Albert, do you not?"

"Yes, yes. Of course, Albert. Good to see you again," Victor said, clasping Bear's hand. Bear quickly introduced the rest of their group. While the aristocrats in her house had quite overawed his wife, Victor seemed unaffected. Looking at the dowager, he screwed up his eyes and asked, "Do I know you, madam?"

Tabitha had to bite her lip to stop herself from laughing. The look on the dowager's face was priceless as she answered, "I do not believe you have had the honour."

If Victor heard the disdain in her voice and noted her words, he certainly didn't seem to care. Instead, he said, "No, no? Well, never mind. Anyway, Phyllis said that you want to ask me something?"

Wolf was happy to return to the point of their visit and drew out the knife that he and Bear had recovered at the murder scene. "We were hoping you might be able to tell us something about this knife, Mr Grund. Bear, I mean Albert, has said that you are quite an expert in the field."

"Well, I am not sure I would say expert. Mr Fishbourne certainly knows far more than I do, but I dabble here and there." With that, he took the knife that Wolf held out and examined it. He turned it over in his hands multiple times, scrutinising the carvings on the handle. Finally, he pronounced, "This is a very interesting knife, known as a Skean. You can see the intricate Celtic knotwork and the Triskelion symbol in the handle, and woven through are the words, Fuil ghlan, which in Gaelic means Pure Blood."

"Have you ever seen a knife like this before?" Tabitha asked.

"I haven't," Victor said. "However, I have read about them quite extensively. This is the motto of the O'Donnell clan, from just outside of Limerick. The clan was quite powerful in the last century and even into the beginning of this one. But they took part in the disastrous rebellion of 1803 led by Robert Emmet. The clan was decimated in the fighting, and many of the men who survived were arrested. Since then, the clan's power and cohesion have become just a faint memory of past glory. The men that were left just slunk back to the farms where they came from."

Victor stared off into the distance, seemingly caught up in the story he was telling. "It was said that these Skeans served as ceremonial pieces in some of the more notorious family rituals."

While Wolf was curious to hear more, he didn't want to get caught up in an elaborate explanation. Instead, he asked, "Is it possible to buy these knives, or is it more likely that the owner of it is descended from the O'Donnell clan?"

"I have never seen one of these for sale," Victor acknowledged. "They are prized family relics, and it would be seen as sacrilegious to allow one to leave the clan, particularly for monetary gain. I would imagine that whoever you got this off has had this knife passed down through generations. I can't imagine his distress at losing it." This was an interesting observation, Tabitha thought. Looking at Wolf, she could see that his thoughts were similar to her own.

Victor Grund didn't have much more to share about the knife. He did offer to show them his workroom, but a quick shake of Bear's head indicated that they shouldn't take him up on the offer. Instead, Wolf said, "Mr Grund, while I would love to see your inventions, I believe that time is of the essence. We must act on the information you have given us."

"No matter, no matter", Victor said cheerfully. "Do come back for tea another day." And with that, he turned and left the room without even bidding his guests farewell.

Phyllis apologised for her husband, "He does not mean to be rude, but when he is working on his contraptions, they are all he can think about."

CHAPTER 21

Back at Chesterton House, the group gathered around their trusty corkboard. Up until recently, there had not been many clues to write up. However, they finally felt that there was some information worth noting. Tabitha and the dowager had forgotten to mention Half-blind Kim's vague recognition of their ginger-haired suspect from Bear's drawing and so that was added to a notecard.

"So, she is going to talk to her girls and get back to you?" Wolf confirmed.

"Indeed. I have no doubt that we will hear from Half-blind Kim tomorrow at the latest," the dowager assured the group. "Meanwhile, let us assume that he is indeed the customer she believes he is." That seemed a fair enough supposition, though it also didn't tell them much beyond that the man had some esoteric personal tastes which no one in the group wished to dive into more than necessary.

Tabitha stood beside the board and looked at the few notecards she had written up and pinned. "What do we know?" she asked of no one in particular.

"Well, we do not even know for sure that this ginger-haired man is our killer," the dowager pointed out.

"True. However, he was seen at the scene of two of the killings, so let us assume that he is involved," Wolf said. "We know that he is an associate of the men who frequent the Spitalfields Working Men's Club, many of whom harbour anti-immigrant, and specifically anti-Semitic feelings and are active in a workers' union. We also know that there are many in the unions who feel similarly about the Jews and believe that they are taking jobs and suppressing wages."

"Surely such feelings are not good reasons to murder innocent girls, merely to rile up popular opinion against the Jews," Tabitha protested. However, even as she said the words, she realised that she had encountered murderers who had killed for less rational reasons over the last seven months or so.

"Let us consider who the victims are," Wolf pointed out. "Jack the Ripper murdered prostitutes, but this killer is not doing that. Instead, he is targeting working-class Irish girls who are far more sympathetic victims. If he wished to do no more than copy Jack the Ripper and strike fear into the hearts of the people of Whitechapel, then why not similarly target prostitutes?"

"Because they engender less sympathy," Tabitha agreed. "Instead, he targeted the daughters and sisters of the average Whitechapel inhabitant. This cannot be an accident." No one disagreed with her conclusion.

Turning back to the corkboard, Tabitha continued, "So, what do we know about our ginger-haired suspect?"

"Apart from his apparent deviant interests?" the dowager pointed out.

"Yes, apart from those, which, at least so far, seem irrelevant to the killings themselves." Even as Tabitha said this, she wondered if it was true. Were they looking at this all wrong, and did their killer have some bizarre perversion that they were overlooking and that he was fulfilling with these murders?" This was certainly a topic that she was most ill-equipped to understand if it were true. However, working on their tried and tested premise that no idea was to be discarded until it was definitively proven to be false, she wrote up a notecard that said, "Are the killings linked to his particular prurient interests?" Wolf raised his eyebrows at her wording but said nothing.

"So, it seems we have two possible lines of inquiry," the dowager stated. "This might be a calculated plot to rile up sentiment against the Jews, or this is a particular perversion playing out that has incidentally put a target on the back of the Jewish community." No one disagreed with this statement, so Tabitha wrote out notecards to reflect these two possible paths.

"Let us lay out what we know about this man," Wolf suggested. "We have good reason to believe that he is Irish. His association with our friends from the Working Men's Club would seem to indicate that, as does the knife. It seems likely that his last name is O'Donnell or that those are his mother's people."

Tabitha thought back to what Victor Grund had said. "If this knife is so sacred, could we use that to our advantage?"

"Whatever do you mean, Tabitha?" the dowager asked.

This line of investigation was interrupted by Talbot announcing dinner. Given that the dowager had not had a chance to return home to dress for dinner, they had agreed to forgo the usual etiquette and to eat informally as a family. Even as they easily agreed to this plan, Tabitha reflected on the dowager's past dictates about the vital importance of maintaining standards around such rituals and considered just how much the woman seemed to have changed over the last few months. Perhaps her fixation on social etiquette had been nothing more than something to fill her hours, and now she had more interesting things to focus on.

The group went into dinner, ignoring any of the usual aristocratic formalities of rank and precedence. Over a delicious meal of Dover sole and then a rack of lamb, they continued to discuss the investigation. Picking up on her earlier thought, Tabitha continued, "What if word got out that we have the knife? Might that not draw the killer out?"

"You wish to bait this man into targeting us?" the dowager said, half horrified and half fascinated by the idea.

"Well, I'm not sure I would use the word 'targeting'. However, perhaps we can draw him out."

Wolf took a sip of claret and considered the idea. Although the idea of luring a ruthless killer into their midst seemed insane, they had no better idea at that moment.

"Let us assume that the killer has no idea who chased him into that alleyway and found the body," Wolf mused. "Might it be possible to draw him out in a way that does not target us specifically?"

"What do you mean?" Bear asked.

"We have some control over this narrative. Perhaps we can use Andrews to release this news." Andrews was a newspaper man who Wolf knew from his thief-taker days and who he considered to have a modicum more decency and morality than the average ink-slinger. He had fed Andrews some news scoops over the past few months, and the man had good reason to help Wolf if he could.

Wolf continued, "We need to concoct a believable story. Who was in that alleyway and why have they gone to the press?"

"Wouldn't the police have taken the knife into custody as evidence," Bear pointed out. Wolf acknowledged that was an issue. The only reason that hadn't actually happened was that they hadn't turned the knife over to the police. However, that was hardly something that could be advertised, certainly not without raising questions.

They fell into silence as they all pondered their conundrum; they wanted to use the knife to lure their killer, but how to explain why they still had it in a way that could be announced publicly?

"Let us put this to the side for the moment," Wolf said. "I think there is a germ of an idea here, and perhaps we all need to sleep on it. What I do believe we can report back to Lord Langley is that this is not the work of someone in the Jewish community. To the extent that proving that and defusing tensions in the neighbourhood is a major concern for the Prime Minister, I believe we can say definitively that the murderer is Irish. Whether or not he is the ginger-haired man, he was carrying an Irish clan knife, which is something that is considered sacred by family members. It is hard to imagine how some random Jew would get his hands on such a weapon."

While they all saw the logic in his argument, it didn't seem as watertight as Wolf would have them believe. Was this really all it would take to convince the general public to stand down from their antagonism towards the Jews? It seemed more likely that this particular animosity was merely a symptom of an underlying longstanding resentment.

Seeing the scepticism on the faces of his friends, Wolf said, "Perhaps this is not enough to go to the Prime Minister with yet. So, what are our next steps?" While they still were waiting for word back from Half-blind Kim, would confirmation of the man's predilections add to their investigation in any meaningful way? Wolf chewed on this worry as he ate.

The group finished a delicious lemon meringue pie in depressed silence. It was unusual for their investigative group to face such a dead end. Even the dowager was subdued.

After dinner, they moved to the comfy parlour for coffee and brandy. The group's spirits were no higher than they had been since they first realised their lack of progress in this investigation. The dowager sat in an armchair by the fire, nursing a brandy, uncharacteristically quiet. Finally, she lifted her head and announced, "We need to talk to Mr Doherty."

"Mickey D?" Wolf asked. "Why?"

"I would imagine there is not much that happens in the Irish community of the East End that he is not aware of. He may know who this O'Donnell character is. Certainly, we should show him the knife and tell him what Mr Grund had to say." It wasn't a bad idea, and undoubtedly, no one had a better one. Finally, they agreed to see if the morning brought a note from Half-blind Kim. Then, they would visit Mickey D and lay their discoveries before him. Wolf hated putting himself in the Irish gang leader's debt yet again. It felt as if every time he disentangled himself from his prior obligations to the man, he turned around to find he had new ones. However, he had no better idea and so agreed with the dowager's plan.

The following morning did not bring any word from Half-blind Kim, and so Wolf made his peace with a visit to Mickey D in Whitechapel. It was well known that Mickey D attended church every Sunday morning and then went home for the family meal that Angie insisted on every sabbath. If the group left it too late in the day, he'd be down The Cock having a pint or two, and Wolf wanted to have this conversation in private. So, after an early lunch, Tabitha and Wolf, with the dowager in tow, set out for Whitechapel.

Angie Doherty was becoming more used to opening her front door to find aristocrats on her doorstep and didn't bat an eyelid at their appearance this time. Instead, she greeted them warmly and led the way into the cosy parlour where Mickey D liked to digest his meal before heading out for a few drinks.

"We need to stop meeting like this, m'lord or people will start to talk," Mickey said sardonically. Wolf considered that he would never be in danger of taking his new aristocratic status too seriously as long as he was keeping company with the Irish gang leader. Perhaps that wasn't such a bad thing, he reflected.

"We need your help, Mr Doherty," the dowager explained.

"Anything for you, Lady P. Will you all have a splash of Irish whiskey?" It was a little too early in the afternoon and they needed to keep clear heads, so they all demurred. "So, what can I do you for?" the man continued.

Wolf gave a brief explanation of the visit to the Working Men's Club. He described following Vicious Scowl and his friends, finally hearing the scream and finding the body.

It was evident from the surprise on Mickey D's face that he wasn't expecting to hear that. "The papers didn't say anything about her being found by a toff."

"Yes, well I did not advertise my rank when I reported the murder and merely dropped Bruiser's name. I told the young constable that Bear chased a man we saw fleeing the scene but that we didn't catch him and couldn't describe him in any meaningful way." Wolf paused, then added, "However, there was something we did not tell the police."

Mickey raised his eyebrows, "Is there now? And what might that be?"

Wolf pulled out the knife, "We found this at the murder scene. We believe the killer intended to use it to mutilate the body as he had the others, but that he dropped it when we interrupted him."

Mickey took the knife and examined it for a few moments. "It's a Celtic Skean from the old country."

"Yes, we already know that. We showed it to someone who is something of a connoisseur of rare weapons and he told us that knives like this have been handed down through families for centuries and hold great significance."

"Aye, in the olden days, when the clans had some power, for sure. I remember my grandda had one that he used to bring out when he told me stories when I was a laddie."

"We were told that this inscription on the handle is the motto of the O'Donnell clan," Tabitha continued. "We hoped that you might have some idea about any O'Donnells living in the East End."

Mickey considered the question and then called for Angie. She came into the room, wiping her hands on her apron. "Who's for tea and ginger biscuits?" she asked. Angie knew that Wolf was very partial to her ginger biscuits and, in fact, had a standing order for some from her every week for the tea trays at Chesterton House.

"Ange luv, do you remember Colin O'Donnell?"

"Well, that name takes me back. I haven't heard hide nor hair of the O'Donnells in over twenty years now. Nasty bunch. Do you remember, must have been twenty-five years ago now, maybe more, that incident with Penny O'Hara back in Ireland? Shocking it was. Well, word was that it was Colin O'Donnell that had done it to her. Of course, he disappeared without a trace and there was no justice for poor Penny. I'd heard tell he'd come to London, but who knows if that was true."

Wolf knew it was grasping at straws, but he asked, "By any chance did this Colin O'Donnell have ginger hair?"

"You mean, was he the man Bear made the drawing of?" Angie asked. "No, he wasn't. I would have said something if I'd recognised him. But the O'Donnells were a large family. I don't think there are any left in the East End now. Some are in prison, one hanged for murder, another was sent to the colonies years ago. Good riddance, I say." If there was any irony in the wife of a notorious leader of a criminal gang saying such a thing about other criminals, it seemed it was lost on Angie Doherty. "A few years ago in passing in a letter, my friend back in Ireland, Marigold, told me that whatever of the family had been left in Limerick had disappeared as well."

"Leave it with me, Wolf," Mickey D promised. "Let me ask around. I haven't heard anything of the O'Donnells around these parts for a very long time but if one of them is back, someone will know."

CHAPTER 22

Arriving back at Chesterton House, Talbot informed them that there had been two telephone calls while they were out. Given the infrequency that anyone other than the dowager telephoned, Wolf and Tabitha were curious to know who their two callers had been. Talbot had taken messages, and Wolf stood in the hallway, reading them both over.

"Jeremy, I do not enjoy being kept in suspense," the dowager said irritably. "Who has telephoned, and are these messages in any way pertinent to the investigation?"

Wolf looked up from reading. "Let us go through to the parlour."

The dowager bristled with impatience and followed, muttering, "At my age, delays such as this are magnified exponentially. I might expire in the next few minutes and will never know who telephoned."

"Mama, I believe you will live for at least a few minutes more and can wait for Wolf to digest what he has read," Tabitha said.

Not two minutes later, settled in their favourite chairs in the parlour, Wolf said, "This first note is from Manning. It seems that your friend, Half-blind Kim, sent around a note this morning." Reading Talbot's transcription of his conversation with the dowager's butler, Wolf said, "It seems that we have a name for our ginger-haired friend. At least as far as your friend's girl knows, he is Wilfred O'Hara. But she says she hasn't seen him in months. He'd mentioned some financial worries the last time he had visited."

"Well, that is real progress," Tabitha said, writing out a notecard. "Will you give this information to the police?"

That was a good question, and Wolf pondered his answer. "We do not have anything more to connect this Wilfred O'Hara to the murders than that two witnesses said they saw a ginger-haired man in proximity to the killings. He may just be a local man who was nearby coincidentally."

"And we cannot overlook that his name is not O'Donnell," Tabitha pointed out.

"Indeed. That is rather disappointing," the dowager said in a deflated voice. "However," she said, perking up at a thought, "perhaps this is not his real name. Mrs Doherty did say that the man was suspected of murder. Perhaps this O'Donnell changed his name to O'Hara to elude capture." It was a reasonable assumption, and no one contradicted her.

"I will tell Bruiser what we know, but unofficially. If this Mr O'Hara lives in Whitechapel, there is a chance that Bruiser will know who he is."

"Who was the second caller?" Tabitha asked, picking up a blank notecard.

"Mr Montagu. It seems that he has had advanced word from a friendly contact on the Edmonton City Council that sentiment is going against his proposed land development. It seems that the anti-Semitism that these killings has stirred up has also riled up some key council members. He has asked that we call on him at our earliest convenience. He is eager to know what progress we have made. He says that he will be at home for the rest of the day."

Wolf considered the information that had suddenly landed in their laps and what needed to be done that afternoon. "I will ask Bear to go to Whitechapel to talk to Bruiser about Wilfred O'Hara. Meanwhile, we should visit Mr Montagu. We owe him an update, at least based on what we know. Perhaps he can use our understanding about the knife's likely provenance to pacify the council members."

Thirty minutes later, Bear was on his way to Whitechapel, and Tabitha, Wolf, and the dowager were back in the Pembroke carriage and on their way to the Montagu residence. That afternoon, the door was opened by a maid. Tabitha realised that with Shabbat over the evening before, the Montagu servants would be back at work again. The maid led them into the drawing room they had been welcomed into two nights before and told them that Mrs Montagu was out, but she would let Mr Montagu know that they were there.

Samuel Montagu came rushing into the room almost immediately, clearly eager to talk with them. "Thank you for coming so promptly, Lord and Ladies Pembroke," the man said. He looked tired, and worry lines etched his face. If possible, it seemed as if he had aged since the Shabbat dinner. Perhaps acknowledging the concern writ clearly on his face, he said, "I received word last night, after Shabbat, about the change in sentiment on the council, and I barely slept last night for worrying over it."

"How did you hear about this?" Wolf asked.

"There is a fellow Jew on the Edmonton Urban City Council. He is how I first came to learn about the parcel of land for sale and to formulate my plan to create affordable housing for the Jews of the East End. He has been keeping a close eye on his fellow councillors and doing his best to sway sentiments in my favour. There is one councillor in particular, a Frederick Holmes, who has been extremely vocal in his opposition."

"He has come out publicly against the Jews?" Tabitha asked, shocked at the idea that a public official might be so brazen in their prejudice.

Samuel Montagu laughed bitterly. "No, Holmes is far too clever for that. Instead, he has talked about land use issues and used the coded language of 'community impact'," Montagu said this very bitterly.

"What does community impact even mean?" the dowager asked.

"People who claim to care about this talk about changing the community character, overcrowding and speak of fears of an increase in crime," Montagu explained. "However, when a not dissimilar development was proposed to bring Irish and Welsh labourers to the district, none of these same concerns were raised. There is no doubt in my mind that such issues are being raised because the planned occupants of my homes will be mostly Jews. Please tell me that you have made some headway in this investigation since we last spoke," the man implored.

Wolf then told Samuel Montagu what they had learned so far and their very strong suspicions that the murderer was Irish. As he had the first time they met, Mr Montagu let him speak without interruption. When Wolf was finished, Samuel Montagu still didn't talk for a few moments.

Instead, he sat back in his chair, his hands linked over his substantial stomach, deep in thought.

Finally, he said, "Would you be prepared to share this information with Mr Holmes?"

Wolf hesitated, then said, "This is all supposition at this point. I would say that the evidence strongly points away from the perpetrator of these crimes being Jewish, but until we have a suspect in hand, I would not want to swear to this."

"Nevertheless, perhaps hearing this from you, an earl, will still Holmes' vicious tongue for a while and allow me to contain the damage amongst the other councillors. Most of them are reasonable men, and I believe that they can be brought to see that not only will a Jewish community in their midst not be a danger, but they will actually be an asset. The Jews of the East End are hardworking and will bring many valuable skills to the community. They are a tight-knit, family-oriented group. Miriam Tuchinsky and her boys aside, the Jewish community is significantly more law-abiding than other ethnic groups in the East End."

Wolf wasn't sure how warranted this slur against the rest of the population of the East End was, but Montagu's point was well-taken; there was no good reason to oppose the housing development for the Jews and yet allow one for other working-class groups. Wolf still had serious doubts about speaking with Frederick Holmes about their limited findings. However, if Montagu believed that doing so would help his cause, Wolf was happy to bring the full force of the earldom to the benefit of such a good cause and attempt to persuade the councilman. He agreed to talk to Frederick Holmes.

"Can I further impose on you, milord, and ask that you speak with him today? There is a council meeting taking place soon, perhaps as early as tomorrow. While I don't believe that the final vote will be happening then, I believe that Holmes intends to use the meeting to stir up more bad feelings against my project."

Wolf had to control the urge to sigh; he was eager to hear what Bear had learned in Whitechapel and didn't feel like gallivanting around the London suburbs. However, catching Tabitha's eye, he realised that they had no choice but to indulge Samuel Montagu. The man truly looked as if he believed they were his last hope for the project that was so dear to his heart.

Montagu continued, "There is a three o'clock train from King's Cross to Edmonton that you should be able to catch." By way of further explanation, he said, "I have taken it myself many times during the exploratory phase of this land development."

Glancing at his pocket watch, Wolf realised that if they were to catch a three o'clock train, they ought to hurry. They made a quick farewell to the Jewish banker and were soon back in the carriage and on the way to the train station.

Despite the traffic on the streets being busier than they might have expected on a Sunday afternoon, they did manage to make the three o'clock train and before they knew it, they were on their way to Edmonton.

"Well, this afternoon turned out to be more exciting than I imagined on waking this morning," the dowager said. At least someone was happy about their expedition, Wolf thought wryly.

Arriving at Edmonton station, they hired a hackney cab to take them to Frederick Holmes' house on Silver Street. Arriving there, Tabitha noted that the man they sought was clearly very comfortably off; the street was lined with substantial semi-detached houses and larger, quite grand detached villas. It seemed that Frederick Holmes' home was one of the latter. The attractive, white-washed house had ornate gables and a large bay window on the ground floor. The front garden was well-maintained and everything about the property announced that this was the home of an affluent man.

The group hadn't discussed how they were going to approach the conversation, but as he looked at the front door they had drawn up in front of, Wolf was inspired. "Lady Pembroke, I believe that the situation we find ourselves in is one that will benefit from your very unique skill set," he said.

"Ha! I believe that the phrase 'unique skill set' is an attempt to make a silk purse out of a sow's ear and that what you really mean is that this Mr Holmes needs to be intimidated in the manner in which I am particularly adept."

Given that was exactly what he meant, Wolf did not contradict her.

Needing no such affirmation, the dowager continued, "However, you are, of course, entirely correct; I am well-practised in putting the uppity men of the middle classes in their place. It will be my absolute pleasure to take the lead in this conversation."

Hearing the dowager say it out loud, Wolf did second-guess his suggestion, but it was too late now. Catching Tabitha's eye, he saw that she was trying hard not to smirk at the predicament he had created. Taking pity on him, she said, "Mama, please bear in mind that we intend to persuade the man, not browbeat him."

"You speak as if there is a difference, Tabitha," the dowager said with the very particular gleam in her eye that she always got when preparing to go into battle. "It is a good thing that I have my special walking cane with me." Alarmed, Tabitha realised that the highly polished mahogany stick with a finely engraved curling handle that the older woman had with her was, in fact, the special sword stick that she had bought in Brighton recently.

"I do not believe that it will be necessary for you to make use of your weapon, Mama. Remember, you can catch more flies with honey than vinegar," Tabitha advised nervously.

"Poppycock! It has been my experience that nothing is ever to be gained by gently stepping around an issue. Now help me down, Jeremy, and let me do what I do best." Oh well, Tabitha thought, the die was cast now. Heaven help Mr Frederick Holmes. He had no idea that his Sunday afternoon was about to take a turn for the worst.

<h1 style="text-align:center">CHAPTER 23</h1>

The dowager's aggressive rap on the door's rather ugly brass knocker made clear that she was ready for battle. This was just the kind of confrontation that made the woman's blood race and soul sing. It was one thing to scratch this particular itch by berating the Archbishop of Canterbury for a perceived infraction by some minor member of his clergy of whom he neither knew nor cared and quite another to be let loose on an unsuspecting villain. Well, maybe he wasn't a total villain, but he was the nemesis to that charming Mr Montagu and that was sufficient reason to bring to bear the full force of her well-honed ability to strike fear into the hearts of men.

A maid opened the door. While the young woman did not know just how illustrious the group on her master's doorstep was, she knew that he was never visited by toffs, and that was clearly what these people were.

Before the young woman had a chance to speak, the dowager commanded imperiously, "You will take us through to whatever reception room this house has and then tell your master that the Dowager Countess of Pembroke is here to see him." As an afterthought, she added, "And the Earl and Countess of Pembroke."

The terrifying little old woman sufficiently overawed the girl that it was likely she would have let the group into the house and taken them

157

into the front room whether or not Frederick Holmes was at home. As it was, she muttered that her master was in his study and she would fetch him immediately, then scurried away.

Looking around the room they had been left in, the dowager sniffed dismissively. As far as she was concerned, everything about this room screamed of social striving that missed the mark. There were paintings on the wall that seemed intended to mimic Turner's landscapes but were obviously painted by a far inferior artist and furnishings whose gaudiness failed to mask substandard workmanship and materials. Everything about the room's decor just missed the mark; the fabric choices clashed, in some cases rather garishly. The pieces of furniture were too large, and the wood stain was too dark for the room size, which gave the entire space a claustrophobic feel. It was not that the decor was old-fashioned; quite the opposite. In fact, it looked as if the whole room had been decorated very recently. There was even a faint odour of new paint lingering in the air.

"Oh, the unfortunate strivings of the nouveau riche," the dowager proclaimed. It was hard to disagree with her in this instance. The room felt oppressive to Tabitha, and she hoped this audience with Frederick Holmes would be brief.

When the man himself entered the room, Tabitha was struck by how ordinary he looked compared to his overly decorated room. He was short with dark hair. He had an unremarkable face, though his nose was too large for it. He was probably in his mid-forties and the beard he sported had some threads of silver in it. His clothing matched his house; it was evident that great effort had been made, probably at a not inconsiderable cost, to dress well. However, somehow, he just missed the mark.

As Tabitha looked at the man, she tried to determine what it was that was so off, but it was hard to put her finger on one item of clothing. Rather, the whole came together discordantly. She could only imagine what Thompson would have made of the decision to pair the yellow cravat with the ochre waistcoat, the two colours similar enough to have probably been intentional but different enough that their juxtaposition was jarring.

His maid had forewarned Frederick Holmes about the unusual guests he had. Nevertheless, he had assumed that in speaking of their grandness, the young, naive local girl had merely been overawed by a bit of good tailoring on a local merchant and had misspoken. However, looking at the fine clothes and jewels of his visitors, as well as that indefinable air of privilege and authority that the upper classes seemed to wear as easily as their diamonds, Holmes had no doubt he was standing before greatness. He just had no idea why. The highest-ranking person he was associated with was a now-retired Edmonton Alderman who had been knighted for services to the community that Holmes believed had been greatly overblown.

Holmes looked at the trio and tried to determine who to greet first. Emily, his maid, had said that there was an earl, a countess and that the old woman was a dowager countess. Holmes didn't really understand the hierarchy of rank within the aristocracy, but he did not doubt that an earl was quite a grand personage. Should he first approach him? On the other hand, it was the tiny but scary old woman who had told Emily to summon him and who had an air about her that seemed it would brook no nonsense.

Finally, the decision was made for him when the dowager countess woman said, "I assume you are Holmes."

Frederick Holmes had risen from nothing by hard work and cunning to run a thriving money-lending business. He had been on the Edmonton Urban Council for more than five years and was a respected member of the community. When people visited his home or office, it was often to seek out his help or to plead their case for an extension of a loan. He had never had someone force their way into his house and then speak to him as if he were a cur, unworthy of even the most basic respect.

Pulling himself up his full five-foot-four, Frederick Holmes said in the cultured accent that he had taken such pains to adopt, "I am Mr Frederick Holmes. I understand from my maid that you are the Dowager Countess of Pembroke and that your associates are the earl and countess." Holmes stated this in a tone that he hoped implied that he was accustomed to visits from such dignitaries. "How may I help you?"

The dowager sniffed, "Well, Mr Frederick Holmes, you may start by telling that so-called maid of yours to bring tea. I have no idea how guests are treated out here in the wilds of Middlesex, but in London, it is customary to offer visitors refreshments."

Frederick Holmes blushed deep red and then quickly paled with anger. How dare this woman talk to him in such a way in his home! He stood, rang the bell, and when Emily entered the room, berated her for not having brought tea yet. The poor maid stammered an apology and quickly departed to rectify her mistake.

Returning to his seat, Holmes tried to compose himself. Glancing over at Wolf, he wondered who this so-called earl was that had not spoken yet and instead allowed this terrible woman to berate him. Wolf saw the man's look and felt for him. However, he knew better than to interrupt the dowager when she was in full battle charge. He had asked her to take the lead, and that's what she was doing. Nothing would be gained by trying to interfere in her process.

Tea ordered, the dowager continued, "Mr Holmes, I believe that you are acquainted with a dear friend of mine, a Mr Samuel Montagu." Holmes' surprise on hearing this was almost comical. If the idiom 'he almost fell off his chair' could ever be truly applied, this would have been one of those times. The dowager didn't wait for Frederick Holmes to confirm the acquaintance and instead continued, "It is my understanding that you are encouraging opposition to Mr Montagu's development of a parcel of land."

Whatever Holmes had thought this conversation might be about, this was not it. Trying to recover himself, he said with all the dignity he could muster, "I am unable to discuss the workings of the Edmonton UDC with persons so entirely unrelated to its business."

"Unrelated to its business! Is that your answer? How dare you speak to me in that manner," the dowager was now jabbing the air with her cane to emphasise her point, and Mr Holmes looked as if he might genuinely fear that she would stand and start attacking him with it. And he had no idea that it was actually a sword stick.

The dowager had worked herself up into a state of high dudgeon, "I am the Dowager Countess of Pembroke. I have the ear of the royal family and of the Prime Minister." Tabitha wasn't sure if cornering the Prime Minister any time she met him at an evening party and berating him for the perceived shortfalls of his government counted as having the man's ear. As for the royal family, Tabitha found it hard to imagine even the dowager imposing herself on the sovereign.

The woman continued, "When I see injustice being perpetrated, I make it my business."

Frederick Holmes tried to gather his wits and take another tack, "Whatever objections I might have to Mr Montagu's planned use of his land are thoroughly justified and are shared by others on the council, I might add."

Despite his resolution not to interfere, Wolf worried that the dowager's methods were only antagonising the man. Clearing his throat enough that both the dowager and Holmes turned to him, he said, "Mr Holmes, we have reason to believe that the foundation for your objections is the recent killings in Whitechapel and the suspicion that has again fallen on the Jewish community because of them."

Holmes didn't acknowledge the truth of that statement, but he also didn't deny it. Ignoring that the dowager's eyes were shooting daggers at him, Wolf continued, "We have been investigating these murders." He could see from the look on Holmes' face the questions he had about why the group of aristocrats might be conducting such an investigation. Despite Holmes' wish to ignore the dowager now that Wolf had taken over, his gaze was drawn irresistibly back to her and that one look at the woman's face convinced the man that he should keep his scepticism to himself.

"While we have yet to make a final determination as to the identity of the killer, we can tell you with high certainty that the man is not a Jew. In fact, we believe he is Irish." As he said this, Wolf noticed a curious emotion play out on the man's face. He tried to put a name to it but couldn't. Perhaps it was nothing more than disappointment at having a good excuse for his bigotry pulled out from under him.

"Are you accusing me of having no basis for my objections to Mr Montagu's plans other than simple prejudice?" Holmes asked indignantly.

Given that this was precisely what they were suggesting, Wolf wasn't sure what to say. Tabitha felt it was time to try to pour oil on the troubled waters that this conversation had quickly devolved into. "Mr Holmes, I am sure that no one meant to imply any such thing. However, it would be entirely understandable if the people of Edmonton, and those who serve in their name, were concerned about the prospect of people moving here from London's East End and perhaps bringing a killer with them. All that we hope to convey is that this will not be the case."

Holmes looked somewhat placated but then observed, "And you believe that you can convey this confidently even though you haven't apprehended this brute yet?" It was a fair question and, indeed, precisely what they had warned Samuel Montagu about.

The dowager did not enjoy being questioned at the best of times, but certainly not by some parvenu. In a tone that would brook no further contradiction, she said, "Lord Pembroke came upon a knife at the scene of the latest murder. Said knife has distinctive Celtic engravings on its handle and includes a family motto that we have been assured is from a family of the name O'Donnell. We have also been told that it would be considered heresy to allow such a family heirloom to leave the clan. There is no doubt the killer dropped the weapon as he fled. Therefore, there is every reason to believe that the murderer is Irish and not Jewish."

Her pronouncement did not invite debate, and Holmes seemed to deduce as much and didn't comment on their deductions. Indeed, he appeared quite stunned by her words. Turning to Wolf, his only response was, "And do the police know about the knife and your assumptions, milord?"

Wolf was still reeling from the dowager's revelation that they had the knife when they had all agreed to keep that information close for now. Instead of answering Holmes' question directly, Wolf replied, "While our investigations are still proceeding, the knife is in my custody." On reflection, that was probably also more information than he should have given out, Wolf thought. However, at this point, the dowager had given so much away that this disclosure seemed minor.

Frederick Holmes wanted this interview to end—very badly. He wanted this awful woman gone from his house, and he hoped never to have to deal with her again. Hoping to indicate the meeting was over, he stood and addressed Wolf. "Milord, I will certainly take your words into consideration when casting my vote."

The dowager looked as if she was about to launch an attack on a second front, but Wolf glared at her, hoping to communicate that further berating of the man was unlikely to persuade him. While she didn't appreciate the glare and would certainly be having words with Jeremy later, even the dowager could see the futility of continuing.

They were a subdued group on the way back to Mayfair from Edmonton. Finally, halfway into the train ride, Tabitha observed, "Beyond his clear prejudice against Jews, there was something about Mr Holmes that I neither like nor trust. However, I cannot quite put my finger on what makes me say that."

"I do not disagree," Wolf replied. "Furthermore, there is something familiar about the man, and I do not know why. I have been wracking my mind trying to think if I know him from my thief-taking days. The man is a moneylender, after all."

"Is that even legal?"

"Well, my understanding is that it is mostly legal, though very much looked down upon. The irony is that it is a commercial activity that has historically been associated with the Jewish people, particularly throughout continental Europe. I do wonder if some of that sits behind Mr Holmes' prejudice: professional rivalry."

"Why do you think you might know him from your old life, Jeremy?"

"Well, when you consider who has to make use of a moneylender's services as opposed to going to a bank such as Mr Montagu's, it is usually those who are unable to receive credit in more formal ways: immigrants, the working class, the kind of people who populate the East End. It would certainly make sense if Frederick Holmes began his business somewhere like Whitechapel." Wolf paused, thought about the interview they just had, and mused, "Moreover, I believe the man is doing his best to cover an Irish accent. Could you not hear it?"

Now that Wolf mentioned it, Tabitha had heard something sitting behind the almost artificially cultured middle-class tone. "Mr Holmes would hardly be the first working-class immigrant to seek to distance himself from his roots," she pointed out.

Their ruminations about Frederick Holmes' true origins did not seem germane to their investigation and so Wolf turned the conversation back to their purpose in visiting the man. "I do not believe that we achieved our aim with Mr Holmes. He seemed unswayed by our assurance that the killer is not Jewish."

The dowager harrumphed. She had been thoroughly disappointed by

Mr Holmes' failure to wither in her presence. "I found his insolence to be insupportable. Why, even Bertie has had the good grace to be cowed in my presence. If the Prince of Wales, a man not known for his humility, can be brought to his knees, figuratively speaking, then I would have expected a jumped-up usurer to have at the very least lowered his eyes in shame."

Tabitha and Wolf had no reply. While they didn't share the dowager's horror at a man's unwillingness to let her tyrannise him, they had hoped that her particular dragooning methods might have yielded better results than they did.

"If there was ever a time to wield my swordstick, I believe that this was it," the woman continued, becoming ever more peeved as she spoke. Tabitha was sitting next to the dowager and so was able to roll her eyes at Wolf sitting opposite without the dowager seeing. Truly, the last thing that they needed was for the woman to feel she had license to brandish weaponry as one of her bullying tactics.

Madison met them with the carriage at King's Cross, and they dropped the dowager off at home before returning to Chesterton House. It had been a long day, and all either Tabitha or Wolf wanted was a quiet dinner followed by an early night.

CHAPTER 24

They were joined for dinner that evening by Bear, who reported back on his visit to Whitechapel. "Well, my conversation with Bruiser didn't yield much. The name Wilfred O'Hara didn't ring any bells. However, he did say they've had some limited success with the drawing of the ginger-haired man. One of the constables who patrol Spitalfields Market thought he recognised the man."

"Does he work on one of the market stalls?" Wolf asked hopefully. It would be a stroke of luck if they could pinpoint where the man might be found.

"The PC thinks so. He says that he's not always there, but he believes he's seen him working a fruit and veg stall on occasion owned by a man called Verde. Says the man has a particularly distinctive way of hawking."

"Then I believe we are visiting Spitalfields tomorrow. Bear, I would like you to join us. If we see this man, I want to ensure that he cannot get away from us." Bear nodded his head, and a plan was made.

"Perhaps we should place a telephone call to Mama and inform her of our plans," Tabitha suggested half-heartedly. While they all had agreed that it was better to include the dowager in their investigation than have her go off half-cocked on her own, and although she was even useful at times, nevertheless, Tabitha felt quite drained from being so constantly in the woman's company.

Wolf saw the reluctance on Tabitha's face and heard it in her voice. "Perhaps we will make this visit on our own," he offered. "After all, I can only imagine the dowager countess' reaction to as plebian a place as Spitalfields Market." Tabitha was grateful for his words but also felt a little guilty at their subterfuge. Heaven help them if the dowager found out.

Tabitha was quite excited about their expedition the following morning. She had never been to a market before, and from the bits and pieces she had heard recently from Wolf and Bear, Spitalfields was a bustling hub of commerce, and she was curious to experience it for herself.

Wolf had advised that a market like Spitalfields was at its most active earlier in the day, and so the group had convened for an early breakfast. The previous evening, they had discussed how low a profile to take at the market. There were definite advantages to flaunting Wolf's rank under certain circumstances, but was this one of those times? Finally, the consensus was that the positives outweighed the negatives, and they had chosen not to wear their usual Whitechapel outfits and to take the Pembroke carriage.

During the ride to Brushfield Street, the main entrance to the market, just off Commercial Street, Tabitha began to have second thoughts about the utility of an earl and countess descending on the market traders of Spitalfields. "How can we possibly explain why we are visiting such a place and asking questions?"

Wolf laughed, "I think that you are looking at this question from the wrong angle; our peers question why we spend our time on investigations. However, my experience of the working classes is that, regardless of what we do, they view our lot as eccentrics with too much money and time on their hands who indulge in all sorts of bizarre activities to amuse themselves. I am sure that they will shake their heads and mutter that it must be nice to have nothing better to do than to harass hardworking common folks."

Tabitha looked somewhat chagrined at this; in many ways, it was not an unfair characterisation of her involvement in the investigations. Before Wolf's appearance at Chesterton House, she did have too much time on her hands and had been bored. Over the last seven months, she'd had sufficient exposure to the harshness of life for the inhabitants of the East End to realise that they did not have the luxury of boredom.

Wolf saw the look on her face and said kindly, "Tabitha, the work we have done together over the past few months has helped people. Think of all the girls now living safely at the Dulwich House or Bobby Charles, who would certainly have been hanged for a murder he did not commit. And let us not forget Maureen Prescott. Who knows what further crimes her deranged mind might have justified committing."

Tabitha gave a small half-smile but didn't seem wholly convinced. Wolf continued, "The people we talk to do not know the good we have done and so it is not surprising if they make hasty judgements based on our clothes and comportment. However, you should never question the value of our investigative activities. Why, it appears that even the Prime Minister now believes that we are doing something worthwhile."

Reflecting on Wolf's words, Tabitha realised that he was correct, and by the time they arrived at Brushfield Street, she was feeling more confident about the task ahead of them. As usually happened when they drove the Pembroke Carriage into the East End, heads turned as Madison pulled up in front of the market. However, the people hurrying in and out, eager to get the best deals and secure their desired wares before they sold out, didn't spend too much time wondering why toffs might sully themselves by shopping for their own food in the East End.

Descending from the carriage, Tabitha looked up at the market. The building was quite new, having been constructed only five years prior, on the site of the old market. It was a large, open structure of brick with decorative ironwork and iron columns supporting a glass roof that let the sunlight of the cold but bright day flood the market floor. It was a good thing that the market had this natural sunlight, because it was crammed with stalls and people and would have felt quite claustrophobic otherwise. As it was, as Tabitha followed Wolf and Bear inside, she felt her senses quite overwhelmed by the noise and the smells. As far as she could see, market stalls displayed colourful fruits and vegetables. There were stalls of pungent-smelling cheeses and some with meat and fish. She saw at least two stalls that were selling what looked and smelled like a fascinating range of herbs and spices.

The market traders and customers were as diverse and interesting as the goods for sale. It was evident that there were a lot of Jews in the market; Tabitha could identify the men by their long beards and skullcaps, but a huge variety of people with a range of skin tones and accents joined them. The buzz of voices adding to the general cacophony of the market seemed to be speaking in a range of languages that Tabitha couldn't begin to identify. As overwhelming as the market was, it was also fascinating, and she would have liked to explore further, but they had work to do.

Wolf realised that there was no easy way to find the Verde stall without guidance, so they stopped at various stalls to ask the surprised and curious traders where they might find it. After a few wrong turns, they finally came upon a large, well-organised stall that was displaying a colourful range of exotic-looking fruits. Tabitha could identify a few of the items on display and wondered if this was where her cook purchased the pineapples and oranges that they often enjoyed at Chesterton House. She'd never really considered before where such items might be bought or, indeed, where any of the food items they enjoyed might come from.

A man was standing next to the Verde stall hawking its goods, but he had dark hair rather than ginger and looked nothing like the man they were seeking. Approaching him, Wolf asked, "Might I have a moment of your time?"

The dark-haired man looked him up and down and didn't seem impressed with what he saw. "'ave the toffs taken to shopping for their own taters and greens now? What is the world coming to?"

It was immediately evident that this conversation wasn't going to be easy. Wolf took out some coins and pointed to some mangos. "I'll have a basket of those and a few minutes of your time."

Mangos were luxury items and were priced accordingly. Selling a whole basket before eleven o'clock in the morning would be a rare success, and the dark-haired man, Billy Peters, wasn't one to look a gift horse in the mouth. Noting that Wolf had no bag with him, Billy handed him the basket and held his hand out for the coins.

Wolf snatched his hand back and said, "I will pay you and add more for some information. We were told that a ginger-haired man sometimes works this stall. Is he here today?"

Billy shook his head. "'E only works occasionally, when the guvnor is short-'anded. 'E was supposed to work today but 'e didn't show, which is why I got landed with doing this."

"What do you know about the man?"

"Not much. Name is Wilfred. 'E keeps to himself. Been working for the guvnor for a couple of months. I don't know anymore. Keeps my 'ead down, I do, and don't ask no questions I don't need to know."

"Where might we find your guvnor?" Tabitha asked.

"Corner of Brushfield and Gun Street. Can't miss it; Verde & Company." With this, the man put out his hand, and Wolf dropped the coins into it.

The group made their way out of the market back towards where the carriage waited. Looking across the street, they could see Verde & Company on the corner, as Billy Peters had described. The shop front was well-maintained, and the clean windows and freshly painted sign spoke of a prosperous business. On both sides of the front door were tables piled high with exotic fruits, similar to the market stall. Just inside the store, there was a neat little man with oiled back hair and an impressively waxed moustache. He was wearing an apron and had a professional air about him that suggested they had found the 'guvnor'.

Elia Francesco Verde looked up as the three well-dressed strangers entered his shop. Elia knew that he supplied many of the great houses of the high and mighty of London society, but he never expected to have them visit his premises in person. An Italian immigrant who had come to London thirty years before with nothing and had worked his way up to owning a thriving business, Elia was proud of what he had built and was thrilled at the prospect that the upper classes of British society might finally be ready to recognise his contribution to the bounty of their tables. The little man stood up straighter and smoothed back hairs that were in no danger of coming free from the copious oil that bound them.

"Good morning. How may I help you?"

While Billy Peters had made his disdain of the upper classes quite evident, Wolf could see immediately that Elia Verde was primed for sycophancy. "Are you the owner of this fine establishment?" Wolf asked.

"I am indeed," the shopkeeper said with an accent that was as heavily Italian as the day he landed in Southampton.

"I am the Earl of Pembroke." Wolf watched the man's face and saw the immediate effect his words had. While it had been evident to Elia Verde from the moment the group walked into his shop that they were quality, as Londoners like to say, never would he have guessed that he might have an earl in his midst. He still didn't fully understand the British systems of aristocratic rank; he barely understood the Italian one. Nevertheless, he understood enough to realise that an earl walking into his shop was a special occurrence.

Elia Verde bowed so low that Tabitha thought he might be about to genuflect. Luckily, he contented himself with the lesser show of obsequiousness and quickly stood upright. "I am honoured to have you grace my humble establishment, your lordship, signor. How may I help you today?"

There were some new exotic fruits that Elia had begun importing that he hoped would take off with the great and good of London. Perhaps this earl could be persuaded to purchase some bananas which Elia had found difficult to market to his customers so far. He could imagine that if this handsome and distinguished nobleman championed the fruit, it would signal to all of London society that Elia Verde was at the forefront of produce innovation. He then noticed the basket of mangos that Wolf had handed off to Bear. "I see that you have already made a purchase from my market stall," the shopkeeper observed.

"Indeed. We spoke to the man you have working the stall. That is in fact why we have come to speak with you."

Elia Verde was immediately on edge at these words; Billy Peters had a mouth on him. Had he offended an earl now? "Your lordship, sir, I apologise for whatever that scemo said to you. I will dismiss him immediately."

"No, no. Your man said nothing wrong," Wolf assured him. "Rather, we asked him about another worker of yours, Wilfred O'Hara, and he suggested that we talk with you."

On hearing the name, Elia Verde shook his head sadly. "Cavolo! I am an immigrant who came to this country with nothing and has built all this," he gestured around the shop. "I am grateful for the help I received along the way and try to lend a helping hand in turn. Sometimes, that hand gets bitten. First, this O'Hara did not show up today, and now it seems he has done something even worse."

Wolf wanted to assure the man that wasn't the case, but he didn't know that was true. If this O'Hara was the killer they were searching for, Elia Verde had harboured a very venomous serpent in his breast. Instead, he asked, "Do you have an address for the man?"

Elia went around the counter at the back of the shop and rummaged until he emerged victorious with a sheet of paper. "I always make sure I know where to find my workers, just in case they end up stealing from me. "He lives on Dorset Street, or at least he did when he first started. When you find him, tell him not to bother returning to work."

CHAPTER 25

Dorset Street was one of the poorest and most dangerous streets in the East End. Located not far from Spitalfields, it had gained notoriety during Jack the Ripper's killing spree when several of the murders had been committed in its vicinity. Even without that gruesome history, Dorset Street was somewhere Wolf would have rather not taken Tabitha. It was true that she had become somewhat accustomed to the deprivation and violence that characterised so much of the East End. Even so, Wolf hoped he might persuade Tabitha that Dorset Street was unlike anything she had witnessed so far. Of course, his attempts to deter her were in vain. Within minutes of leaving Verde & Company, they found themselves in the crowded street with its plethora of dilapidated boarding houses, most of which lacked basic facilities, further contributing to its rampant poor sanitation and ensuant disease.

While Tabitha had been determined to join the outing to Dorset Street and had opposed Wolf's attempts to shield her with her usual indignation, when they actually arrived, and she saw the desperation all around her, she did second guess her decision. Prostitutes seemed to be everywhere, despondency as much a part of their persons as their garish makeup and shockingly revealing clothing. Malnourished, filthy children, their eyes deadened with hopelessness, some as young as Melody, broke Tabitha's heart.

The appearance of the Pembroke carriage caused even more of a stir on Dorset Street than it usually did in the East End. As Wolf stepped down before Tabitha and Bear, a woman who looked past her prime, though perhaps that was just the result of her years on the street, approached him.

"Alright, my luv. 'ow do you fancy a bit of fun and games?"

Wolf answered politely, "No, thank you, miss."

"Miss? Can't remember the last time I was called that." She held out a rather grubby hand, "Me name's Katie Barclay. Me regulars know me as Kissing Katie. Though I'll do a lot more than kissing, if you know what I mean." Katie Barclay winked lasciviously.

Tabitha, hearing voices outside the carriage, now exited it and came face-to-face with the prostitute. "Oh!" was all she could say.

"This your missus then?" Katie asked. "She's pretty enough I guess, if you like them tall and skinny." And as she said this, Katie grabbed her own bountiful assets and pushed them up.

"Wolf..." Tabitha said, not sure how to handle the situation.

"Yes, yes. Miss Barclay, please excuse us but we are in something of a hurry and have some business to conduct."

Katie Barclay laughed, "The likes of you 'ave business around 'ere? Wonders will never cease. If you change your mind, luv, you know where to find me. I'm 'appy to take it up against the wall, I am. No need for nothing fancy for Katie Barclay."

Bear followed Tabitha out of the carriage, and Katie Barclay's eyes almost popped out of her head, "Well, aren't you a big one, luv! I might have to charge double to manage you."

Tabitha wasn't sure she had ever seen Bear blush, but he did then. She had come to realise over the past few months that the man's enormous size and terrifying visage masked a very sensitive soul.

Finally able to extricate themselves from Katie Barclay, the group made their way to number 42. Even by the standards of Dorset Street, the boarding house was dilapidated, with filthy windows and a front door that was more peeling paint than anything. There was no knocker, so Wolf rapped on the door with his knuckles.

There was no answer for at least a minute, and then the door was opened by a haggard, middle-aged woman with a pock-marked face and watery eyes. Her hair was greasy and straggly, and Wolf worked hard to suppress his gag response to the awful rotten smell emanating from her. As it was, he took a step back as the woman opened a mouth full of blackened teeth and said, "Wot you want?"

"We are looking for a boarder here, a Mr Wilfred O'Hara."

"We got no one by that name here," the woman asserted, though her shifty look suggested she was lying.

Even as she said these words, Wolf heard a door slam behind her and jerked his head towards Bear. The pair had a lot of experience from their thief-taking days in situations such as this one: knocking on the door of someone who wished to elude them. They wordlessly fell back into the routine that had served them well for many years and Bear dashed off around the alley to the back of the house.

"We were told by Mr O'Hara's employer that he had given this address," Wolf said.

"Don't know nuffink about that, do I?" the woman continued. She wasn't sure why that handsome Mr O'Hara wanted to escape these toffs, but he usually paid on time and would bring her some leftover veggies from the market, and that was enough to win Lucy Grove's loyalty.

It was evident that they would be getting nothing out of the landlady, so Wolf thanked her for her time and said to Tabitha, "I am taking you back to the safety of the carriage and then will go to see if Bear needs help." Tabitha's first instinct was to insist that she did not need an escort for the few hundred yards back to the carriage. However, that instinct was quickly superseded by a stronger survival one that told her that perhaps she should accept Wolf's protection on Dorset Street.

They were not even halfway to the carriage when Bear emerged on the street holding a ginger-haired man in his iron grip. As they'd been told, Wilfred O'Hara was not a large man; he was probably barely five-feet-two and likely didn't weigh more than ten stone. Bear didn't have to make much of an effort to keep the man in his grasp.

"Caught this one trying to jump the high wall at the dead end of the alleyway," Bear said with a chuckle. "He might have got away if he'd been taller and stronger."

"I've done nothing wrong," Wilfred O'Hara protested in a very pronounced Irish accent.

"Men who have done nothing wrong do not usually flee," Wolf pointed out.

"Who says I was fleeing?" the man continued to protest in the face of incontrovertible evidence that he was doing precisely that.

"What do you want to do with him?" Bear asked, holding the man with one hand as if it were no more difficult than controlling a recalcitrant cat.

Wolf considered the question: what should they do with him? The most obvious thing to do was to drive him to Whitechapel Police Station and turn him over to Bruiser and his men. However, Wolf wanted to question him fully before doing that. They could certainly do so in the carriage, but the man didn't smell a lot better than his landlady, and Wolf preferred not to subject Tabitha to that in a confined space. Finally, he said, "Let us take him to Mickey D's." Even as he said this, Wolf sighed inwardly; yet another obligation he was putting himself under to the gang leader. Would he ever be able to get out from under the burden he seemed to keep exacerbating?

It was fortunate that the trip to Mickey D's home was brief because Wolf had not overly anticipated how awful it might be to be cooped up in the carriage with Wilfred O'Hara. The carriage had barely come to a stop outside Mickey D's house when Wolf threw open the door, stepped out and quickly put a hand out to help Tabitha escape. Bear followed with the malodorous Wilfred O'Hara still in his grip.

Wolf knocked on the front door and, as usual, it was opened by Angie. "He's not here, Wolf," she said before Wolf could even speak. "And I don't know where he's gone, I'm sorry to say."

Then, noticing the man Bear had in his grasp, she said, "Is that the man you've been searching for?"

"It is," Wolf confirmed. "Mr Wilfred O'Hara."

"I haven't heard that name for a while," Angie said, peering more intently at their captive. "And he looks a lot different since I last saw him, more than thirty years ago."

"You recognise this man?" Wolf asked incredulously.

"Well, I know who he is. I should have looked at the drawing you gave

Mick more closely. But now I see him in person, I'm sure I know him. You better come in. No need to keep talking on the doorstep just to give the neighbours something to chinwag about."

Angie led the way into the parlour and indicated that they should all sit. Bear released his grip on Wilfred O'Hara, who hadn't said a word since his capture, but pulled out his revolver and kept it trained on the man.

"Willy O'Hara, is that really you?" Angie asked in amazement. She admitted to no one in particular, "I used to be quite sweet on this one, back in Ireland. He's a year or two older than me and didn't give me a second glance, of course." Then pausing, she turned to Wolf and said, "Remember I mentioned poor Penny O'Hara?"

Wolf didn't remember, and seeing this from his expression, Angie continued, "I was friends with Penny O'Hara, his sister, back in Limerick. We came over here together, in fact."

Now Wolf remembered the mention of Penny O'Hara. "I do recall now, Angie. You mentioned that something had happened to her and that a Colin O'Donnell was to blame."

At this, Wilfred O'Hara jerked his head up and spat, "That animal O'Donnell raped and murdered my sister."

They all looked at Angie, who confirmed, "Certainly, someone did. There was never proof that it was Colin O'Donnell, but he disappeared right after and hasn't been heard from since."

"Of course it was him. He was always obsessed with her, even back in Ireland but she never had any interest in him. When she came over here to get away from him, he followed her. A month later, she was dead."

"Perhaps if you O'Haras had taken her seriously, this never would have happened," Angie said bitterly. "But oh no, your father said she had an overactive imagination and what would a grown man like O'Donnell want with a wisp of a lass like her?"

Wilfred looked shamefaced at her words. "Aye, you're right there, Angie. Da didn't take our Pen seriously, and so we boys didn't. We should have horsewhipped O'Donnell and made sure that he never looked at her again, but he was a good friend of our Liam, and he swore up and down for the man. When Pen said she wanted to go to London with you, Mam and Da agreed that perhaps it was for the best. She was never meant to be a farm girl, that was for sure. We didn't think much of it when Colin O'Donnell left a few weeks later."

"I know that Penny wrote to you that he had followed her," Angie said in the same accusing tone.

"By the time we got the letter, she was dead, and no one has heard hide nor hair of O'Donnell since."

Tabitha glanced at Wolf and raised her eyebrows slightly. This was interesting but unrelated to the investigation at hand, and the look he gave her indicated he agreed.

Attempting to get their interview back on track, Wolf asked, "Angie, would it be too much to ask for a pot of tea and some sandwiches?"

"Course, my luv. What was I thinking? I'll be back in a jiffy."

With Angie out of the room, Wolf turned back to Wilfred O'Hara and said, "Why did you run today?"

"In my experience, when some fancy strangers come asking for you, it's never a good thing," the man answered defensively. "I'd heard word around Whitechapel that a picture of me was being handed about and that I was being blamed for them murders of those girls."

"If you knew this, why did you not come forward? If you are innocent, you have nothing to fear," Tabitha said.

Wilfred O'Hara laughed bitterly. "If you are innocent, or maybe even if you're guilty, you have nothing to fear," he pointed out with emphasis. "Me? An Irishman with barely a few pennies to his name, barely managing to pay for a rat-infested cesspit in one of the worst streets in London? The coppers aren't usually inclined to a presumption of innocence for the likes of me."

The man had a point, and neither Tabitha nor Wolf could really argue with him. Of course, another reason that he ran could be because he was guilty. Angie's identification of the man did muddy the waters of what they had suspected so far after Victor Grund's explanation of the significance of the knife and the O'Donnell clan. Nevertheless, perhaps Wilfred O'Hara had come into possession of the knife at some point and had wanted to point the finger of blame at the family he hated.

"You spoke to one of the victims perhaps minutes before her murder and were seen in the vicinity of another," Tabitha noted. "How do you explain that?"

"Well, I stopped the lass because I was looking for Fournier Street and I'd got turned around. She was walking up Brick Lane and looked like she was a local. There's no crime in asking for directions, is there?"

"Why were you looking for Fournier Street? Wolf asked. He had a pretty good idea of what the man was looking for, but he wanted him to confirm it.

"Not that it's any business of yours, but I was looking for the Working Men's Club. One of Verde's workers, Billy Peters, is a member, and he invited me to join him for a pint." Wolf considered the man's words and realised that this must have been when Sean had spotted Wilfred O'Hara.

"And what of the other victim?" Tabitha asked. "Why were you following her?"

For a few moments, it seemed as if Wilfred O'Hara wasn't going to answer. Everything about his sullen face and tightly coiled posture indicated that the man had secrets he wasn't willing to share. However, finally, he slumped forward somewhat and seemed to have come, however unwillingly, to a decision. "I wasn't following her. I was following O'Donnell."

"Colin O'Donnell?" Angie exclaimed, entering the room with a tray laden high with sandwiches, cake, and ginger biscuits. "Colin O'Donnell is back in London?"

"I don't know," Wilfred said with a shrug. "But his brother Tommy is. I caught sight of him that night at the Working Men's Club. I haven't seen the man in more than twenty-five years; he left Limerick even before you and Penny went. But I'd know that weaselly look anywhere. I never liked or trusted the man, even back then. We'd heard that he disappeared around the same time his brother did, but I guess he must have come back to London. That night in Fournier Street was the first I'd thought of an O'Donnell in a long time. He didn't recognise me, and I kept a low profile. I tried to follow him that night but lost track of him around Lamb Street."

The man paused and looked longingly at the sandwiches. Taking pity on him, Wolf indicated that he should help himself. The next few minutes were spent with the seemingly ravenous man eating a plate of sandwiches so quickly that Tabitha worried he would choke. The rest of the group used the opportunity to help themselves to food. It had been a long morning, and they had missed luncheon.

Sipping on her tea and nibbling a cheese sandwich, Tabitha pondered Wilfred O'Hara's words. Finally, noticing a slowdown in the man's eating that indicated at least an initial satiating of his hunger, she asked, "Were you hoping that this Tommy O'Donnell might lead you to his brother?"

Finishing up the last sandwich on his plate, Wilfred nodded. "Aye. I wouldn't say I had much of a plan. Maybe the man has no idea where Colin went to. But my family has been waiting to avenge our Pen for a long time, and when I saw an opportunity, I took it. That little weasel Tommy used to be almost as much a bad 'un as his brother."

Wolf considered the evening he had spent at the Spitalfields Working Men's Club, and the men gathered in the bar that night and wondered if this Tommy O'Donnell had been amongst them. He described some of the men most prominently involved in the heated debate that evening. When he described Bulbous Nose, Wilfred said, "Aye, that's Tommy. I'd recognise that nose anywhere, even if it looks a lot worse than it did all those years ago."

Well, that was helpful, Wolf thought. They had an O'Donnell clan knife, which there was reason to believe belonged to their killer, and there was a man called O'Donnell apparently living in the East End. Of course, there were probably a lot of Irishmen called O'Donnell in London, so this was hardly conclusive evidence of anything, but it was a lead. However, just because Victor Grund had been convinced that an O'Donnell would never willingly let a clan knife out of his possession didn't mean that wasn't exactly what had happened. It was not enough proof to arrest a man who happened to be called O'Donnell. This seemed particularly the case when they had a different suspect who had been seen just prior to two of the murders.

Tabitha considered what Finn O'Brien had told them days before and asked, "What were you carrying in the carpetbag you had with you when our witness saw you?"

"Everything I own," Wilfred admitted. "I'd had to move boarding houses that day and had taken the few things I had with me to Verde's. I had no idea where I would go, so I took Billy Peters up on his invitation because he said that there was usually free food at the club, and I couldn't afford to turn that down. While I was there, he told me about the boarding house on Dorset Street. When he'd first come to London, he'd stayed there for a bit. Told me how cheap it was and that if I kept on the right side of the landlady, I might even get some porridge thrown in first thing. So, after I lost sight of O'Donnell, I made my way there and took the room."

Wolf reflected on the man's words. Wilfred O'Hara was a pitiful sight. Wolf was curious about the man's history and how he had ended up in such dire straits, but it didn't seem relevant to their investigation, at least for now. Instead, he turned to Bear and said, "You believe that you caught sight of the killer. I know you weren't sure at the time what you saw, but casting your mind back, could this have been the man?"

Bear pondered the question. He'd reflected a lot on what he thought he had seen in the alleyway on the night of the murder. "I wasn't sure then what I'd seen, but if I had to say, I think I saw a man in a top hat and a cape that had a red lining."

They all looked at the man in front of them; it seemed highly unlikely that his wardrobe contained such items. Finally, realising they could not leave this stone unturned, particularly given the paucity of other evidence, Wolf said, "Tabitha, I would like you to take the carriage and return home." Seeing her open her mouth to protest, Wolf put up a hand and said, "This is not about protecting you. But you saw that boarding house. I plan to return with Mr O'Hara and search his possessions. If we find anything suspicious, we will turn him over to the police. If we don't, we will return home immediately. This is not a job that needs three people."

Tabitha narrowed her eyes suspiciously; while Wolf's explanation was reasonable enough, she still felt that he was trying to shield her. On the other hand, having seen the outside of 42 Dorset Street and its landlady, she had to admit that she had no desire to explore the revolting boarding house any further.

Chapter 26

Talbot opened the front door of Chesterton House with a nervous look on his face that was almost as alarming as the one he had worn when Lady Jameson had visited. "Is my mother here again?" Tabitha asked anxiously, assuming the worst.

"I am happy to say that, while you have an aggrieved visitor, it is not Lady Jameson," the butler intoned.

Tabitha rolled her eyes; there could only be one other person who might consider herself aggrieved and feel she had the right to impose herself on them with no notice. "I assume the dowager countess is in the drawing room."

"Indeed, milady. It may be worth mentioning that she has been here for almost an hour. Also, that she had telephoned an hour before that and demanded that I tell her where you had gone. Luckily, I did not know."

"Thank you for the warning, Talbot. Please send in some fresh tea."

"I delivered a fresh pot no more than five minutes ago, m'lady."

Tabitha nodded, handed him her outerwear, and steeled herself for the likely diatribe. She knew the dowager well enough to know that the woman rarely expressed her most extreme displeasure with heated discourse. Given this, Tabitha was immediately on alert when the dowager said in a voice as cold as ice, "How nice of you to return finally, Tabitha."

Tabitha's first inclination was to pour a sherry to fortify herself against the likely onslaught. However, her mother's words from two days before rang in her ears, and she resisted the urge. Instead, she poured herself a cup of tea. Neither woman said a word.

Finally, seated with her tea in hand, Tabitha lied, "If I had known you were intending to visit, I would have returned sooner."

"Is that the case?" the dowager said, her voice dripping with sarcasm. "Talbot informed me that Jeremy and Mr Bear were also out. Is it unreasonable of me to assume that the three of you were investigating without me?"

There it was. Tabitha was surprised that the old woman hadn't drawn it out for longer. Perhaps she was too impatient to know what they had discovered.

Tabitha considered how much she wanted to placate the dowager and finally said, "Mama, we made a decision late last night to visit the Spitalfields Market early this morning. We did not want to risk waking you last night, and we all know how you feel about activities too early in the morning. At the time, we did not believe the outing would be as interesting and fruitful as it turned out to be."

This wasn't the entire truth; they had made the decision over dinner, and there was no reason to believe that the dowager would be asleep at nine o'clock at night. And, of course, they could have left word with Manning. It was evident that the dowager was appropriately sceptical of this explanation. The woman seemed to be fighting an internal battle as to how much to continue berating Tabitha and how much to move on from her grievance in the interest of being brought up to speed.

Finally, a decision was made. The dowager sniffed once, then said, "Fine. It is true that I prefer not to bestir myself in the early hours of the morning. Though, next time, I would prefer to be given the choice."

Tabitha schooled her face for sufficient contriteness and said, "Of course, Mama. We will remember that in the future." After taking another sip of tea, she then put the woman out of her misery and told her about their day.

Sitting back in amazement, the dowager exclaimed, "My my. So, you believe that this O'Hara is not our killer after all?"

"Well, Wolf and Bear have gone to search his room, but we do not believe so. Honestly, the man was rather sad and pathetic. There was nothing about him to indicate a vicious murderer."

"What would indicate a vicious murderer, my dear?" the dowager asked acerbically.

"You know what I mean, Mama. Think about Miss Prescott. In hindsight, it was quite evident that she was a little unhinged. Just consider her initial behaviour towards us both. It was not unbelievable when we discovered just how far her unhinged behaviour had gone." The dowager acknowledged the truth of her words, and Tabitha continued, "We have dealt with crimes of passion for the most part. Maureen Prescott was the first killer whose activities were premeditated. I think it takes a certain kind of person to plan the death of another, let alone a brutal death. There was nothing about Mr O'Hara that suggested he was that kind of person."

"What now? He was our only suspect. If we strike him off the list, we do not have much else."

Tabitha acknowledged the woman's words; it was quite frustrating to think that all the supposed evidence they had collected over the last few days could be for nothing. However, running her mind back over those clues, she pointed out, "Not all of what we have learned is useless. What we know about the knife is still important.

"Maybe. However, we have got no further along in tracing its owner. If Jeremy believes that he saw this Tommy O'Donnell at the club for the working classes, why do we not ask for the man there?"

At her words, Tabitha stood up. "Mama, you are a genius!"

"Well, I am glad to have you finally acknowledge that. Which particular part of what I said is so brilliant?"

"The man that Wilfred O'Hara was following is an O'Donnell. The knife could belong to him. We know this man is a member of the Working Men's Club. The Club will have a record of where we can find this O'Donnell."

The dowager considered her words for a moment, then said, "I really am quite a genius, am I not?"

Both women could barely sit and wait for Wolf and Bear to return. The wait might have been interminable if they hadn't heard Melody's voice outside of the drawing room. Tabitha called out for Melody's nursery maid, Mary and moments later, the door opened, and the young woman and her precocious charge entered the room. Mary then curtsied and excused herself.

"Granny!" Melody squealed, running up to the dowager gleefully. "Why are you here? I'm going to see Uncle Maxi."

Remembering that Mondays were one of Langley's days with Melody, and suddenly conscious that she had missed a couple of her afternoons that week because of the investigation, the dowager patted the spot on the sofa next to her. Melody climbed up and leaned over to kiss the old woman on the cheek. Tabitha was still amazed by how fond of the dowager the little girl was. Even more extraordinary was that the affection was reciprocated. Even learning of Melody's history and her origins as the child of poverty-stricken parents in Whitechapel who had lived on the streets with her brother when they were orphaned had not diminished the dowager's genuine delight in the child.

"I am sorry that we missed our visits this week, Melly," the dowager said in a sweet and loving tone that Tabitha had never heard her use towards her own children and grandchildren. "I promise that I will make it up to you. I may need a few more days, but then I promise we will go to Hamleys, and I will buy you a present."

Under other circumstances, Tabitha might have disapproved of spoiling a child in such a way. However, given the harsh conditions of the first four years of Melody's life, she could hardly begrudge the child a treat now and then.

Rat, Melody's brother, had been unsure of exactly when either of their birthdays were. Tabitha and Wolf had decided to celebrate Rat's on Christmas Eve. Talking with Rat about what he remembered from when Melody had been born, he had spoken about there being some blossoms on the trees. Wolf had then consulted the Almanac from that year and had determined that it had been a very warm and dry month, so the blossoms would have been on the trees early. Given this, they had decided that Melody's birthday would be March first. Thinking of this, Tabitha said, "Perhaps you can look at what you might want for your birthday, Melody, from Wolfie and me and Granny."

The dowager looked as if she was inclined to argue against this compromise but, in the end, thought better of it. For all her bluster, the dowager was aware that the time she spent with the child was at Tabitha's discretion.

"What a splendid idea, Melly! We will have tea at Lyon's Tea Shop after that."

Melody clapped her hands in delight. "I love you, Granny!" she exclaimed.

The dowager took one of the little girl's hands and said, "I love you too, Melly." Tabitha could have sworn that the woman's eyes were even a little wet as she said this. As extraordinary as it was, Melody was perhaps the only living soul the dowager seemed to care for deeply.

As touching as the scene was, Tabitha was cognisant that Lord Langley was expecting Melody. "Mama, we should let Mary and Melody make their way over to Langley House."

"Pish posh. Maxwell can cool his heels. I have not seen the child in days." The fact that this was entirely through her choice to be involved in every aspect of the investigation seemed unnecessary to point out. The dowager continued, "Have Talbot telephone to say that Melody will be late."

Bowing to the inevitable, Tabitha rang for her butler and asked him to relay the information to his cousin, Langley's butler, the other Talbot. She made a point of emphasising that the older Lady Pembroke was spending time with Melody at Chesterton House. Tabitha was sure that Langley would read between the lines.

Over the next fifteen minutes, Melody chattered away about nothing in particular. The dowager engaged in the childish conversation with a genuine enthusiasm that she rarely brought, even to her conversations with the Prime Minister. Of course, if this had been pointed out to her, the dowager would likely have noted that if the Prime Minister was even half as entertaining as the child, then he might also get her undivided attention.

There was a knock at the drawing room door, and Mary returned with a very excited Dodo. While Tabitha had been no fan of the puppy when she had first come to live at Chesterton House, the Cavalier King Charles Spaniel had slowly won her over. This change was largely due to the dog's significant role in saving Tabitha from a killer's grasp in Brighton and then following Rat's scent to where the insane Maureen Prescott was holding him and another boy hostage in Wales.

The beautiful, silky-haired puppy was more than six months old now and had calmed down somewhat. Rat had been working with the puppy, and she seemed to understand and occasionally obey basic commands. Unfortunately, neither maturity nor training seemed to have cured the dog of her more destructive tendencies, and she would still rip apart any shoes she managed to get hold of.

Despite Tabitha's genuine warming towards the dog, she still insisted that Dodo accompany Melody to every visit with Lord Langley if only to impress upon the man the burden he had inflicted, unasked, upon their household when he had given the child the puppy during her unplanned and prolonged stay at Langley House. While Tabitha had forgiven Langley, for the most part, for his abduction of Melody and had developed a genuine affection for the man, she nevertheless would never let him forget that he had compounded the sin of kidnapping with the canine imposition.

"M'lady, I thought it best to get Dodo and take her outside to relieve herself while Miss Melody was in here," Mary explained.

"That was a very sensible idea, Mary," Tabitha replied. "Lord Langley has been alerted that your visit will be delayed, so why don't you take Dodo back to the kitchen until Miss Melody is ready to go?" The dowager was perhaps even less of a fan of dogs than Tabitha, always associating them with her horse and hound-loving deceased husband, never a pleasant association for the woman.

Thirty minutes later, the dowager was finally persuaded that Melody should be allowed to go to Langley House. With the little girl gone, the dowager said rather ominously, "Tabitha, there is something I have been meaning to talk to you about for some time. It is about Melody."

Tabitha's eyes widened and she felt her heart rate increase at these words. She had taken Melody in and had established her as her ward. Nevertheless, she was aware that her hold on the child was tenuous and that it might be challenged at any moment, particularly if any other family members suddenly surfaced. Apart from anything else, Tabitha had promised Wolf and Rat that if the latter, at any point, decided on a change in his sister's situation, she would honour it. While Tabitha had genuinely intended to honour that promise when she made it, it had become increasingly evident how unbearable it would be to have the child taken from her. Her primary concern with Melody spending so much time with Lord Langley was that the little girl might come to prefer Langley to Chesterton House. While Langley swore he would never take the child from Tabitha's arms, she couldn't quite shake her insecurities. Was the dowager about to challenge the current living situation?

"Yes, Mama. What about Melody?" Tabitha asked hesitantly.

"I have spoken to my solicitor, Mr Peabody," Tabitha's heart sank. She was right; the dowager was going to suggest that Melody live with her. "I have spoken to Mr Peabody about how you might best formalise Melody's situation as your ward," the dowager finished. Tabitha could not have been more surprised; whatever she had expected her erstwhile mother-in-law to say, that wasn't it.

Perhaps noting Tabitha's reaction, the dowager continued, "What did you expect me to say? That Melody should come and live with me?" Given that was what Tabitha had been thinking, she made no reply. Luckily, the dowager rarely needed a response, and now was no different. "As much as I love the child and cherish the time I spend with her, I am an old woman and have neither the patience nor the energy to mother a young child."

She paused, then adopting a softer tone than she usually used with anyone, let alone Tabitha, said, "Melody is a very lucky little girl to have you as her mother." At this, Tabitha's eyes filled with tears, but she didn't respond. In truth, she was too overwhelmed to say anything. "One can only imagine what might have become of the child if you had not taken her in. Despite Rat's herculean efforts to protect and provide for his sister, he is just a child himself. As we have all seen over the last few months, the streets of the East End are a harsh and brutal place for anyone, let alone an orphaned child."

Finally able to control her emotions and speak, Tabitha asked, "What did Mr Peabody suggest?"

"He said that we should appeal to the Court of Probate to appoint you and dear Jeremy as her guardians. I should mention that I have set up a fund for the child that she will be able to draw from when she is eighteen years old."

"A dowry?" Tabitha asked.

"Nothing of the kind. I have no desire to have aristocratic ne'er-do-wells and their impoverished offspring importuning Melody merely for a dowry that they will then be the main beneficiaries of. No! As a young woman, she will have free access to the funds for whatever she chooses to do with her life. If she wishes to further her studies, travel, or devote herself to good causes, that will be her choice."

Tabitha couldn't have been more shocked. The dowager's granddaughter, Lady Lily, wished to study botany and one of the major voices insisting that she should instead marry well had been the dowager's. However, Tabitha had no desire to point the contradiction out to the woman in the face of such a genuinely kind and generous act. Whatever her reasons for feeling differently about Melody's future than she did about her granddaughter's, Tabitha was grateful for her words.

The dowager continued to explain, "If I should die before Melody turns eighteen, management of the fund would need to be handled. I do not want to run the risk that some miscreant male relative of Melody's suddenly appears and takes control of her money. If you, and particularly Jeremy, are her guardians, I can ensure that management of the fund passes to you. Of course, such an arrangement will need your consent before the Court of Probate."

This was such a sensible, obvious plan, and now that it had been said out loud, Tabitha couldn't believe neither she nor Wolf had considered such an action.

"Thank you, Mama, for suggesting this. It is a wonderful idea, and, of course, Wolf and I will be happy to do whatever is necessary to safeguard Melody's future." Truly, wonders would never cease.

CHAPTER 27

Wolf and Bear walked the short distance from Mickey D's back to Dorset Street, their captive in tow. Bear had let go of the man but assured him that he had his gun in hand and any attempt to escape would fail. As it happened, Wilfred O'Hara seemed happy enough to escort them back to his boarding house, another indication that he was, in fact, innocent.

Turning the corner onto Dorset Street, they came face-to-face with Katie Barclay. "Back again so soon, my luv? You just can't keep away, can you?" the prostitute chuckled at her joke, demonstrating just how many of her teeth were either missing or rotten.

Noticing that Tabitha was now absent, Katie said in what she mistakenly believed was a seductive voice, "Got rid of the missus, did you, my luv? You know, I might even do you for free; you're quite the looker, you is."

Wolf was not as flattered by the compliment as Katie hoped and said gently but firmly, "Miss Barclay, I must refuse the offer."

Suddenly noticing Wilfred O'Hara, Katie Barclay said, "Wot you want with 'im?"

"Do you know this man?" Wolf inquired, genuinely curious what, if anything, the prostitute might know about Wilfred.

"I know 'im alright," Katie confirmed. "Got some right nasty tastes 'e does. Not that I wasn't up for it. As long as there's coin, I'm up for most things." Realising the import of her words, the prostitute hastily added, "Except for you, my luv. You can 'ave it for free. At least once or twice." She winked lasciviously at Wolf.

Realising that this conversation was unlikely to get them anywhere, Wolf thanked Katie Barclay again for the offer but declined, more vehemently, this time.

"No bovver, my luv. You know where to find Katie Barclay when you change your mind." With that, the prostitute sauntered off, being sure to sway her ample hips as she went.

Wilfred O'Hara had a key to the front door, so there was no need to deal with his landlady again. His room was on the ground floor, at the back of the house. It was a shoebox of a room, barely large enough for the narrow bed and small wardrobe that took up most of it. There was a small table at the far corner that had a plate of half-eaten food on it. It seemed that they had interrupted Wilfred's meagre lunch when they had called earlier.

"I'll search the wardrobe, and you look everywhere else," Wolf suggested to Bear. While they began their search of his home, Wilfred stood awkwardly in the corner of the room. Bear searched under the bed, then pulled up the thin, lumpy mattress to see if there was anything hidden there. Finding nothing, he went over to the table, but it was immediately obvious that there was nothing but the plate with a stale crust of bread and a small piece of unappealing-looking cheese. Bear turned and looked around the room, but there were not many places where something might be hidden.

Wolf wasn't having much more luck with the wardrobe; Wilfred O'Hara seemed to own few clothes beyond those on his back. There was a threadbare winter jacket that he hadn't had time to don before fleeing and one shirt that had been patched and mended so many times that Wolf wondered how much of the original shirt there still was. What there wasn't was anything that might have passed for a cloak and top hat.

The entire search took less than ten minutes. "There's nothing here," Wolf said, voicing the obvious.

"I told you there wouldn't be," Wilfred O'Hara said defensively. "I don't have a pot to piss in. The few pennies that I get from old Verde barely cover the money I spend on this rat's nest."

Out of curiosity more than anything, Wolf asked, "From what we have heard, you have fallen down on your luck recently. What happened?"

"I came to London three years ago. Things have been rough in Ireland and, at least from what I'd heard from others who'd come over, there were jobs aplenty for anyone prepared to work hard. Turns out it's not true. I came over with a bit of money and ran through most of it before I found a job at the docks. But I got into a spat with another worker a couple of months ago, and the guvnor took his side, and I was out on my arse. Since then, I've not been able to find anything permanent, just whatever hours Verde throws my way."

Given this, Wolf was tempted to ask why the man had jeopardised the job by not turning up for work that morning. However, he'd known lots of men like Wilfred O'Hara in his years as a thief-taker, men who would swear up and down that the cards were stacked against them and that their bad luck had nothing to do with anything they had done. Whatever the man's shortcomings were, it didn't seem, at least for the time being, that they had any bearing on their investigation, and so Wolf kept his question to himself.

Instead, he said, "I am sorry for what happened to your sister. What is your plan if you manage to track this Colin O'Donnell down?"

"I'm going to cut the man's throat, just like he did to our Pen," Wilfred said unapologetically. While Wolf didn't condone street justice, he had a hard time blaming Wilfred O'Hara for his words. Unsure what to say given this, Wolf merely nodded his head and said, "We will bid you farewell, Mr O'Hara, at least for now. I will tell our contacts with the Metropolitan Police that we have tracked you down and that you do not appear to be the killer." Wilfred didn't bother to question why the police might stand down based on Wolf's word. It was obvious enough to a poor Irish farmer that a rich, titled Englishman might be powerful enough to command law enforcement.

Soon enough, Wolf and Bear were walking through Whitechapel, hoping to find a hackney cab at some point. They had done the walk back enough times and were prepared to do it again if necessary. Luckily, just beyond Smithfield Meat Market, they saw a cab and, fifteen minutes later, were back at Chesterton House.

Walking into the drawing room, Wolf was surprised to be confronted with the dowager enjoying tea and cake and even more surprised when Tabitha jumped to her feet expectantly, saying, "Thank goodness you're back, Wolf. Mama had the greatest idea."

"Indeed, I did, dear Jeremy. It was an idea even beyond my usual wisdom and insight," the dowager proclaimed. She was tempted to launch back into her grievances at being left out of the morning's activities. Still, she did not want to say anything that might detract from the general acknowledgement of the enormous contribution she had made to cracking the case.

"I cannot wait to hear this great idea," Wolf said, going to pour himself a cup of tea. Settled in an armchair with tea and a plate of biscuits, Wolf indicated that he was ready to be amazed.

"Before we tell you, did Mr O'Hara's room turn up anything useful?" Tabitha asked, irritating the dowager who had been all ready to astound.

"It did not," Wolf acknowledged. "At least for the time being, there seems no reason to believe the man is guilty of the murders."

"Wonderful! Moving on," the dowager said impatiently. "My brilliant insight was that Mr O'Hara has been following a Mr O'Donnell and that our knife may belong to him and so we should focus on this club as a way to find the man that Mr O'Hara spotted."

Wolf sipped on his tea and considered the dowager's words. It was true that discovering Wilfred O'Hara had caused them to concentrate less on the provenance of the knife; eyewitnesses who could put the man at the scene of two of the killings had seemed to trump Victor Grund's explanation of the importance of the engravings on the weapon. However, now that they were reasonably certain that O'Hara was not their man and given that he had spotted and followed a man named O'Donnell, it seemed to make sense to refocus their attention there.

While Wolf wouldn't necessarily have categorised this as a brilliant insight that he and Tabitha wouldn't have likely come to quite quickly themselves, he understood the dowager well enough to know that nothing short of unequivocal acclaim would satisfy the woman. "Lady Pembroke, whatever would we do without you?" he gushed, causing Tabitha to roll her eyes. While she understood why he felt the need to lavish praise on the woman, she still couldn't help her response even though she had been the first to commend the dowager for the idea.

"I hope you will remember that sentiment, Jeremy, the next time you are tempted to pursue an investigative strand without me," the dowager said caustically.

Wolf glanced at Tabitha who gave a little shake of her head; this was not worth arguing again. Instead, he answered, "Indeed, I will remember."

Unsatisfied by this response but keen to move on to their next steps, the dowager asked, "And so what is our plan?"

Therein lay the rub; what was their plan? They all thought for a few moments, and then Tabitha said, "Well, as Mama pointed out, we know that this O'Donnell belongs to the Spitalfields Working Men's Club. Surely someone there will know where we might find him."

"That is an excellent idea. I will ask Bear to find Mickey D's nephew, Sean and see what he knows. If nothing else, he can go back to the club and ask the doorman, Jack." Wolf felt bad sending Bear back to Whitechapel so soon after they had arrived home and decided to let the man eat something before asking him to make another round trip to the East End.

"So, is that it? What do we do meanwhile?" the dowager demanded.

"I suggest that you return home and that we all wait and see what Bear can turn up. For myself, I am quite exhausted from our adventures today and would like nothing more than to wash the grime of the East End off me and have an early dinner." The dowager was tempted to protest at the suggestion that she leave. Still, she had accepted an invitation to a dinner party that evening, which she had every reason to expect Lady Hartley to attend. She could not pass up an opportunity to publicly chastise the woman for the gossiping that had led Lady Jameson to London to berate her daughter.

CHAPTER 28

An hour later, Wolf had bathed, changed his clothes and made his way downstairs. He had spoken with Bear before he had made his way up to his bath, and his stalwart friend, who never complained no matter what the task he was set, willingly agreed to return to the East End and seek out information about Mr O'Donnell.

Talbot informed Wolf that Tabitha was still dressing for dinner, so he went into the drawing room and poured himself a brandy. During the walk from Dorset Street to Smithfield Market with Bear, Wolf had brought up the topic that he had discussed with Langley days earlier. In the chaos of the investigation they had found themselves thrust into, he had not found an opportunity to make the request of his old friend. Bear had declared himself honoured and delighted to take on the responsibilities and so now all that was left was to lay out the plan for Tabitha.

Wolf had gone to great lengths to investigate what might be done legally to set Tabitha's mind at ease regarding marriage and was doing everything he was able under the law, as it was currently, to protect her. Nevertheless, he realised that it might still not be enough. He could not assure the woman he loved that there was no risk in giving up her independence and putting herself once more in a man's power. He didn't know all the horrors of Tabitha's brief marriage to his cousin, Jonathan, but he knew enough to understand her reluctance ever to marry again. However, he also realised that their current living situation wasn't tenable in the long term. Perhaps it might have been before they acknowledged their mutual feelings, but not now. At some point, their passion would spill over into something more, and he refused to make Tabitha his mistress.

Wolf wasn't sure how long he had been sitting lost in thought when he realised that he was no longer alone in the drawing room. "A penny for your thoughts?" Tabitha teased, gracing him with the beautiful, gentle smile he so loved.

"Let us go into dinner and talk then," Wolf said, surprising her with the seriousness of his tone.

Talbot was the most discreet and also the most sensitive of butlers. He could sense that his master wished for privacy, and after the soup was served, he shooed the footmen out of the dining room, saying that he would return in twenty minutes to serve the fish course.

Tabitha smiled at the butler's retreating form, "Whatever you wish to speak about, even Talbot has picked up on its seriousness."

Wolf was sitting at the head of the long dining table, and Tabitha was diagonally opposite him, as they usually were when dining alone. He reached out and took one of her hands, stroking it gently before saying, "Tabitha, you know that I love and wish to marry you."

Tabitha looked into his open, honest, handsome face. It was a face she had grown to love more than she had ever thought possible. "I know that Wolf, and you know that I love you in return."

Wolf caught her gaze and looked into her beautiful hazel eyes, flecked with gold. "I know that you love me, Tabitha. I also understand your hesitancy to ever put yourself in a man's power again."

"Wolf, you know that is not because I do not trust you."

He squeezed the hand he was holding, "You do not have to explain yourself. I understand fully that, at least the way the law stands today, once you marry me you are effectively becoming my property. If I should decide to beat you one day, as my cousin did, you would have no more recourse than you did then."

"Wolf, I do not believe you will ever raise your hand to me," Tabitha assured him. "You must know that."

"I do. However, if I was to hit my head one day and turn into the kind of monster who would raise his hand to a woman, there would be little the law or society would do to stop or even censure me." Tabitha acknowledged the truth of this hypothetical statement.

"When we were in Wales, I promised you that the next time I spoke of marriage, I would address and banish every fear you have. I have taken steps to try to do just that." Wolf felt Tabitha tense in anticipation of his words. "Having spoken extensively to my solicitor, it has become clear that there is nothing I can put in place now to prevent my future self from choosing to use my wife as a punching bag and being allowed to without the law turning a mostly blind eye."

Tabitha tried her hardest not to show her disappointment. She hadn't been sure what she thought Wolf would be able to put in place, so she had no reason to feel despondent, and yet she did. Seeing these emotions play out on her face, Wolf rushed to continue, "However, there are some things I can put in place. My solicitor informed me that thanks to the act of Parliament in 1882, which was further strengthened five years ago, it is no longer the case that whatever property and fortune you enter marriage with automatically become your husband's."

This was news to Tabitha. Certainly, no one had explained to her before her marriage to Jonathan that this was the situation. Not that she had anything besides her dowry at the time. Even if she had, it was such a social convention that a husband became master over his wife in mind, body, and every other way that she couldn't imagine ever having challenged Jonathan or having mustered up the courage to leave him.

Wolf continued, "However, my solicitor confessed that the enforcement of this act is spotty and might very much depend on how conservatively a particular judge chose to uphold the law. Again, I am trying to take into consideration a hypothetical future where I am not the man I am today and, for whatever reason, behave entirely counter to how I would like to believe I will. What he did point out is that, as an earl, I would likely get deferred to far more than the average husband might."

"So, what did he suggest?" Tabitha asked, unsure where this explanation was leading.

"He suggested that before any marriage takes place, you put your fortune into a trust that is managed on your behalf by a trustee. You could set this trust up to allow you to access your money at will and in whatever amounts you choose. The trustee might also be entrusted with the power to dissolve the trust, for example, on my death or if the law progresses to the point where it is no longer needed."

"That is a lot of power to bestow on any trustee."

"Indeed. For this reason, and in case of death, my solicitor suggested that there be two trustees assigned."

Thinking back to Wolf's mysterious outing a few days before, Tabitha guessed, "Would I be correct that you have asked Lord Langley to be one of those trustees?"

"I did." Wolf hurried to add, "I hope that I did not act out of turn in speaking with Langley before speaking with you, but I wanted to make sure that I had everything in order before I presented you with this plan."

"I can imagine no man besides you, who I trust more," Tabitha assured him. Even as she said these words, she marvelled to herself at how her feelings about the man had changed in not much more than six months. It wasn't that long ago that Tabitha had considered that Langley left a cold, almost reptilian impression. Now, she couldn't even remember why she had felt that way.

Turning back to the matter at hand, Tabitha noted, "You said that there would be two trustees. Who will the other be?"

"I asked Bear if he would consider the role."

"What a wonderful choice. I do not know why I did not consider him immediately."

"Does this mean that you are amenable to such a trust?" Wolf asked with a note of desperation in his voice that squeezed Tabitha's heart. Why did they even have to be in such a situation? Was she being irrational to put the man she loved and trusted through this?

"I trust you, Wolf. If you believe that this will best protect me, I will do it willingly."

"That is not all," Wolf admitted. He then told her the second request he had made of Langley and Bear regarding any children they might have and why.

Tabitha sighed and said sorrowfully, "You are assuming that this will be an issue, Wolf. I have given up all hope of a successful delivery of a baby."

Wolf now took both her hands, "I have not given up such hope. Not for myself. Truly, I will not mind if you are not able to bear me a child, but for you, because I know how much you want this. And if we are able to have children, I want to ensure that you and they are protected, and this seems the best way I can do that." Tabitha acknowledged his words, though she found his sentiments about the protection of children she did not believe she would ever bear to be merely wishful thinking.

However, Wolf's words did remind Tabitha of her earlier conversation with the dowager. Before she could relay it, Talbot and a footman re-entered the room with their fish course. The plates were safely distributed, and the servants silently glided out of the room again.

"I had the most extraordinary conversation with Mama today," Tabitha told Wolf. An extraordinary conversation with the Dowager Countess of Pembroke might cover a multitude of sins and so Wolf was ready for anything. However, he was not prepared for Tabitha's next words, "Mama has created a substantial trust fund for Melody."

"Has she?" Wolf asked in surprise.

"Oh wait, that is not the most remarkable part. She has set it up so that Melody can access it at eighteen for any reason, be it marriage, travel or to continue her education."

Wolf almost choked on the wine he had just taken a sip of. "To continue her education? The dowager countess has setup a trust so that Melody might choose to continue her education instead of marrying?"

"Indeed, the irony was not lost on me. Though I believe it is entirely lost on her. Mama has made a request of us that we apply to the Court of Probate to be Melody's legal guardians. She is concerned that if she dies before Melody reaches her majority, some unscrupulous relative of Rat and Melody's might surface and try to gain control of the money. Of course, as soon as she said this, I realised that regardless of whether this might happen, she is correct, we should become Melody's legal guardians. We need to ensure she is protected no matter what becomes of us."

"Indeed. In fact, part of my proposal regarding your trust was to be that I add to it to provide for Melody regardless of what happens between us," Wolf admitted.

"Well, that may not be necessary now. I believe that Mama inherited quite a bit of money after my father-in-law died and is a wealthy woman in her own right. Of course, we should confirm how much she plans to place into trust, but she led me to believe that Melody will never want for anything."

"Then I will contact my solicitor tomorrow and have him begin the process of applying to the court. I think it is a wonderful idea, and I agree; I do not know why we did not think of it sooner." Tabitha had some idea why they hadn't but didn't comment on what a sea change there had been in Wolf's attitude to Melody and her place in their lives. Instead, she just smiled at him gratefully. "And once she is our legal ward, any protections we put in place for the guardianship of our natural children after my death will automatically flow to Melody, and that will be a relief."

Suddenly, Wolf put down his fork, and he stole a shy look at Tabitha. "Does your consent to my plans mean that you will also consent to be my wife?"

Tabitha laughed, "Well, you have not asked me formally yet. We will not know until that happens."

Wolf placed his serviette on the table, stood, moved in front of Tabitha and then bent down on one knee. She turned towards him, already so choked up with emotion that she wasn't sure she would be able to reply to his question. He took the signet ring he wore on his pinkie finger and held it out to her. "Tabitha, I love you with all my heart. Will you do me the honour of being my wife?"

With tears of joy rolling down her face, Tabitha nodded, then managed to croak, "I will. I will marry you, Wolf."

"I apologise for not being better prepared and I promise to replace this with a more appropriate ring. However, for now, please accept this as a token of our betrothal."

As Wolf said these words, Talbot entered the dining room, the footman on his heel. He saw his master on one knee and promptly turned and pushed the footman back out the way they had come.

Standing and pulling Tabitha to her feet with him, Wolf called out, "You may come back, Talbot and congratulate us. Lady Pembroke has agreed to be... well, she's agreed to continue to be Lady Pembroke."

"May I be the first to extend my sincere congratulations to you both on behalf of the entire staff. I know that I speak for all of them when I say how happy we are for you." Talbot might have mentioned that this was a day the staff had all been expectantly waiting for. However, it was not for a butler to tell his master and mistress that they'd taken their time getting to a point their servants had been anticipating for weeks if not months.

The Dover sole was replaced with guinea fowl, and Tabitha and Wolf retook their places at the table. They had eaten many meals together, sitting just as they were, including many once they had declared their love for each other. Yet something felt different for Tabitha; now she was sitting next to her future husband, and her place at Chesterton House was beyond doubt.

Reflecting on this caused Tabitha to realise that, in the midst of all the running around they had been doing over the last couple of days, she had omitted to tell Wolf about her mother's visit. Lady Jameson's words were even more pertinent now than they had been two days before. Unwilling to break the magical mood but aware that she wanted no secrets between her and her newly betrothed, Tabitha told Wolf about her mother's visit and demands.

"When she ordered me to leave this house a betrothal was still hypothetical. Now that it is not, I cannot help wondering if she is correct." As much as it pained Tabitha to acknowledge this, Lady Jameson's words hung over what otherwise should have been the most wonderful evening of Tabitha's life.

"Correct that you should move to be with her in Cambridgeshire?" Wolf asked incredulously. "You cannot possibly be serious."

"Heavens no! There is nothing that will compel me to live under the same roof as my mother ever again. However, Mama's suggestion that I live with her is a practical solution; she lives nearby, and I could continue to run this household. There need not be any change in Melody's schedule."

"But why, Tabitha? You have stated many times that you do not care what society thinks of you. Why begin now?"

"I do not care for myself. I do care for you." Seeing Wolf about to interrupt, Tabitha put up a hand and continued, "I know that you do not care for yourself. However, you should care for the title. While I do not believe I will be able to fall pregnant, if I were to do so, and if the child were to be male, it is of the utmost importance that there be no doubt as to his legitimacy. The only way to ensure this is for me to remove myself to Mama's before the announcement of engagement is made public."

Wolf wanted to argue, and yet he couldn't deny the truth of her words. He just hated the thought that she would leave Chesterton House, even for a few weeks.

Chapter 29

When dinner was finished, and Tabitha and Wolf had retired to the parlour for brandy and coffee, Bear returned to Chesterton House and joined them.

"It wasn't as easy to try to hunt this O'Donnell down as I hoped it would be," he acknowledged. "It took me a while to find Sean, and when I did, he didn't have much to tell. They do keep records of members at the club, but he doubts they would just open them up when asked, especially for the likes of me. This may be a job for the Earl of Pembroke," he said to Wolf with a smirk. After ten years of friendship, of working, living, fighting, and sometimes starving together, Bear was able to tease his dearest friend about his new rank and wealth in a way that might have been unbearable coming from almost anyone else.

"I then went and talked to the doorman, Jack, but he wasn't a lot more useful. He suggested that perhaps this O'Donnell is a new member, which is why he doesn't know who he is. I'm sorry to say that I came up short at the end of the day."

"You did your best, my friend. We will return there tomorrow, and I will subject the powers that be at that club to the full deference and obedience that nine generations of an earldom can make a man feel entitled to." Wolf paused. He and Tabitha hadn't discussed how and when to reveal the changed status of their relationship. However, whatever they choose to say to the world in general, Bear was family, and it didn't feel right keeping this momentous news from him. Anyway, if Talbot and the footmen knew, it was hard to believe that the entire household wouldn't soon as well and the last thing that Wolf wanted was for Bear to hear the news from anyone but him.

Glancing at Tabitha and receiving a smile and a nod, he said, "Bear, Tabitha and I have news."

The words were barely out of his mouth when his friend had leapt out of his chair and bounded across the room to shake his hand. "I have not told you what the news is," Wolf pointed out, laughing.

"What else could it be? And after our conversation earlier, it was clear this was something you were planning to do. We've all been waiting for you two to get around to it."

"All? Who is 'all'?" Tabitha asked, genuinely curious.

"Everyone; the servants, the dowager countess, Lady Lily definitely. The dowager's butler, Manning, asked me about it casually a few weeks ago. And I know that the lad has been waiting very impatiently."

"What would make everyone assume that we were going to get betrothed?" Wolf asked. Bear just laughed in reply.

Changing the subject, Tabitha said, "I suggest that we call Mama and tell her about our plans for tomorrow. I assume that even if women cannot enter the club during evening hours, there is no reason we cannot breach its walls in the morning? I would imagine they have women in the building doing all manner of cleaning and cooking, after all."

"Are you suggesting that the dowager countess join us?" Wolf asked.

"After the tongue-lashing I had today, yes, I am. I propose that we first go there and tell her our news. We will never hear the end of it if she hears it from someone else. As I have now come to learn that Lady Hartley was able to pick up enough gossip about us from someone that she managed to relay news of our supposed betrothal back to my mother, I do not want to assume that our servants' hall is impervious to leaks."

Wolf knew that Tabitha was right and rose to make the telephone call himself. Returning a few minutes later, he sighed and said, "There really is no pleasing the woman. She was far from happy to hear that we intended to call on her before eleven o'clock in the morning, yet when I suggested that she was welcome to sit out this part of the investigation, she was even unhappier. Anyway, the upshot is that she will be joining us, even if she spends the entire time griping about how unnecessary it is to set out at such an ungodly hour."

The following morning, Wolf informed Thompson that he would be dressing in full aristocratic splendour that day. Thompson was comfortable enough with his employer that he didn't bother to control his facial expressions and his feelings about the constant oscillating between Wolf wanting to blend in when visiting the East End and wanting to ensure that his status as earl was immediately known.

"Yes, I know, Thompson, these things are sent to try you," Wolf said teasingly.

"Indeed, milord."

Wolf had relayed his sartorial intentions to Tabitha the night before, and she had matched him in grandeur. They had not felt the need similarly to inform the dowager; they were always grateful if she controlled herself enough not to wear her diamonds to Whitechapel. Just after ten o'clock, they were in the Pembroke carriage and on their way to the dowager's home.

Manning answered the door and showed them through to the drawing room, where a visibly irritated dowager awaited them. "Is there any reason this trip could not have waited for an hour or two?"

Tabitha and Wolf each took a seat and ignored the question. There was really no point in reminding the dowager that just the day before, she had claimed that an earlier hour than she was accustomed to was not an excuse for excluding her from investigative activities. Instead, Wolf said, "Before we leave for Whitechapel, Tabitha and I have news." At this, he shot Tabitha a shy, affectionate look that the dowager didn't miss.

"Finally! Really, I cannot imagine what the shilly-shallying was about. In my day, you barely had to know a prospective spouse for a few days for a marriage proposal to be forthcoming."

Tabitha decided not to mention to the dowager that such norms were what led to the kind of abusive marriages that they had both suffered and that perhaps getting to know a man before choosing to shackle yourself to him for life was sensible.

The old woman continued, "Anyway, the deed is finally done, and I wish you both congratulations. Tabitha, I assume that you intend to move in with me for the weeks it will take for the banns to be read. Or will you wait for a late summer wedding? June is such a delightful time to be wed."

"I will take you up on your very kind offer, Mama. However, our plan is to apply for a special license and to wed as soon as possible." Tabitha paused, unsure how the dowager would take the news of Wolf's plan to protect her as much as he was able by setting up the trust. "There are some legal issues that Wolf intends to take care of before we can wed." Tabitha then gave the dowager a brief overview of Wolf's plans for her fortune, Melody, and any future children.

Whatever Tabitha and Wolf had expected the dowager to say, it wasn't to answer with a full-throated endorsement of the plan. "What a wonderful idea, dear Jeremy," the dowager gushed. "If my great aunt had died while Philip was alive but before the act of 1882, my entire inheritance would have immediately become his to fritter away on whores and horses. I was never more grateful for an act of parliament than I was for that one, even if it was passed by a Liberal. Indeed, that may have been the only thing that I applaud Gladstone for, but it was not an insignificant change for the better as far as I am concerned."

Of course, it was not surprising that the dowager looked at all social progress only through the lens of how it might directly impact her. Tabitha did not doubt that if the Married Women's Property Act had not benefited the woman herself, she might have very different views on it.

Tabitha kept these thoughts to herself, and the dowager continued, "I am particularly happy to hear of the provisions you have made to protect Melody. As you know, I have known Maxwell since he was in short trousers and, of course, have not always approved of his behaviour. However, I will acknowledge that he is an honest and trustworthy man, that one unfortunate incident aside. Certainly, I believe that Maxwell and Mr Bear will have nothing but the child's best interests at heart."

The dowager thought for a moment, then said, "Special licenses are not as easy to get as is often portrayed in novels. Even earls are supposed to present a compelling reason not to wait to hear the banns read. After all, if it were simple, every Tom, Dick, and Harry, would get one and then what would be the point of insisting otherwise?"

Where was she going with this, Wolf wondered. He didn't have to wait long to have that answered. "Special licenses are issued through the Archbishop of Canterbury's office. You may leave this with me, and you will have one within twenty-four hours." The dowager's constant beratement of the Archbishop whenever she encountered him socially on topics as wide-ranging as the length of the average service to supposedly blasphemous teachings being promulgated by his clergy, at least according to her, was well known. Neither Tabitha nor Wolf had any doubt that the man would do whatever the woman asked just to get himself out of her line of fire.

"I will tell Manning to inform my housekeeper and the rest of the staff that you will be arriving tonight and staying for an indeterminate amount of time," the dowager said.

Tabitha started at her words; that night? While she knew that she needed to live with the dowager until she and Wolf could marry, that had been a vague concept. She had hoped that perhaps she could take a few days to prepare herself and that perhaps by then, it was possible that everything would be arranged, and the stay would not even be necessary.

Seeing Tabitha's hesitation, the dowager said in a surprisingly kind voice, "You know that this is for the best, Tabitha. If not for you, then for the title." Given that this was precisely the argument Tabitha had used with Wolf, she had no choice but to nod in agreement.

"Let me telephone Chesterton House before we leave and instruct Talbot to speak to Ginny and have her begin packing." Tabitha hesitated, then added, "Talbot and one of the footmen walked in on Wolf's proposal, so I do not doubt that the household has some awareness of the situation."

"Then that is even more reason not to delay. If your staff know, then this news will be circulating through the servant halls of the best homes in London before you know it. You must be out of that house before it does."

Thirty minutes later, they were nearing Spitalfields Market. Given that the dowager had not visited the market with Tabitha and Wolf the previous day, she was in no way prepared for the frenetic energy of the place nor the sounds and smells. Driving down Fournier Street to the Spitalfields Working Men's Club, she peered out of the carriage window, fascinated.

"And you say you walked through this market yesterday and actually spoke to a vendor, Tabitha? I wonder whether Cook knows about this place."

Tabitha did not doubt that the dowager's staff did not need their mistress making "helpful" suggestions as to where they might shop. "It is very well known, Mama. I am sure she is fully aware of its existence."

"I will make mention of it regardless. One can never be too sure when it comes to the servant class."

They pulled up outside of the unassuming, red-bricked building. The dowager sniffed, "This is a club? It is not very imposing, is it?"

"It is a club for the workers in and around the market, Lady Pembroke, not White's," Wolf pointed out.

Thinking about the notion of men of all classes having spaces to which they might retreat for social, intellectual, and leisure pursuits, Tabitha turned to the dowager, "Have you considered joining the new Empress Club, Mama? Apparently, it has the blessing of Queen Victoria herself."

"Why would I need yet another place with which to mix with the harpies who make up most of aristocratic society?" the dowager sneered.

Luckily, by this time, the carriage had come to a stop on Fournier Street, preventing the dowager from further expounding on the subject. Wolf noted that Jack Geraghty was not outside. It was before noon, so not really surprising. He knocked at the door, and after a brief wait, it was answered by a woman who seemed, by her dress and the fact that she was carrying a broom, to be a maid of sorts.

Wolf didn't believe he would need the full Earl of Pembroke persona to convince the woman to let them in. Instead, he said in something akin to his normal voice, "Is there a manager of sorts we might speak with?"

The woman looked at the group in front of her and shrugged her shoulders as if to indicate that her job was only to ensure the building was clean, not to be a gatekeeper evaluating visitors. She stepped back and indicated that they should follow her. The woman led the way to a plain-looking door with a little brass plaque on it that said, "Manager," and knocked.

On being hailed to enter, the woman opened the door and said in a broad cockney accent, "Bunch of swells to see ye, Mr 'ayes." And with that, she turned and left.

Tabitha looked into the office and saw a small, bare space with a grimy window that seemed to look out onto a gloomy alleyway. The only furniture in the room was an old, battered desk with one chair behind it and two in front and a large filing cabinet that took up almost a quarter of the room. Behind the desk sat a small, mousey-looking man. The few wispy strands of hair on his head seemed unwilling to be smoothed down and stood up at odd angles. The man had a neat little moustache that sat above a small, thin-lipped mouth. His eyes were beady and, at that moment, screwed up in confusion at the maid's words.

Wolf stepped into the room, fully embodied his late grandfather, and pronounced, "I am the Earl of Pembroke." He then gestured to Tabitha and the dowager and gave their titles.

The small, mousey man sitting behind the desk, Mr Hayes, jumped out of his seat at their entrance. He had run the Spitalfields Working Men's Club for the past five years. Before that, he had been a clerk at the market. Archie Hayes was a working-class man through and through, as his father and his father before him had been. He had been born, raised, and had raised his children within spitting distance of the market that had provided for so many generations of the Hayes family. Archie was a proud supporter of the Labour Party and the trade union movement. He had always held great disdain for the upper classes. This disdain was even greater towards those who had inherited their wealth and power. Yet, when face-to-face with an aristocrat for the first time in his life, all those genuinely held beliefs flew out of the window and he could barely mutter a "M'lord."

For his part, Wolf was always equal parts baffled, amused, and grateful for the effect that his title seemed to have on people, particularly those in the lower classes. He was the same man he had been a year before when he was merely Wolf the thief-taker and he used to spend his days and nights amongst people who now almost genuflected at the mere sight of him. He was no more insightful, compassionate or honest. The only things he was now more of were powerful and wealthy, and those seemed a poor way to judge the worth of a man and how much respect he was due.

Nevertheless, whatever his private feelings on the level of awe his rank routinely inspired, Wolf had made his peace with how useful a tool it could be in investigations and was happy to discover that Mr Archie Hayes was no exception. In contrast, the dowager expected nothing less than veneration from the lower classes. She swept into the room and sat on one of the two chairs in front of the desk. Tabitha had followed the dowager into the room and took the other chair. If nothing else, the office was too small for her and Wolf both to stand. The dowager then demanded, "And who are you, sir?"

"Hayes, Archibald Hayes, m'lady," the man stuttered. He had heard some rumours of a couple of toffs coming through the market the day before, but he'd thought it was probably the typical hyperbole of market vendors. He'd imagined that the truth had been no more than a particularly well-dressed merchant and his wife. However, now he realised how wrong he had been for surely these were the very same people.

"Well Mr Archibald Hayes, we have need of some information," the dowager proclaimed. Wolf hadn't really expected that the dowager would let him take the lead in the interview; she didn't usually. Still, he'd hoped that she might at least allow him to make the initial request. Shaking his head resignedly, he questioned why he'd been so naive.

Archie Hayes didn't reply to the dowager's request, but he nodded his head solemnly. "We need the address of a member of this establishment, a Thomas O'Donnell, perhaps known by the absurdly childish nickname Tommy."

Mr Hayes blinked a few times. While, to his knowledge, no member of the club was currently wanted for criminal activities, it was his nature to assume the worst of those in authority. These people did not seem as if they were associated with the police – two of them were women, after all, and the man was an earl – but you couldn't be too careful. Given this natural resistance towards sharing information about members, he was happy to be able to say with great certainty, "We have no member by that name, m'lady."

"Do you have anyone with the last name O'Donnell?" Tabitha asked. The man shook his head. "Anyone who goes by the name Tommy?" Tabitha pressed, now clutching at straws.

"We have no members called Thomas, Tom, or Tommy," Archie Hayes assured them with relief. As he had previously to Wilfred, Wolf described the man, Bulbous Nose, he had seen the night he had visited the club. It was evident from the surprised look on Archie Hayes' face that he wanted to ask why a peer of the realm had felt compelled to spend an evening in a club in Spitalfields. He also had no idea why such a man would lower himself to seeking out one of the club's members. Archie may have wondered all these things, but all he said was, "Yes, we do have a member who matches that description, but his name is not Tommy O'Donnell."

At last, they were getting somewhere. Tabitha asked far more patiently than she imagined the dowager would if she had asked the question first, "What name does this man go by, Mr Hayes?"

Archie hesitated; personally he had no love for the man in question, who held some extreme views and was a troublemaker. If it hadn't been that he had been recommended for membership by one of the officers of the club, Archie wouldn't have moved his membership forward. Suitably overawed by his visitors' magnificence, which won an internal battle with his sincerely held political opinions, Archie said, "The man's name is Harry Brady. He's a newish member, maybe three months ago now. My understanding is that he's a tailor of some sort."

"And would you have this Mr Brady's address?" Tabitha asked.

Archie Hayes shook his head. "We don't take the addresses of our members. A lot of them are living in boarding houses and move around a lot, so there wouldn't be much point. As long as they pay their dues and their bar bill, that's all we need."

Archie might have mentioned that he did know the address of the member who had recommended Harry Brady. However, he was not so overpowered by their presence that he felt the need to volunteer information, and his visitors didn't think to ask such a question. Instead, the dowager stood and said dismissively, "Well, this certainly was somewhat of a disappointment, Mr Hayes. I suggest that you improve your record-keeping in the future."

Chapter 30

Back in the carriage, Wolf said, "Well, I suppose we have a name now, at least. However, forgive the tailoring pun, but I feel we are looking for a needle in a haystack."

"Very droll, Jeremy. However, I believe that I know where we might start." The dowager paused for effect, relishing the suspense her pronouncement had produced.

"Where?" Tabitha finally asked, irritated by the woman's need to draw out the moment.

"Really, Tabitha! Have some patience. I believe that we should talk to Tuchinsky. After all, the front for her professional activities is a tailor's shop, and I assume the gentleman who sits in it sewing has some professional association with the trade."

Tabitha looked at Wolf; that really was a very good idea. Realising how much it would cost Tabitha to have to give the dowager her dues, Wolf answered, "I believe you are correct, Lady Pembroke. After all, when I saw this Harry Brady. he was railing against Jews siphoning off employment opportunities. If he belongs to this club, he must live locally. He is a tailor, the Jewish community has come to dominate the garment industry and Brick Lane is just down the street from here. If our man is such an agitator against Jewish workers, it wouldn't be surprising if there had been some altercations. And nothing happens around here that Tuchinsky does not know about."

Brick Lane abutted Fournier Street, so it was barely worth taking the carriage. However, neither Tabitha nor Wolf was in any doubt as to the dowager's feelings about walking the streets of London, let alone those of the East End. In fact, given how busy Brick Lane was with market vendors, children playing in the street, and locals bustling here and there, it would have been quicker to walk. Nevertheless, five minutes later, they had pulled up outside of the tailor's shop that was the public face of Tuchinsky's criminal enterprise.

Brick Lane was even more interesting to Tabitha than the rest of the East End. The smells were enticing, and the Jews busy shopping, gossiping, and working up and down the street were exotically interesting. Tabitha had spent a few days living above the tailor's shop when Wolf had been shot protecting Tuchinsky's grandmother, Bubbe, but she'd spent all of that time by Wolf's side and hadn't seen much of the local inhabitants. Looking around her now, she wished they had time to explore.

The dowager led the way into the shop. Sitting where he had been when they were there previously was the same old man with a long grey beard, still wearing the funny little round cap on the top of his head. He always seemed to be sewing something, though it wasn't clear to Tabitha that the store functioned as a tailoring establishment anymore.

The old man recognised them, put his sewing down, stood up and said, "So, the fancy goyim are back. I'll let the guvnor know you're here."

Almost immediately, the man was back and gestured that they should follow him. The man led them through the shop's back room with its three tables, each with a sewing machine that stood as a silent testament to when the shop had really been the bustling hub of the Tuchinsky tailoring business. He led them up the stairs to the flat that Tuchinsky shared with her bubbe and zaide and down the corridor to the kitchen.

During her stay in the Tuchinsky household the past November, Tabitha had noticed that the smell of Bubbe's chicken soup seemed to linger in the air even when she was not cooking it. It was as if years of making the delicious soup, usually multiple times a week, had caused every piece of fabric in the home to absorb its scent. Tabitha reflected that this wasn't an unpleasant experience and that she could be blindfolded and walked into this flat and immediately know she was at the Tuchinsky's. From the different smells emanating from the kitchen, it seemed as if chicken soup was not on the menu for lunch that day. The cooking odours made Tabitha's stomach rumble and she was happy in the knowledge that, if Bubbe were in the kitchen, she would insist that they eat.

The old man leading the way called out ahead of him. He then pointed the way to the kitchen, saying, "You know which way to go," then turned and left. The dowager led the way with Tabitha and Wolf following.

The group walked into the kitchen where Tuchinsky was eating lunch with her cousin, Shlomo. Bubbe was hovering around, stirring a pot on the stove while keeping a watchful eye on how much her granddaughter was eating. They all looked up at their visitor's entrance. Bubbe's face lit up with a beaming smile, "Your ladyship, what a lovely surprise." Turning to her granddaughter, she scolded, "Miri, why didn't you tell me we were having guests? I would have made enough food for everyone."

Given that the table was laden with enough food for them all and a few more people, Wolf laughed as he went over to kiss the old woman on the cheek. "Bubbe, Tuchinsky had no idea that we were coming, but even if she had, there is always enough food at your table."

Bubbe patted his cheek and replied, "You look much better than the last time I saw you, bubbelah. All that chicken soup did its job." It was an article of faith in the Tuchinsky family, and beyond that, Bubbe's chicken soup could cure most ills. She had plied Wolf with it daily when he had been recovering in her home. "I'm sorry, I don't have any ready today. Do you like gefilte fish?"

"I have never tried it, Bubbe, but have no doubt it will be delicious."

"Then sit and eat." Turning to greet Tabitha, Bubbe said, "You, in particular, dolly. You need to put some more meat on that tuchus." Tabitha laughed but happily sat down. The dowager and Wolf joined her. Bubbe immediately began loading up three more plates with little fried balls that turned out to be minced, slightly sweet white fish, and some kind of baked potato dish that Bubbe informed them was kugel. There were also beigels, the delicious round bread rolls with a hole in the middle. There was fish in various forms in dishes on the table; something Bubbe referred to as schmaltz herring, whatever that was and another kind of herring that was pickled. Bubbe heaped plenty of it all on plates for her visitors.

As Bubbe served up lunch, Miriam turned to the dowager and asked, "Have you come to tell me you've solved the case?"

"Well, I would not characterise where we are as a solution, but we have definitely made progress." She then told Tuchinsky all they had learned, including the name they had got from the reluctant Archie Hayes.

"So, you're sure this butcher isn't a Jew?" Tuchinsky asked hopefully.

"We are as sure as we can be at this point. We plan to inform our government connection of this fact, and we have told Samuel Montagu," Wolf explained.

"And yet Jews are still being attacked, and synagogues are being dese-crated," Tuchinsky said bitterly. "Did you see the Illustrated Police News?"

"We did. Nasty stuff, but, unfortunately, that is the kind of muckraking a rag like that loves to print."

Tuchinsky shook her head, "It's a miracle that no one has been killed yet. Well, besides those poor girls, of course. But tensions are high, and it's only a matter of time. Things were hard enough for us before this. It took years for the community to feel safe after everything that happened in eighty-eight. We were just starting to feel like we were being accepted and were safe here, and then this." Miriam Tuchinsky prided herself on keeping tight control over her emotions, believing it was the only way she stood a chance of being respected and feared amongst the men of London's underworld. However, she could not keep the desperation out of her voice and prevent the slight quiver of her chin as she spoke.

"We know, dear," the dowager said gently. "That is why we have come to you for help now." She then finished their story with what they knew about Harry Brady.

When they were done, the dowager asked if Tuchinsky knew the man. "Well, I don't, but someone around here must." Turning to Shlomo, Tuchinsky said, "Go tell your father to come back up here."

A few minutes later, the old tailor from the front of the store had returned. Tabitha turned to Wolf with the silent question, "So this is her uncle?" Wolf's slight cock of his head and raising of one eyebrow answered that it must be.

"Uncle Solly, do you know a Harry Brady? He's a tailor who works around here somewhere. He's been mouthing off a lot lately about Jews taking jobs. Perhaps even more than mouthing off. I know there's been some trouble recently. I even sent the boys down to make sure it didn't happen again.

The old man pulled up a free chair and sat. Helping himself to some of the fish balls, Uncle Solly considered the question. "I don't know what those fools were thinking, coming onto your patch and causing tsuris for people you protect."

"Well, Shlomo and the boys think they've made sure it won't happen again. But was this Harry Brady one of them?"

"He's quite distinctive looking," Wolf said and then described Bulbous Nose.

"That sounds like the ringleader Joshie was describing. Nasty piece of work, he said."

"Can you ask around, Uncle Solly, and see if anyone knows where he lives or works?" Tuchinsky asked. Uncle Solly assured her he'd do that immediately and then left the kitchen, taking his plate of food with him.

Their business out of the way, everyone resumed their lunch. Bubbe ensured that no one's teacup was ever empty and, at the end of their meal, pulled out an unlabelled bottle.

"Ah, now you're in for a treat!" Tuchinsky said, fetching some small glasses. "Bubbe's homemade schnapps!" Tuchinsky poured them all a small glass of the clear liquid. Tabitha didn't want to offend Bubbe, so she took a small sip. The fiery liquid burned her throat, and she almost choked. Looking at the dowager, it seemed the other woman's experience was similar.

Tuchinsky laughed, "It'll put hairs on your chest. Bubbe won't be insulted if you don't finish it." Grateful for these words, the dowager and Tabitha both pushed their glasses away from them. Wolf copied Tuchinsky and downed his in a shot.

An hour later, they left the Tuchinsky home laden with a bottle of schnapps, a basket of the fish balls, which really had been delicious, and an assurance that they were welcome back anytime. They left through the tailor's shop where Uncle Solly told them where Harry Brady could be found.

Chapter 31

The address they had been given was on Commercial Road, about a quarter of a mile from Spitalfields Market. As it pulled up outside the plain storefront, the Pembroke carriage caused a similar curiosity and head-turning as it had on Brick Lane. On the brief drive there, Wolf had considered whether their current course of action was the correct one. He'd have preferred to have Bear with him and the dowager and Tabitha safely at home. If Harry Brady was the killer they sought, then he was a dangerous man. The only reason Wolf hadn't made such a suggestion was the certainty of how it would have been received. At least he'd had the foresight to slip his revolver into his boot before they left home.

Before Wolf descended from the carriage, he said in a very serious tone, predominantly to the dowager, "I must insist that I be allowed to take the lead in this interview and that the two of you stay back. I would ask that you stay in the carriage, but I know that is unlikely to happen."

The dowager and Tabitha both shot him looks that made clear what they thought of that suggestion but conceded that he would take the lead. Walking into the shop, they were greeted by a jovial-looking man in his fifties. With a quick shake of his head in their direction, Wolf indicated to the dowager and Tabitha that this was not Harry Brady. The man was, in fact, a Mr Hildebrand who had long aspired to have his establishment be on par, or at least in competition with Saville Row. As the well-dressed group entered his establishment, Mr Hildebrand's hopes soared that perhaps this was the day his dreams became a reality.

Wolf immediately shattered those dreams by inquiring whether a Harry Brady was employed there. Trying to hide his disappointment, Mr Hildebrand nodded and disappeared into the back, returning a few moments later with Bulbous Nose, known as Harry Brady.

Harry Brady didn't like Jews, but he didn't like toffs either. He looked Wolf up and down with suspicion. He could have sworn he'd seen the man before but couldn't put his finger on where or when.

"Are you Harry Brady?" Wolf asked.

"Who's asking?" Harry said with a sneer. His accent was clearly Irish, though Wolf didn't know enough to be sure if he was from Limerick.

"I am the Earl of Pembroke," Wolf said imperiously.

Harry Brady laughed, a nasty, grating sound. "Sure you are. Earls and dukes love to slum it down Commercial Street."

Mr Hildebrand was immediately alert to the possibility of scaring off the closest thing he had ever had to an upper-class clientele. "Harry, watch your lip. If this gentleman says he's an earl, then I'm sure he is." Realising that he was leaving these important people to have their conversation in the front of his store, he quickly offered, "Would you like to go through to my office to talk to Harry in private?"

Harry seemed like he had little interest in this proposition, but Wolf immediately accepted. A few minutes later, they were all seated in a small but neat office with the door closed. Wolf withdrew the knife that he had secreted in his other boot. Tabitha hadn't realised that he'd brought it along, and her surprise showed on her face.

"Do you know what this is, Mr Brady?" Wolf asked.

"Looks like a knife to me," Harry answered in a begrudging tone as if even that acknowledgement was too much trouble. However, there was a look in his eyes that suggested that he was far more interested in the knife than he was letting on.

"Indeed," Wolf continued. "In fact, our understanding is that it is a Skean and that the engravings on the handle of this one suggest that it belongs to the O'Donnell clan." At this, Harry Brady visibly started, but still he said nothing.

"What would I know about that? You think that all us Irish are related, do you?"

"Not at all, Mr Brady. Or should I say, Mr O'Donnell?"

"Don't know what you're talking about. My name is Harry Brady," the man insisted with a snarl.

"But I believe that it is not. In fact, I have good reason to believe that your name is Thomas O'Donnell, known as Tommy."

"And who did you hear this from then? Huh?"

"A Wilfred O'Hara in fact. I believe he knew you from back in Limerick. It seems he is eager to speak to your brother."

Harry Brady visibly paled at Wilfred O'Hara's name. If they hadn't been sure that they had the right man before, they certainly were now.

"What do you want?"

"This knife was found next to the most recent East End murder victim. I myself found the body before her killer had a chance to mutilate her," Wolf explained.

Harry Brady stood up, "I'm no killer and I won't have the likes of you saying I am and putting a noose around my neck."

"Sit down, Mr Brady," Wolf commanded, drawing his revolver out of his boot. "Or I will make you sit down." Harry Brady complied, and Wolf continued, "I was informed that a clan knife, such as this one, is a treasured item and that no O'Donnell would willing give one away or sell it. So, it is highly likely that whoever dropped this knife is an O'Donnell."

Harry Brady seemed to have collected himself somewhat and resumed his cockiness, "O'Donnell's a common enough name, so it is. Limerick's full of them."

"So, you are from Limerick, just like the man Wilfred O'Hara is seeking?"

Realising his slipup, Harry Brady shrugged and said, "What if I am?"

Realising the man was not going to be so easy to crack, Wolf said, "From what we have heard, this Thomas O'Donnell is brother to a Colin O'Donnell who raped and murdered Mr O'Hara's sister."

"The little slut didn't get raped," Harry spat out. "She was gagging for it, she was."

"So, you do know what I am talking about," Wolf said triumphantly.

"Everyone knew about Penny O'Hara, and lots of men were well acquainted with her, if you know what I mean," Harry said with a nasty sneer and a leering wink.

"And so she deserved to be murdered by your brother?" Wolf immediately retorted.

A host of emotions washed over Harry Brady's face. It was very evident that he had admitted more than he'd intended. Now, he seemed to be battling with how much to continue to deny. Finally, apparently realising that the jig was up, he conceded, "Fine, so I'm Tommy O'Donnell. It's not a crime to get a fresh start, is it?"

"It depends on why you feel the need for that fresh start. Are you also admitting that this knife belongs to someone in your family?"

The man's eyes were wide now, and he seemed to be sweating. "Yes, it's an O'Donnell Skean, but it's not mine. I swear," he said, his voice now filled with fear and desperation.

Tabitha suddenly remembered the story Angie had told and interjected, "But it is your brother, Colin's, isn't it?" They didn't need the man to answer; his expression told the whole truth. Of course, a man who has brutally raped and murdered a young girl once would think nothing of killing again. Now that Tabitha had said it out loud, she couldn't believe they hadn't pieced it all together sooner.

Wolf realised the truth of Tabitha's words and pointed the revolver at Harry Brady, or as they now knew he was, Tommy O'Donnell. "Where might we find your brother, Tommy?"

Wolf had seen enough people lie over the years to recognise the signs that Tommy was about to do so. "No idea. Haven't seen him in years."

"Is that a fact?" Wolf asked, not even trying to hide his scepticism.

"Yeah. It is." With that, Bulbous Nose stood, "Is that all you'll be needing then? Some of us have work to do." It didn't seem as if they were going to get any more out of the man, and so they let him go.

Back in the carriage again, this time heading back to Chesterton House, the dowager demanded, "Is that it? We just take his word for it?"

"Not at all. I have a plan."

"Jeremy, I am not one of those ridiculous people who enjoys being kept in suspense. Spit it out, whatever this plan is."

"Can we all agree that Tommy O'Donnell is lying and that he knows exactly where his brother is to be found?" Wolf asked. The women nodded their heads in agreement. "Then I do not doubt that the man's next actions will be to warn his brother that we are looking for him. And more to the point, to warn him that Wilfred O'Hara is. O'Donnell is tied to his job for the next few hours, so I believe we have some time. On our return, I am going to telephone Langley House and ask if Rat will watch the man and follow him to see where he goes."

"Absolutely not!" Tabitha said immediately and forcefully. "I thought we had come to an agreement about using Rat in investigations. If nothing else, his near brush with death in Wales should have shown us all," and at this, she glared pointedly at the dowager, "how dangerous such activities can be for a boy his age."

Wolf sighed; he had been expecting this response. "Tabitha, I promise that I will not put Rat in harm's way."

"Why cannot Bear do this surveillance?" Tabitha demanded, her anger white hot at what she perceived as Wolf's reneging on their agreement.

"Bear is the ideal choice for any part of an investigation that needs brute strength or the threat of violence. However, no one his size can be good at shadowing a man, but Rat is perfect for this. The boy is quick and slight. He can blend into the shadows and, wearing his old clothes, no one will bat an eyelid at a vagabond child hanging out on the street, hoping to catch a few pennies from somewhere. I promise, all I want him to do is to follow the man, nothing more. I will make very clear that if there is even a suggestion that O'Donnell knows he's being followed, then Rat is to abort."

Tabitha's posture and expression made clear that she would not be coaxed into agreement. Wolf tried again, this time using what he hoped was his most persuasive tone, "Tabitha, young girls are being brutally murdered. It has been days since the last killing. This monster never seems to leave long between the murders. We do not have time to waste." He could tell from the slumping of Tabitha's shoulders that this had been the decisive argument.

"Promise me that all Rat will be doing is watching O'Donnell and discreetly following him from a distance."

"I swear that is all I will ask the boy to do. I will have Langley give him some money in case the man takes an omnibus and he has to follow. But that is all."

Grudgingly accepting Wolf's words, Tabitha nodded. However, the rest of the ride back to Chesterton House was marked by a distinct chill in the air.

As soon as they returned, Wolf put a telephone call through to Langley House. He spoke to Langley and then to Rat. Finally, he came into the parlour where the women were waiting for him. "Rat will change his clothes and leave right away. Langley's carriage will drop him on the edge of the East End to save time and he can walk the rest of the way to Commercial Street. I have warned him that he is to do no more than follow O'Donnell and that he is to abort at the first sign he has been detected or of any other trouble."

Tabitha nodded stiffly but didn't reply.

CHAPTER 32

Rat was thrilled at Wolf's request. He had been worried that his run-in with Maureen Prescott in Wales and her attempt to kill him had put paid to any further involvement in investigations, at least if Milady Tabby Cat had anything to do with it. Rat assured Wolf that he had clothes that, if not quite as ragged and dirty as those he had worn when living on the streets of Whitechapel, were plain enough that they wouldn't attract attention in the East End. Wolf told him that Lord Langley would give him some money in case he had to travel across London and, most importantly, impressed upon him that at the first hint of danger or detection, he was to abandon his tailing of O'Donnell and return home.

If Wolf could have seen down the phone, he would have been amused at the wide grin Rat wore when he promised that he understood and would be careful. More than anyone except perhaps Bear, Wolf understood that as much as Rat appreciated the new life he led, not worrying about where his next meal would come from or whether he would have to sleep out in the cold, he had made sacrifices in moving to Mayfair. There had been adventure and excitement in the work he had previously done during Wolf's thief-taking days. Now, Rat's days were taken up with studying and practising the manners he would need in the new life ahead of him. It never occurred to him for a moment to leave Langley House and return to the streets of Whitechapel, if not for his own sake, for Melody's. Even so, the prospect of an afternoon back helping Wolf on an investigation made the young boy very happy indeed.

Rat quickly changed into the clothes that would be less conspicuous in the East End. The Langley carriage dropped him about a quarter of a mile from the tailor's shop on Commercial Street. It was a sunny day, warm enough that the promise of Spring was in the air. Rat walked towards Commercial Street whistling.

As he walked, Rat saw plenty of children who reminded him of himself less than a year before. Perhaps they had been sent out by their parents to scrounge for a few pennies to buy bread. Possibly, like Rat and Melody, they had no parents and were making do for themselves. As he watched these children, there was no doubt in Rat's mind that his life was better, much better now. More importantly, Melody's was. His mother's dying words to him had been to take care of his sister. He had only been seven at the time. Back then, Rat's only thought had been to keep his sister safe and well. Now, she lived in a grand house with her own maid, was never hungry and wore lovely clean dresses every day. She was going to grow up to be a fine lady, just like Milady Tabby Cat. Whatever sacrifices his new life brought, it was all worth it for what it meant for Melody. And for himself, well, he enjoyed his studies and enjoyed living with Lord Langley for whom he had great respect.

Before Rat knew it, he was at the tailor's shop that Wolf had described. He found himself a nearby doorway from where he could sit and watch the shop. He knew that no one would think twice about a young boy hanging around, perhaps hoping for a pocket to pick or a stale loaf of bread at the end of the day.

Wolf hadn't indicated what time the man he was watching, Tommy O'Donnell, would be done working. Rat didn't even know what the time was, just that he'd been waiting a while. People came in and out of the shop, but none of them matched the description he'd been given. Just when he was starting to get very stiff sitting in the same position, a man exited the shop. Rat only caught a glimpse of his face, but the nose was unmistakable. Jumping to his feet, Rat began to follow the man at enough of a distance not to be noticed, but close enough that he didn't lose him on the narrow streets.

The man walked down Commercial Street, then turned right and made his way to Aldgate station. When Langley had given Rat money, he'd told the boy to follow the man long enough to find out where he went. The money was for if he had to travel across London, so it seemed that the London Underground train, which it appeared the man was going to take, fell into that category.

Rat was excited; he'd never been able to afford to ride the London Underground when he had lived in Whitechapel, and since coming to Mayfair, he had a carriage at his disposal and had no need. He followed O'Donnell into the station, overheard him say that he was going to King's Cross, and saw him buy a ticket. Rat then went to the ticket office, said the same thing, and paid his penny for a ticket.

The stairway down to the platform was lit by gaslight but was still quite gloomy and a little scary, if Rat was honest. He descended to the platform, which was next to a huge tunnel cut into the earth. Rat had heard about the underground train, but nothing had prepared him to be on a platform waiting for one. All around, he could hear the rumble of trains. The air was heavy with soot and smoke.

Rat saw the man walk halfway along the platform and then sit on a bench, and so he followed him, staying close to the wall. They only had to wait a few minutes for the great steam-powered train to come through the tunnel. Since moving to Mayfair, Rat had been on quite a few locomotive trains, but the novelty and excitement still hadn't worn off. He was so in awe of the train that he almost forgot that he was supposed to be keeping an eye on the man.

O'Donnell got into the third-class carriage, and Rat followed him, taking a seat a few rows behind. The trip from Aldgate to King's Cross wasn't far, and it wasn't long before the man stood and prepared to get off. When the doors opened, Rat followed him up the stairs, out of the tube station and into the majestic splendour of King's Cross Station.

Looking around the train station, Rat wondered if he should continue to follow the man. Who knew where he was going? Certainly, everyone would be worried about Rat if he wasn't back that evening and for all he knew, the man could be going to Scotland. In the end, Rat decided to follow the man to the ticket office and try to discover where he was buying a ticket for. Then he would look at the map and if it seemed not far, he'd also buy a ticket and follow him. If not, he'd return to Chesterton House and report back what he knew.

If Tommy O'Donnell had noticed the small boy hanging around, he would have found him indistinguishable from all the other children on the streets, begging or stealing. Wolf had explained to Rat why he wanted him to follow the man and not Bear, and the boy had immediately realised the truth in Wolf's words; no one paid attention to children.

Loitering near enough to the ticket office that he could hear what the man said, he overheard him asking for a ticket to a place he'd never heard of. There was a train map on the wall, and Rat went over and tried to find the town. Eventually, he located it and realised that it was far enough that everyone would be worried if he followed, and he wasn't even sure if he could get a train home that night.

Abandoning his shadowing of the man, Rat looked at the London Underground map to see how he could get back close to Mayfair. He was very glad that he could read now; the names of the stations would have meant nothing to him a year ago. From what he could see, he had to get back on the Metropolitan Line and continue to Baker Street, and he could walk to Mayfair from there.

Rat didn't need to worry now about keeping an eye on someone and was able to enjoy his second ride on the underground train fully. From the first time he had ridden on one going to Scotland with Lord Langley, the boy had been fascinated by trains. Given the freedom he was allowed at Langley House to come and go as he pleased as long as his studies were complete for the day, he determined to explore the London Underground system when he had time.

Finally arriving at Chesterton House, Rat was shown into the parlour, where an anxious Tabitha had been unable to settle into any activity because she was worried about him. As soon as he entered the room, she jumped up and ran to embrace him.

"Oh, Rat! I am so happy that you are safe. I have been so worried."

The boy disentangled himself from her arms. "Milady Tabby Cat, I'm fine. No need to worry. I know what I'm doing."

Tabitha looked at him. Rat had shot up in height in the more than six months he had been living in Mayfair and, with regular meals, he had filled out and no longer was the scrawny ragamuffin she had first met. His time with Lord Langley had evened out his speech so that he no longer sounded like a cockney from the East End, and the boy had a more assured air about him. However, he was still a child, and Tabitha cared deeply about his well-being.

Realising that her outburst of emotion had embarrassed the lad, Tabitha stepped back and answered, "I know you are very capable Rat. Far more capable than most boys your age. Please do not ever doubt that."

Wolf, who had been almost equally anxious awaiting the boy's return, intervened and said, "Come in and tell us what happened."

There was a pot of tea and a plate of biscuits and cake on the table, and Rat eagerly helped himself to food before settling on the sofa. As impatient as Tabitha and Wolf were to hear what the boy had to say, he'd been out for hours and was clearly starving. They let him satiate the worst of his hunger.

After what felt like an eternity but was in reality no more than five minutes, the boy said, "So, I followed him, and he took the London Underground train, and so did I." Tabitha started at this. Still, a sharp look from Wolf stopped her from commenting on the boy taking the train alone. "He took the train to King's Cross and bought a ticket. I listened to where he was going and looked at the map. It wasn't so far away but far enough that I wasn't sure I could get there and back in time not to worry you all. I didn't follow him anymore and came back."

"That was very sensible, Rat," Tabitha commended. "Where was the ticket to?"

"A place called Edmonton."

Wolf and Tabitha both sat up straight at the name. "Edmonton? You are sure of that?" Wolf asked.

"Yeah, because I went and looked at the train map to see where it was."

Wolf stared off into the distance for a moment, lost in thought. Then he snapped his fingers and stood. "I know who Mr O'Donnell's brother is!"

"You do?"

"Remember when we went to Edmonton, and I said that Frederick Holmes looked familiar but I could not think why? It is because he reminded me of Tommy O'Donnell, or as I then thought of him, Bulbous Nose."

"You think that Colin O'Donnell assumed a new name and became Frederick Holmes and has been living as a councilman in Edmonton all this time?" Tabitha asked. Even as she voiced the question, it all began to make sense. The corkboard was propped up on a sideboard against the wall, and she stood and went and looked at it now. As she did so, a diabolical pattern began to emerge.

Turning back to Wolf, she said, "Could anyone really be wicked enough to murder innocent girls merely to influence a council vote?"

Wolf realised what Tabitha had pieced together and replied, "Someone who had already raped and murdered an innocent girl might think nothing of doing such a thing again. We know that Holmes hates the Jews. It must have infuriated him to think of having a large group of them as his neighbours in Edmonton. His position on the Edmonton Urban Council gave him insight into the members who were wavering in their support of Samuel Montagu's plans to develop his land. Holmes must have realised that those council members could be persuaded. The anti-Semitism that the Ripper killings caused in 1888 must have given him an idea for how to tilt the vote."

"What do we do now? We have no proof that Holmes is really Colin O'Donnell, and we have no real proof that either he or Tommy owns the knife. It is all pure speculation," Tabitha said, her voice filled with frustration.

"I might approach Bruiser with this information if our suspect were not a powerful councilman. There is no way that the Metropolitan Police will arrest a man of Holmes' stature on such circumstantial evidence." Wolf was as frustrated as Tabitha. There was no doubt in his mind that they had correctly identified the killer and that they had a credible motive. Wolf was usually the one to point out the difference between legal recourse and justice, but in this case, he wasn't sure how to achieve either one.

Rat had another slice of cake and then left for Langley House. Tabitha and Wolf sat in dejected silence.

CHAPTER 33

When Wolf had initially put the telephone call through to Langley House to ask for Rat's assistance, the dowager had considered remaining at Chesterton House to wait for his return. However, after an hour, she had become bored and returned home. The woman's parting words to Tabitha had been, "I will tell Manning to expect you tonight, Tabitha."

Now Tabitha said with some reluctance, "We should call Mama and let her know what we believe we have discovered, or perhaps I will update her later. I will be leaving here tonight, after all."

Wolf replied, "Well, regardless of when we tell Lady Pembroke, we also need to tell Langley."

They were saved the decision of which to communicate to first by Langley's appearance in the parlour.

"I am sorry to barge in, but Rat told me that you believe you have discovered the killer," the man said apologetically.

Given that Langley House was a five-minute walk and that a carriage ride would likely have taken as long, the brief period between Langley learning what Rat had to say and then appearing in their parlour was impressive. It also made the decision about who to telephone first redundant.

Wolf rose and left the room, returning a couple of minutes later to say, "Manning says that Lady Pembroke has gone out for the evening. Given this, I think we can safely proceed with telling Lord Langley what we know."

They then walked Langley through everything they had discovered since they had last reported on their findings. They ended with their conclusion as to the identity of the killer and his motive.

"And you are sure of this?" Langley asked.

"As sure as we can be," Wolf assured him.

"Then let me take this away and make some inquiries. I will contact you tomorrow when I know more."

After Langley had left, Tabitha thought about what the man had said. "Tomorrow may be too late. We know that Tommy O'Donnell has gone to warn his brother. Frederick Holmes, I mean Colin O'Donnell, fled from a murder accusation years ago. He may do so again."

Wolf considered her words. "Of course, all those years ago, the man had little to lose. Now he has a home, a business, a reputation. He may decide to brazen it out. He probably realises that we have no concrete evidence to tie him to the murders."

"But we can prove that he is Colin O'Donnell. Apart from Wilfred O'Hara, Angie Doherty can identify him as the man who raped and murdered a girl all those years ago."

"All those years ago in Ireland," Wolf pointed out. "I truly doubt that the Metropolitan Police are going to arrest a prominent member of the community for something that Mickey D's wife claims happened a long time ago, over in Limerick."

Tabitha thought about Wolf's words. "We need to go to Edmonton and ensure that he does not escape before Langley has a chance to formulate a plan."

"Wolf looked at the clock on the mantelpiece. It was already seven o'clock at night. He had no idea what time the last train was. More to the point, if O'Donnell tried to flee, they needed to be able to follow him. "I think we need to take the carriage, even though the ride will be at least an hour and a half," he said.

"We might be too late."

"We might be. However, as I said, the man has a life now. I doubt that he will abandon that with nothing more than the clothes on his back. If Rat returned here thirty minutes ago, then it is fair to say that Tommy O'Donnell is on his way but may not even have arrived at his brother's house yet. Perhaps Colin O'Donnell is not at home, and Tommy will have to wait. Even then, he has to persuade his brother that we are onto him. Then, Colin needs to prepare to leave. There is a chance that we will be there in time. I think it is a chance we must take. However, there is no time to change. Grab a cloak, and I will call for the carriage."

Tabitha had changed into a day dress on their return from Spitalfields earlier, but she knew that Wolf was right. Wolf had not changed his clothes, but he had put his gun away and so he went to retrieve that and to find Bear. There was no doubt that his presence would be very helpful if there were a confrontation of any sort.

Within ten minutes, they were on their way to Edmonton. During the ride, Tabitha and Wolf brought Bear up to date on what they had learned and deduced that day. When they'd finished, Bear asked, "So you think this man is going to do a runner?"

"He has done it before," Wolf pointed out. "He may believe that he can stay and bluff it out and he may realise what we have: that no one is going to arrest him for the murder of an Irish girl more than twenty years ago on the word of an Irish gang leader's wife. Nevertheless, he may be spooked enough and decide not to try his luck. We cannot take that chance."

They didn't speak much for most of the journey to Edmonton, each lost in their thoughts about what they had learned. As they drove into the town, Bear asked, "So, what is the plan?"

Wolf considered the question. It had consumed his thoughts for most of the trip, and yet he still didn't have a solid scheme. "I am not sure," he admitted.

"Well, let us work on the assumption that by the time we arrive, Tommy O'Donnell is either there or has been there. We suspect that he has gone to tell his brother about our suspicions. So, why do we not knock on the man's door and express them ourselves?" Tabitha suggested. "We may find him obviously preparing to leave and can question why, or we may find Tommy still there, and there will be no point in either of them denying their connection."

Wolf wouldn't exactly call that a fully formed plan, but he had no better suggestion, so they agreed to knock on Frederick Holmes' door and confront the man in his front room.

The carriage pulled up outside Holmes' house, which was mostly dark except for a faint light coming through the glass in the front door. Edmonton was not Mayfair, and so it was likely that the maid they had encountered on their last visit and any other servants didn't live in. If the master of the house was at home, he might well be in his study, which was probably at the back of the house. Regardless, there was no time to be lost, and they all descended from the carriage.

Wolf led the way to the front door and rapped on the ugly brass knocker. There was no answer. "I think I heard a noise from within," Bear said. "I can't be sure though."

"I thought I heard it too," Tabitha said.

Wolf knocked again. When it was clear no one was coming to open the door, he said, "Let's make our way around the back. Kitchen door locks are much easier to pick." The house was a two-storey detached villa and there was a red-bricked path leading to a side gate that led to the back garden. They walked through the gate and around to the kitchen door, only to find the door open. It seemed that whoever they had heard inside had fled.

Looking around the garden, Bear said, "The wall at the back isn't high. It wouldn't be hard to jump over it."

"Go and see if you can catch whoever it is," Wolf directed. "I will go inside and see if anyone is still there." Bear did as Wolf asked. Wolf turned to Tabitha. "I want you to stay out here." Seeing the refusal on her face before she had uttered a word, he held up a hand and said, "Please. I have no idea what I will find in there. Perhaps nothing. It was probably Holmes, or should I say, O'Donnell, who fled. But we cannot be sure."

Reluctantly, Tabitha agreed, and Wolf entered the house alone. He was hardly gone a minute or two when he returned. "Holmes is dead. Someone has cut his throat. It is a rather gruesome scene. I saw a police call box on the corner of the road. I am going to go and report the crime. You should wait in the kitchen for Bear to return. Just do not go into the study. Trust me, it is not a pretty scene."

Tabitha did as Wolf asked, and a few minutes later, Bear walked into the house. He hadn't had any luck catching whoever had fled. Tabitha told him about the dead body in the study, and Bear went to check for himself. Tabitha chastised herself for her unwillingness to see the body. However, as much as she insisted to Wolf that there was no reason to protect her and that she could handle anything he could, she was glad that she hadn't been the one to discover the corpse.

Bear came back into the kitchen. "Nasty. Whoever did that was angry."

"How can you tell?"

"It wasn't just a clean slashing of the throat. The body had multiple puncture wounds even though if his throat had been cut first, he was likely already dead. Whoever killed him wanted to mutilate his body."

Tabitha reflected on Bear's words. "It must have been Wilfred O'Hara. He must have followed Tommy O'Donnell when Rat did. The boy would have had no reason to pay attention to any man other than the one he had been asked to shadow. O'Hara only wanted to find Tommy in order to get to Colin and finally get revenge for his sister's death."

Wolf returned from using the police box and Tabitha told him her theory. "But how did O'Hara know where to find Tommy?"

"Well, you rolled up to the Spitalfields Working Men's Club in the carriage and then made stops around the neighbourhood. I'm sure that didn't go unnoticed by the locals," Bear pointed out. "O'Hara must have heard gossip and followed your trail."

"So, we led him to Tommy and then here to murder a man in cold blood," Tabitha said, horrified, and instinctively clutching her throat.

"Well, we led him to brutally murder a man who was a brutal murderer. I am not going to lose any sleep over this," Wolf assured her.

"And what do we tell the police when they arrive?" Tabitha asked.

Wolf considered the question. "What do you think we should tell them? After all, we do not know for certain that Wilfred O'Hara had anything to do with this. All we have is speculation."

Tabitha thought about all they had learned during this investigation and their earlier acknowledgement of how difficult it would be to prove their suspicions against the man known as Frederick Holmes. "I believe that justice has been served and the world is a better place without Colin O'Donnell in it. We have no reason to believe that Wilfred O'Hara poses a threat to anyone else now that the man who raped and murdered his sister is dead."

Smiling at how much more nuanced Tabitha's thinking had become over the last six months, Wolf said, "I could not agree with you more. Justice has indeed been served."

By the time the police had come, interviewed them and then let them leave, they were all glad that they had brought the carriage rather than taking the train. Tabitha leaned against Wolf's shoulder and slept most of the way back to Chesterton House. He knew that he should take her to the dowager's home, but it was late, and he didn't want to answer questions from the old woman about where they had been. There would be time enough the next day for all that.

CHAPTER 34

The following morning, Tabitha met Wolf at the breakfast table. "You should have taken me to the dowager's house last night," she said in a voice that was more lovingly teasing than rebuking.

"You were so tired, I had to carry you in and find Mary to help undress you. I cannot imagine what a stir it would have caused if I'd carried you through the dowager's home to your bedchamber."

Tabitha acknowledged the truth of his words, then asked, "Has there been any word from the Edmonton police or Lord Langley?"

"Nothing, but it is still early. I did call Langley House last night to give an update of our evening, so I'm sure we will hear something at some point. Meanwhile, you should use this time to ensure you have all you need to have with you for your time away and then we can take the carriage and go and give the dowager an update."

"You know that we will be receiving a tongue lashing, both for investigating without her and for my absence last night."

Wolf sighed, "Yes, I know. However, we need to take our punishment bravely rather than compounding our crimes by making her wait to hear our news."

An hour later, Wolf left word with Talbot that, if Lord Langley were to telephone, he should be directed to the dowager's home.

During their investigation, neither of them had seen anything of Lady Lily. Now that she was officially betrothed to Viscount Tobias, the two had been free to spend as much chaperoned time together as they wished. Lady Lily used this new freedom to explore every museum in London and to attend every scientific talk where women's attendance was tolerated.

That morning, however, they found her in the dowager's drawing room, playing the piano. Lady Lily's mother, Jane, was an accomplished pianist. Her daughter was merely a dilettante by comparison. Nevertheless, Lily enjoyed playing and found it was often a good counterweight to her scientific ponderings.

When Tabitha and Wolf entered the drawing room, Lady Lily stopped playing and stood to greet them. "I am sorry we interrupted you. Please do not stop on our account," Tabitha said, accepting the younger woman's warm embrace.

"I was only tinkering. To be honest, I have neglected my playing of late and I know that Mama will be appalled when next I see her. But I have been having such a wonderful time exploring all the intellectual opportunities that London has to offer with Toby, that my music has been quite neglected."

Tabitha smiled, but behind the smile was the nagging worry that she always had whenever she thought about Lily's engagement to Viscount Tobias. There seemed little doubt that the young man adored Lily, but the extent to which it was reciprocated was another matter. Tabitha was sure that Lily liked Tobias as a friend, perhaps even a little more than that. However, it had been Lily herself who had confided that her real inducement to wed the viscount was that she considered him sufficiently malleable, at least for the time being, and surprisingly open to her academic pursuits.

While this arrangement suited the intellectually inclined Lily's immediate goals – to escape from her family's single-minded plan for her to marry well – Tabitha worried about what the future would bring. Would Viscount Tobias always be willing to indulge his wife's eccentricities? Tabitha had voiced these concerns already and realised that, at this point, there was little more she could do. Nevertheless, a disquietude was always in the background of her interactions with the young woman she had grown very fond of.

They sat and chatted with Lady Lily about a talk she had attended recently at the Royal Society by a proponent of Charles Darwin's theories, Joseph Dalton Hooker. Tabitha had only the most superficial understanding of Darwin's work, but Wolf seemed sufficiently informed to at least hold up their end of the conversation with the highly intelligent Lily.

After thirty minutes, the door to the drawing room opened, and the dowager entered, her eyes narrowed suspiciously. "Two early morning visits from you both in a row; what do you have to confess today?" She went and sat in her preferred chair and continued, "More to the point, Tabitha, why are you visiting this morning instead of walking down the stairs from your assigned bedchamber to greet your betrothed?"

Because the dowager was always inclined to blame Tabitha and forgive Wolf, he took the lead in explaining their activities of the previous evening. Uncharacteristically, the dowager didn't interrupt, though the expression on her face spoke of her displeasure at being excluded. However, Wolf's telephone call before they had left for Edmonton when Manning had told him that the dowager had left for a dinner provided them with an excuse that even the always happily pugnacious woman had a difficult time seeing her way around.

When Wolf had finished the narrative, the dowager's only response was a particularly vehement harrumph. That this was her only indication of displeasure was evidence enough that she knew her plan for self-righteous high dudgeon had been thwarted.

Whatever else the dowager might have wanted to say was interrupted by the arrival of Lord Langley at the drawing room door.

"Talbot told me that you were all in here," Langley explained. It seemed expeditious to come myself rather than telephoning here. I have news." At this, Lady Lily excused herself. Despite the young woman's interest in most intellectual pursuits, she found the investigations that her grandmother, cousin and aunt insisted on becoming involved with to be tremendously boring.

As the door closed behind Lady Lily, the dowager said impatiently, "Out with it Maxwell. I am not a young woman and do not have time for this dilly dallying. When one reaches my age, there is always the possibility that one might not live long enough to hear the end of a story that is being needlessly drawn out."

"Well, as I suspect Lord and Lady Pembroke have informed you, Colin O'Donnell, or as he was known these days, Frederick Holmes, was killed last night. The police do not have any suspects nor leads and are therefore categorising it as a burglary attempt that was interrupted when Lord Pembroke knocked on the front door." When Wolf had telephoned Langley House the previous evening, he had not left any details out and had trusted Langley's innate sense of right and wrong would enable the man to see the justice of the situation for what it was.

"However, there has been an interesting development this morning that I thought you should know about." As Langley said this, he could see from the look on the dowager's face that if he didn't immediately get to the point, he would yet again be berated for his circumlocutions and so quickly said, "Colin O'Donnell was wanted by the Metropolitan Police in Whitechapel for the rape and murder of a young woman twenty years ago. He escaped capture at the time and disappeared from the East End. The case against him was apparently solid enough that the man would undoubtedly have been convicted and hanged for the murder. Given this, it seems that whoever killed him last night, merely expedited the work of the judicial system."

Tabitha considered his words. "Lord Langley, there has always been more to this investigation than catching a murderer. How do we ensure that there is a clear understanding by the public that these killings had nothing to do with the Jewish population?"

Langley nodded in acknowledgement of the truth at the heart of Tabitha's question. "Do not worry; that is in hand. The Prime Minister has been informed of your suspicions about this Colin O'Donnell and certainly, what we now know about the man's prior murderous activities, only bolsters your claims. The government is extremely good at leaking stories to the press that have no obvious fingerprints on them. This will be taken care of."

Langley then paused, "However, any negating of the suspicions and accusations against the Jewish community in the East End for these murders will come too late for our friend Mr Montagu. I understand that the Edmonton Urban Council called an unplanned meeting yesterday at the behest of our Mr O'Donnell, otherwise known as Mr Holmes. They voted against Samuel Montagu's proposal for the development of his land."

"But surely now that the truth is out about who Holmes really was and what he did to stir up prejudice against the Jews, the council can be forced to take another vote," Tabitha protested.

"Perhaps. However, anti-Semitism is more than a superficial preference that might be easily countered with what we now know. I suspect that O'Donnell's actions merely bolstered many of the council members deeply held prejudices and allowed them to justify their vote. Whatever else Montagu is able to do with his land in Edmonton, I suspect that he will not be seeing this particular dream for his people come to fruition."

EPILOGUE

Tabitha had been staying with the dowager for more than a week and she was growing wearier and wearier of the experience with every passing day. In many ways, it could have been worse; the dowager hadn't changed her schedule at all to accommodate her houseguest and so she and Tabitha did not spend an enormous amount of time together. Tabitha ate breakfast alone every morning. At least half of the evenings, the dowager had social plans to which she didn't invite Tabitha to join. Because Lady Lily spent most of her evenings with Viscount Tobias out somewhere, this meant that Tabitha also ate dinner alone frequently.

If it had been left to her, Tabitha would have done nothing more than sleep in the dowager's home and would have spent most of the days and evenings back at Chesterton House. However, the dowager and Wolf had both pointed out that if she were there from morning to night, the neighbours and local gossips would hardly be able to tell the difference from before Tabitha moved out. If this happened, it would scupper their objective: to put paid to any post-marital whisperings about the legitimacy of an heir. Then leaving would have been for nothing.

Instead, Tabitha usually didn't return to Chesterton House until at least noon, when she and Wolf usually had lunch together. After that, she spent time with Mrs Jenkins, the housekeeper and finally spent at least an hour with Melody in the nursery. She would then return to the dowager's home before dinner.

On the morning of the eighth day Tabitha was shocked to see the dowager up and at the breakfast table by nine o'clock in the morning.

"Ah Tabitha, nice of you to join me," the dowager said breezily as if she was not the one who rarely left her boudoir before eleven. "Lady Lily and I are planning to discuss wedding preparations this morning and I thought that you might want to join us."

Whether or not Tabitha did want to join, she knew that she couldn't leave Lily to her grandmother's machinations with no support. By all rights, organising the wedding fell to Lily's parents. However, even if they hadn't lived in Scotland, no one expected the dowager to leave the planning of such a socially important event to her daughter. Tobias' mother, Lady Williams, might have hoped to have a significant hand in the planning, particularly given that the wedding breakfast was to take place in her home. Again, no one expected that the dowager would give over control to anyone else. Given this, it was unlikely to be an enjoyable conversation, but she couldn't leave Lily to suffer alone.

An hour late, the three women were in the dowager's morning room and the discussion was underway. As Tabitha listened to the dowager make pronouncements and force her opinion on her granddaughter, Tabitha reflected that discussion was not the right word for what she was subjecting herself to. In fact, she wasn't sure why the dowager had even asked her to join.

Finally, the dowager seemed to have exhausted all she had to say on the topic of wedding planning, at least for the time being. Just when Tabitha thought that she could finally excuse herself and make her way to Chesterton House, the dowager said casually, "Oh, Tabitha, I forgot to mention, we have been invited to take tea with the Duchess of Somerset this afternoon."

"We have? I wish you had given me more notice; I had promised Melody that I would spend time with her this afternoon before she goes to Langley House."

"That will not be an issue. Lily and I will accompany you earlier and will visit with Melody and then we will all make our way to Rowley House afterwards. Oh, and Tabitha, please remember that we are visiting a duchess and dress accordingly."

Tabitha clenched her jaw; how dare the woman insinuate that she ever underdressed? She would show her! Tabitha fumed through lunch and continued to be irritated as she went up to her room to change. After telling Ginny what the dowager had the audacity to say, she announced determinedly, "I want to wear the pink Worth dress that recently came from Paris. I will show the woman that I do not need to be told to dress accordingly." Ginny didn't reply but went and retrieved the gown that she had luckily thought to bring with them from Chesterton House. She hadn't packed all of Tabitha's jewellery but had brought a delicate sapphire necklace and matching earrings that would beautifully complement the dress.

Thirty minutes later, the dowager, Lady Lily, and Tabitha were in the carriage, making their way the short distance to Chesterton House. Tabitha was already second-guessing the expedition; the Worth gown, while beautiful and sophisticated, was hardly made for sitting on the floor and playing with a child. However, it was too late now, she realised. She and Melly would just have to sit quietly and read.

When they pulled up outside Chesterton House, Tabitha was surprised to see Lord Langley's carriage standing there. Surely, Wolf would have mentioned if the other earl wanted to talk about a new investigation. Perhaps Wolf had asked him for advice on estate business.

Entering the house, Tabitha was prepared to go straight to the nursery. If Wolf was with Langley in the study, she didn't want to interrupt them. She assumed that the dowager and Lily would accompany her to see Melody as planned.

"Milady," Talbot intoned, "His lordship has asked for you to join him in the drawing room."

What on earth has happened? Tabitha thought. Wolf found the drawing room far too stuffy and formal and always preferred to spend time in the comfy parlour or his study unless they had guests. Of course, Lord Langley was with him. Did he count as a guest at this point? Tabitha considered the question as she led the way into the room.

Opening the door, the first thing that Tabitha noticed was that the room was full of people. Looking around, she realised that all the staff, including Ginny, were in there. How had Ginny managed to get over to Chesterton House so quickly after helping Tabitha dress? And why?

Suddenly, her legs were grasped at the knees. "Tabby Cat, you look so pretty."

Tabitha looked down to see Melody hugging her. Then, she noticed a very dignified man with a shock of white hair, complemented by a white beard, standing talking to Lord Langley. The man seemed to be a clergy-man. In fact, based on his purple robes, he was a bishop. Tabitha did a double-take when she realised who he was. Why was Frederick Temple, the Archbishop of Canterbury, in the drawing room at Chesterton House? What was going on?

She looked back at the dowager and Lily, who both had absurd grins plastered across their faces. Then she looked back and found Wolf standing in front of her. He was dressed as smartly as she'd ever seen him look and had even trimmed his hair.

"You look beautiful, Tabitha," Wolf said, taking both of her hands in his.

"What is going on, Wolf? Why is the Archbishop of Canterbury here?" Out of the corner of her eye, she realised that Bear's mother, Mrs Caruthers, was sitting on the sofa talking with Anthony Rowley, the Duke of Somerset. Anthony caught her eye and smiled broadly. It was as if everyone Tabitha most cared about was in the drawing room. It occurred to her that perhaps she was dreaming. Yet, her hands in Wolf's felt very real.

"The trust has been set up and all the necessary legalities have been concluded. I have the special license. All that is left is for us to pledge our undying love to each other. If that is acceptable to you, that is."

Tabitha's eyes filled with tears. Suddenly rehashing the events of the morning, she turned to the dowager and asked, "Is this why you insulted me? To goad me into wearing my best dress?"

"What else would you believe my motives to have been, my dear? I am hardly someone known for passing judgment for no good reason," the dowager said with her usual blithe lack of self-awareness that never ceased to amaze Tabitha. However, for once, she was willing to overlook the woman's obliviousness to her character and behaviour.

Turning back to Wolf, she asked, "And we are to be married by the Archbishop of Canterbury? Does the man not have better things to do with his time?"

Wolf laughed, "You may thank Lady Pembroke for that."

"Indeed, Tabitha. Better things to do? What nonsense. I cannot imagine what the man spends his days doing, but he certainly has no better way to spend his time than marrying members of my family. Now, are we ready? I believe we have all waited long enough for this wedding to happen, and I, for one, am ready to move on to cake and champagne."

Wolf leaned in and whispered in Tabitha's ear, "I am very ready to move on to other things as well." She blushed prettily at his words but didn't disagree.

❧

WOLF AND BEAR, THE DUO YOU'VE GROWN TO LOVE, HAVE A friendship and business partnership spanning over a decade. Curious about the beginning of their journey? Find the link at sarahfnoel.com.

❧

FINALLY, TABITHA AND WOLF ARE MARRIED AND THEY couldn't be happier. The last thing either of them wants is to be sucked back into a murder investigation. However, when Christopher "Kit" Bailey reappears and asks for help, they're unable to refuse. As you can imagine, the dowager wants nothing to do with her nemesis. However, her stance changes when she realises that this case might unearth another of her well-kept secrets, a revelation she cannot afford. **Order** Book 8, An Intrepid Woman now!

❧

MELODY AND RAT ARE THE ADORABLE WHITECHAPEL STREET urchins Tabitha has taken under her wing. Would you love to know what they're like as young adults? Never fear, my new series, **The Continental Capers of Melody Chesterton**, will reveal all. Book 1, A Venetian Escapade, is available for **order!**

Keep reading for a sneak peak...

May 1911

Approaching the Venezia Santa Lucia train station, Melody had caught glimpses of Venice. Actually, what she was really looking at, for the most part, were the many small islands, such as San Michele and Murano, that dotted the Venetian Lagoon. Just as the train was coming into the station, Melody was able to see the northern edge of the Cannaregio district, one of the city's six sestieri, as the Venetians call them.

Descending from the train, Melody was too impatient to wait for Mary and Rat or to worry about their luggage. Instead, she almost ran down the platform in a very unladylike way and burst out of the station. None of her reading about the city or studying paintings and even photographs of Venice had prepared her to exit the station and find herself confronted by the Grand Canal.

The first thing that struck Melody was how bustling the area surrounding the train station was. It was not so very different from the streets around King's Cross station, with Venetians hurrying about their business, street vendors hawking their wares, and gawking tourists clogging up the Fondamenta Santa Lucia running each side of the Grand Canal. Opposite the station was a beautiful building that Melody assumed was a church. Its ornate facade and striking green copper dome dominated the skyline.

As far as Melody could see, beautiful, colourful buildings with a distinctive ornate architectural style lined the canal. Perhaps the most striking thing about the view was the myriad of long, thin boats, gondolas, with their gondoliers standing and using a single, long oar to steer and propel the boats. All the gondoliers were dressed in similar outfits: striped shirts, either black and white or blue and white, dark trousers and wide straw hats adorned with colourful ribbons.

Melody thought she could have stared at the view in front of her forever.

"It is glorious, is it not?" a suave, English-accented voice said from slightly behind her.

Startled out of her reverie, Melody turned to see the very handsome stranger from the train just slightly behind her. Up close, he was even more attractive than he had seemed from a distance. Despite his very cultured English accent with the modulated lilt and rounded vowels that indicated an upper-class upbringing and education, the man had a distinctively foreign look about him. His olive skin tone and jet-black hair were far more indicative of the Mediterranean than of the home counties. Apart from perfectly even features marked by the most patrician of noses, the most striking thing about the man were the startling green eyes, whose colour seemed almost unnatural. In an unfair endowment of natural charms, those eyes were framed by thick, dark, curling lashes. Melody's first thought was what she would give to have similar eyes.

Melody realised that rather than staring at the man with her mouth agape, she should be answering him. "It is, sir," was all she could stammer out.

"The Conte Alessandro Foscari di Villa Foscari, at your service," the man said, executing a neat little bow.

Melody tried to remember what Granny had said about introductions by strange men. She had never paid much attention during the tedious etiquette and deportment lessons. Still, she vaguely remembered something about it being improper for a man to introduce himself directly to a woman without a formal introduction by a family member or close acquaintance. She also remembered thinking at the time how silly such a rule was.

Finally, deciding that any such social rules were from a different century and did not apply to a young, modern woman in 1911, Melody boldly held out her hand and said, "Melody Chesterton. It is very nice to meet you Conte Foscari."

The man took the outstretched hand, raised it to his lips, then held it long past when it was socially acceptable to do so and said in a sultry voice, "Please, call me Alessandro." This was the sight that met Mary and Rat as they hurried out of the station, a porter in tow with their luggage, anxious to find where Melody had disappeared to.

"Melody!" Rat said sternly, "Why did you disappear like that? We had no idea where you had gone to." Then, realising the scene he had interrupted, he said in a mature, almost paternal tone that was belied by his very youthful appearance, "And who is the gentleman holding your hand?"

Author Note

Samuel Montagu was a real person and his efforts to use his land in Edmonton to create decent housing for the Jews of the East End was really denied by the city council. The council actually turned down his proposal a little later in the year, but I took some artistic license for the purposes of the story.

Afterword

Thank you for reading An Indomitable Woman. I hope you enjoyed it. If you'd like to see what's coming next for Tabitha & Wolf, here are some ways to stay in touch:

SarahFNoel.com
Facebook
@sarahfNoelAuthor on Bluesky
sfnoel on Instagram
@sfnoel on Threads

If you enjoyed this book, I'd very much appreciate a review (but, please no spoilers).

About Sarah F. Noel

Originally from London, Sarah F. Noel now spends most of her time in Grenada in the Caribbean. Sarah loves reading historical mysteries with strong female characters. The Tabitha & Wolf Mystery Series and its spin-off, The Continental Capers of Melody Chesterton, are exactly the kind of books she loves to curl up with on a lazy Sunday.

Visit Sarah's website (sarahfnoel.com/) to join her mailing list, connect with her on social media, and see what's coming next!